A Host of Angels

Angel Sisters, Book 1

Catherine Lampshire

Dad, thanks for all your support. You have always been there for me through thick and thin. Thanks to your efforts, you are making my dream come true. I am proud to have you for a dad.

Contents

Chapter 1

Present Day

Seraphima Angel (Sera)

"What's happening?" I ask groggily, coming out of a drugged sleep with an unsteady jolt. Smacking my lips as if that will ward off the chemical taste in my cotton-dry mouth. The lingering queasiness from the drug makes me want to hurl.

"Shut up," Peter replies testily over his shoulder before returning his focus to his cell phone.

Turning my face away I look out the window of the private jet plane Frank's piloting. Turbulence rocks the small expanded four seater. It's not making my already upset stomach feel any better. The contents of my stomach surges into my throat. I clamp shut my eyes as tightly as my lips. If I've learned anything in the last forty-eight hours it's to not poke serpents when they're coiled and ready to strike.

If wishes were dreams and dreams came true I wouldn't be in this nightmare.

Pressing a white knuckled fist to my lips, I choke back a sob while the accompanying tears threaten to escape. I've survived up to now. I can endure a little more. Once my feet are on the ground I'll make a plan of escape.

What I need is a miracle. But I don't think I believe in them any more. I do, however, believe in monsters. They're real. Three of them are right here. No need to pinch myself. This is no dream I'm in. This is a nightmare of Biblical proportions.

Hell is a real place and I'm sitting across from a minion of Satan himself. From underneath my lashes I peek at Peter. Though he may look like a Grecian god, I know he isn't. He's evil itself in human form. I wish on all that is holy that I'd never met him.

My mom always said never to judge a book by its cover. Boy, she sure had that one right.

I whimper in fear as the plane shudders and shakes as we hit more turbulence. It's coming more and more often. Knocking and jostling the tiny plane in ways none can anticipate. Outside the window I can see dark clouds looming across the horizon. We're heading straight for them.

God help us. Help me. I say a silent prayer to any deity that may be listening and keen to lend a hand.

"I'm going to be sick." I gulp.

"In there, you stupid bitch." Peter indicates a compartment where I find barf bags.

I snag a couple to keep at the ready.

"You had better not puke all over the plane or you'll be the one cleaning it up—with your tongue," he warns icily.

Frank, one of Peter's bodyguards and the pilot of this plane, smirks. Peter is up front riding shotgun, while I'm stuck in the back with George.

I quickly look away, not wanting to see the evil that lurks in Peter's eyes. It matches the venom in his voice, the darkness of his soul. Peter returns his attention to his cellphone. I'm glad I'm no longer the center of his attention. I go back to looking out the window.

Images reflecting there only intensify the queasiness of my stomach. Vaguely, I see the other henchman fumbling for his own barf bag. Sweat beads on his brow. His adam's apple bobs as he swallows convulsively, attempting to keep down his rising gorge. Thank goodness he finds one in time. The stench of his puke fills the interior of the plane. I pinch my nose shut with my fingers and breath through my teeth.

"Fuck, George get rid of that before you make the rest of us ill," Peter orders, giving him a look of disgust.

It's my turn to smirk. George blushes before turning his mean eyes on me. The promise of pain is written all over his face. Yeah, this guy would love to hurt me. He's the kind that gets off on causing others misery. George does as he's told. On slightly unsteady feet, he pushes himself out of his seat and lumbers to the dinky wash closet located just behind Peter's seat. The noise of suction and a pressured *woosh* sounds as George flushes the barf bag.

For a moment I watch all the color tones and textures of grey and white that seem layered in the darkening sky. In its own way, it's quite beautiful. Maybe it's like they say about the calm before the storm. There is beauty in the ugly like there is light in the dark. Peter is like that but not in a good way. He has a beautiful face and body but with the heart of a monster. It's how he traps his prey, his victims. And now I'm one. I shudder.

"Cold?" George asks. As if he genuinely cares. "Slide right over here, Angel, and I'll warm you up fast," he says, leering at me.

He licks his lips and flares his nostrils. Now I'm *really* going to be sick. I pretend to gag in his direction, getting a thrill when he jumps back to avoid the fountain of vomit he thinks is coming his way. I give him a disgusted look then turn away, but I catch the ugly look he throws back. Some guys just can't handle rejection.

"You'll pay for that, bitch," he threatens under his breath.

Looking out the window, I can see we're flying directly into the storm.

What are storms but a mixture of the two competing forces? A battle that unites and creates something awesomely terrifying in its strength and power. Destructive and cleansing at the same time. Oh, how I long to cleanse away all the filth that has entered my life of late. Maybe the heavens will open up and do me a favor.

How I wish to possess some of that passionate power.

My passion has always been directed toward helping those in need. That's why I became a doctor. Instead of working in a hospital network or having my own private practice, I work for Global Medicine, an NGO funded through generous private donations. A team of doctors who routinely visit places where quality medical care is limited.

I'm a general practitioner with additional training and certification as an OBGYN. I'm not a plastic surgeon or any other kind of specialist. I might not conduct extreme lifesaving or life altering surgeries that get the lion's share of media attention, but I do make a difference.

Delivering babies, helping pregnant women, administering prenatal care and inoculations, and treating illnesses within my repertoire are just as necessary for a high quality of life. Besides, it frees up others to do their important work.

How ironic that it's that passion for my work and the difference my team and I make that got me where I am, here, stuck on this plane, a prisoner.

Unlike David, my former fiancé, I don't come from money. My family isn't wealthy. What we are rich in is love and determination. No strangers to hard work and perseverance. Good grades got me scholarships and acceptance into a good college and medical program. Working several jobs enabled me to support myself so I wouldn't be a financial burden to my family. One of those jobs is modeling. I fell into it as a youth and have continued with it, working on the side when I'm not traveling the world with Global Medicine.

For the past several years, Global Medicine has been my life. We live and work on an outdated and refurbished cruise ship donated by one of the cruise lines. Each member of the team has their own cabin unless people want to share. The ship has been outfitted to serve as a floating hospital complete with several surgical theaters, waitingrooms, rooms to house overnight patients, and rooms in which to see and treat patients.

Sometimes there is more space onboard than we use. Knowing this, Peter wanted to use it for his own purposes. Actually, I should say, for his boss's. Peter works for a man who operates a drug cartel, among other things. He's constantly looking for mules or methods to transport illegal drugs to key destinations.

We're medical professionals. As such, rarely are we scrutinized by government agencies searching for illegal contraband. That might all change once the issue with David goes public. Who would suspect a floating hospital of concealing and transporting illegal drugs? Right? That's what Peter counted on. We already have numerous controlled substances on board, but all are for medical purposes.

I know some among my team with lower ethical standards may be tempted. Heck, the pay Peter, or his boss, promises is alluring, but once you sign up there's no getting out. You've just sold your soul.

David discovered this the hard way.

The only way to call it quits is to die. Should you get caught with the junk? Not even heaven can help you avoid retribution.

Depending on where exactly one gets caught, death may come knocking on the door any way. Or worse, a person may spend years behind bars in a third world country. Even if they're lucky and get a reprieve, they'll lose their medical license and never work in the field again. Think of the wasted years and dollars spent. In the end, it just isn't worth it. At least by my way of thinking. Not so for others...

Best bet, in my estimation—stick with your ethical standards and personal code of integrity. Don't get involved.

Thing is, I have moral fiber. I'm not bragging. It's what it is. My parents taught my sisters and I right from wrong. For goodness sakes, they named me Seraphima Angel. You know like in seraphim. The Seraphim are the angels that sit closest to the throne of God and sing holy holy holy.

The Seraphim are the highest-ranking order of angels according to many Christian faiths. They are celestial beings filled with passion for doing God's holy work. Some claim them to be six-winged divine messengers. A few ancient texts describe seraphim as winged dragons or serpents, even phoenixes, and 'flying elements of the sun.' All my sisters's names have to do with the goodness and purity of angels.

Living up to our name was mandatory in my parent's household. My sisters and I did not dare disappoint our parents. We were always expected to act like angels because we were Angels. It sounds a bit tongue in cheek but for my parents, they were serious. They weren't evangelical uber conservative in their faith. They were quirky people who had high expectations and saw things in black and white when it came to raising their daughters.

As a result, I was never a problem child. Never has my integrity, my honesty been questioned. Doing the right thing is what got me into trouble. Go figure.

The problem? My fiancé didn't possess those same ethical standards. Or if he did, he failed to heed them. By the time David fully realized just what sort of trouble he'd gotten himself into, he'd lost the power to say no. Once you've bargained with the Devil there's no out clause.

Call me blind, but I wasn't aware of what he'd done until it was too late.

I'd begun noticing odd behaviors and mood swings. He was increasingly showing signs of stress and anxiety. His blood pressure was elevated, requiring medication. David never seemed to get a full night's rest. Often, he would complain of stomach ailments.

He was always popping antacids, particularly when we were arriving into ports of call. David had scary outbursts. People other than myself were noticing. I became worried. We started to fight. Constantly. Finally, I'd had enough. When he realized I was walking away, ending our relationship, that was when he finally came clean—to me that is.

Once I heard it all, I sat in shock.

"Why?" I asked, aghast that he would or could be so stupid, so gullible, so…weak.

"David you're a brilliant surgeon. Why would you get involved with anything that would jeopardize that? You've put your entire life and career at risk, and now us," I said.

"Don't you think I know that?" he had fumed, pacing around his messy cabin. Dark circles under his eyes gave him a haunted appearance. He'd gone unshaven and looked rumpled and exhausted. When was the last time he showered?

"What were you thinking?" I demanded.

If he thought I would assuage his guilt, he was dead wrong. I would comfort him later. How naïve I was to think, at first, that we'd work together to find a solution. Frankly, I knew he was screwed. Back then, I needed to hear all of it and he needed to own up to his one whopper of a mistake.

"I was thinking of all the money I could bank. We're getting married soon and I thought the extra cash would go a long way toward making our lives together more comfortable. We've both got debts that need to be paid off..."

"What debts?" I asked, cutting him off. His should be zero. His wealthy family paid for all of his school and living expenses, within reason. If he was meaning me... There was no way I was going to allow him to foist off his problem onto my shoulders. This wasn't *my* or *our* doing. I refused to feel guilty over *his* actions, his wrong-doing.

"All I have are my student loans from med school. I don't have any other debts. All my plastic gets paid off with each statement. I even manage to save a good portion of my income."

One of the perks of this job was free room and board. Sure, additional snacks, sundries, and clothing expenses came out of our pockets. But that applied to him too.

"I live well within my means which is sure tighter than yours, David. Sure, we might get paid peanuts working for Global Medicine, but we, at least I, don't do it for the bucks," I told him. "That isn't what the program's about. We knew this going in."

"Do *you* have other debts?" I had asked.

He shouldn't. David's trust fund took care of everything. College, car... He even lived in a swank apartment in Chicago, also courtesy of said trust fund. David loved quality clothing, but what he took in from his regular practice as a plastic surgeon was more than adequate to cover it and the lifestyle he chose.

His hesitation scared me. "Tell me, David. I need to know it all," I had urged.

That was when he came totally clean. Evidently the David I knew was not the person I thought he was. Seems David liked gambling. Indulged in it a *lot*. A closet gambler. Those conferences he'd told me he attended? Gambling jaunts.

Unfortunately, David wasn't as good at cards and the roulette wheel as he was with a scalpel. Luck had not been a lady to him. It had been one mean, fucked-up bitch. Another problem—David didn't know when to quit.

To pay off his gambling debts, he borrowed money from some shady people. He didn't want his family to know. Typical. As if that wasn't worse. There's no figuring out stupidity born from desperation and addiction. Habits being what they are, he didn't quit. Instead, he got deeper into debt until repaying what he owed became nearly impossible along with the mounting interest accruing on that substantial debt.

Through all this, did he seek help for his addiction? No! He continued and even increased his frequency at the casinos and the size of his bets.

Out of desperation, he said yes when approached with a deal to smuggle drugs or other illegal contraband. He planned to do this until all of his debt plus interest was paid off. He was just now realizing that the first time he said yes to any shady shenanigans was the moment he had sold his soul. There was no going back. "No" would never be a word he could say again, ever.

"David..." I had said, mournfully. I buried my face in my hands. What was there to say?

∞ ∞ ∞

I lean down to insert a finger between my ankles and the zip tie that binds them.

"*Ah ah ah*, Dr. Angel," George warns menacingly.

"What's the bitch doing now?" Peter barks.

"She's fiddling with her ankle ties, boss," George tells him.

"Hey asshole, it's too tight. It's cutting off my circulation. Look." I indicate my lower limbs. "My feet, ankles, and calves are starting to swell and discolor. If this keeps up, I'll not be walking down the aisle or anywhere," I retort.

"George..." Peter huffs with irritation as he rubs his fingers on the spot between his eyes.

George takes that as permission to belt me one. My head snaps back from the blow across my cheek, plowing me heavily into the seat. I bring my likewise bound hands up in a defensive move, dabbing at my split lip. My tongue flicks over the wound. I can taste the metallic flavor of blood as it begins to bleed.

"Watch your mouth, bitch," he growls. He pulls back as if to strike another blow.

"What the fuck, George!" Peter admonishes. "I didn't mean belt her one. Christ almighty, I meant cut her bindings."

"Boss?" George questions, but puts down his cocked hand.

I breathe a sigh of relief. I've already received many cuts and bruises from these brutes.

"Cut the fucking bindings, George. There isn't anywhere

for her to go," he says.

"But she's an Angel, a seraphim angel," George says. "Maybe she's got wings hidden under that dress of hers. When we aren't looking or least expecting it, she'll jump from the plane and simply fly away," he chuckles darkly. He gives me the once over, looking me up and down, winging his eyebrows the way a wolf appreciates the lamb he is about to slaughter.

Frank shakes his head then huffs out a bit of a laugh.

Peter just gives him the stink eye as he pauses in his flight-long communion with his cellphone. To my relief, George takes out his pocket knife and severes my bound ankles. He shakes his head *no* when I hold my wrists out for the same.

At least my ankles are now free. Closer examination reveals that the plastic of the zip tie has cut into my flesh, making deep furrows and scratches. Purplish skin indicates there is some bruising along with the bleeding. But finally I can feel the blood begin to circulate. I rub the sore areas, moaning silently in relief.

I close my eyes hoping it will make me less airsick. It will at least keep me from having to look at these thugs and worrying about what's to come. God, I've never been so scared in my life.

Before David came to me with his unique problem, I figured it was my role to stand by my man. I believe in that vow of 'for better or for worse.' When engaged to be married, that vow was implied before the final "'I dos'." This had to be the worst. If our relationship endured this then it could pretty much handle anything.

Wow, was I naïve!

My sister Faith says our natural naiveté, or gullibility, is somewhat derived from our parents never permitting us to watch television. We never had one in the house while we were growing up. What did we do for entertainment? We played, read, listened to music, and spent lots of time in the great outdoors.

Camping was a cheap and common weekend or holiday event. Dad taught all his Angel babies how to fish and hunt and survive in the wilderness that was our land or in a national park. He wasn't a prepper, but he wasn't far from it. He was a farmer.

If I hadn't gone into medicine, I might have studied botany as did my sister Grace or gotten a degree in conservation and wildlife management like my sister Heavenleigh. Faith, another sister, is an environmental engineer. My other sister, Precious, is a farm-to-table chef who owns her own restaurant preparing meals with produce and protein she and Grace raise and grow on the family upstate New York farm. The farm has been in our family since the first Angel arrived.

When on leave from Global Medicine I took the opportunity to spend time with my other sisters. It was also a chance to earn a bit more money by modeling. Now, I'm no Twiggy or Kate Moss. Next time your thumbing through a wedding magazine, take a closer look at the bridal gown models. You'll see very few of them are your typical runway model. Sure some are skinny but most have meat on their bones and curves.

Gals with a noticeable bust and curves look best in bridal photos. With my long natural-blonde loose-curling hair, fair complexion, and blue eyes, I was a natural. Or so Henri told me when he spotted me when I was barely sixteen.

Henri, a photographer for a bridal designer, "discovered" me when I was having dinner with my parents. He gave my parents his business card. Mom and Dad talked about it for days before discussing it with me. Mom made an appointment with the agency Henri suggested and next thing I knew I had a new source of income. My parents made sure I deposited my earnings in an account reserved for my college fund.

It's amazing how the threads of one's life that seem so disconnected from one another finally come together. This is what happened and eventually brought me to where I am now. Odd how my side job as a bridal gown model, my relationship with my fiancé, combined with my medical work would lead me to this point.

I snort, earning odd or quizzical looks from George and Peter. Mentally I chastise myself for drawing their attention. I need to better school my thoughts.

Once again, my mind wanders back to the events that brought me to this point.

∞∞∞

"David, the only way to make this nightmare go away is to wake up. You need to go to the authorities. The longer you delay the greater the chance that either you'll get caught or that this...Peter guy will come after you," I told him.

"Neither option is appealing," David whined.

"What did you expect?" I challenged in return. "You broke the law. Not only did you break the law, but you're involved with drug lords, organized crime. What about all this doesn't tell you this was a stupid thing to do?"

David hung his head cradling it in his hands. He moaned and cried. Yeah, he actually shed tears. Thing is, I wasn't sure if the tears were out of fear, regret, or atonement. I think they were just a part of his selfish nature that was more and more coming to light.

Though I was worried and definitely scared for David, pity was something I lacked. It was like I was seeing a different person, one that I neither knew nor particularly liked, let alone loved. My heart squeezed painfully. It felt like I was in mourning, like learning my lover was dead. For all practical purposes, my relationship was clearly coming to an abrupt end.

"What am I gonna do?" he whispered sorrowfully.

"You need to go to the authorities. Contact them now. The sooner the better. You can tell them that you weren't thinking straight due to your gambling addiction, get some help for that and throw yourself on the mercy of the court and the medical ethics investigative team. You may lose your license to practice but you could always teach," I reasoned.

David gave me a face that let me know he didn't like my idea.

"How about going to your contact person on a bent knee, saying something like…oh, I don't know…how about, 'Mr. Badguy, I've changed my mind. Though I really want the money, I've thought it through and think working for you is wrong and totally out of the question. So here are your drugs back and instead I'll send you monthly instalments to repay my loan'."

"Seraphima, that isn't funny. This isn't a joke," he thundered.

"No shit, Sherlock." That got me the stink eye.

"But seriously, what'll happen if you tell this creepy bad guy that you've changed your mind? Then go to your dad and tell him all and see if he won't loan you the money. Maybe he has connections and know how that will help you out."

"Are you crazy?" he stormed. "For starters, if I tell my contact thanks but no thanks, I'm dead. Dead! If he doesn't kill me, he'll have someone do the dirty work for him. If by some chance he says yes, my dad will kill me," he screamed.

Yup, soon I would be in mourning. I already was at that point. I could wear black for a full year. I could do it.

"So either way you're toast. Either jail and lose your license or die. Those are your choices," I summarized.

David just looked at me. "Some help," he finally mumbled, causing me to open my eyes wide on a number of things.

Screw Tammy Wynette when she sings that shit about standing by your man. David might have put a ring on it, but, baby, I could damn well take it off and toss it right back in his friggin' face. Where was *I* when he was having his fun? Did I or us even register when he was out indulging himself? Did he ever stop to think about what he was doing to me? To us?

"Okay, here," I said, unscrewing my engagement ring from my finger and handing it out to him.

"What's this?" he demanded darkly.

"Pawn it. The cash can go toward repaying your debt. Until this matter is cleared up, I am not going to marry you."

"You're breaking up with me?" he asked, incredulous. "I'm going through some rough shit and your response is to make it worse by breaking up? Seriously, you're just going to walk away?" he demanded.

"Making me feel guilty isn't going to work, David. Truth is, I don't love you anymore. The man I fell in love with, is not the person who is before me now. I want to find that other David. If he's gone for good, I need to get to know the new David before becoming his wife and living the rest of my life with him." On this I was firm.

David just looked at me, thunderstruck.

I waggled the ring at him until he reached out and took it none too gently, nearly ripping it from my hand. He looked at it and then slipped it into his pocket. Yeah, just what I thought, selfish jerk.

"You cut me deep, Seraphima," he said in a hoarse voice.

"Answer me this, David. Have you quit gambling?"

"Huh?"

I crossed my arms. It was my "I'm not taking any of your bullshit" position. I could see his neck starting to turn red. Damn.

"When was the last time you gambled?" I rephrased the question.

His hesitation was answer enough.

"I know you and some of the guys got together last night. Care to enlighten me as to what you did?" I asked.

"What? Now you're my warden? I gotta check in with you so you can keep tabs on me?" he scoffed.

"Do I?" I challenged. "Cause, David, if I do then this relationship is ended for keeps."

Silence.

"David?"

"Don't you trust me?" he weedled.

"Seriously? You're asking me that? David, I *know* what you did. Others were with you. Robert sent pictures from his cell to Bethany and she showed them to me." I snorted in disgust when he gave me that fish-face blank surprise look.

"I think you're sick, David. You're not thinking straight. You're in a serious situation with no easy outcome and your answer is to continue doing the exact behavior that got you into this mess? David, are you an idiot or is this suicide by proxy?"

"What does that mean?" he demanded.

"David, what you are involved in can get you killed. You said so yourself. The fact that you're still gambling and ratcheting up more debt tells me you want someone to stop you, and the only way is jail or death. I don't think you want to spend years behind bars so I assume you want death. Too chicken to do yourself in, you are behaving in such a way to get someone to do it for you."

"Bitch," he muttered.

I arch a brow. "Hmmm. Well I'm not going to stand around and watch it happen. Consider our relationship over. I'm out of here." I turned toward the door.

David stepped in front of me, blocking me from the door. "Please don't go. Give me another chance."

His pleading almost did me in. Nearly caved. Love can make you stupid sometimes. It must have been the grace of God, but I was spared that time.

"David," I breathed out wearily. "If you want me in your life then you need to do the right thing..."

"And turn myself in," he finished.

"Yes. I won't be in a relationship with a man who puts an addiction before all else, his career, his ethics, and his potential future wife."

"Okay," he relented with a whisper.

"Okay? Okay what?" I wanted him to say it plain, say it clearly. There could be no mistake in what he will do, what he meant. Tough love is really—tough. Not just on the one in peril but on ones administering it.

"You win. I'll turn myself in."

I let out a breath of relief and closed my eyes hoping that some of my topsy turvy world will right itself a bit more.

"How do I begin?" he asked.

"Well, I think we start by going and speaking with Dr. Anderson." Dr. Anderson is the man in charge of our team. "He should be the first to know and then with his advice, we'll take it from there."

"Are we back together now?" he asked.

"Nope, not until this is alllllll cleared up. You are just getting started," I told him.

This was in fact the beginning of the end, a very quick end. I could see images of guillotines in my head. Sharp, with an edge, and lethal. Chop and it's all over.

As I expected, Dr Anderson didn't like what David had to tell him, but it was better coming from David than finding out that the floating medical ship was routinely being used to smuggle illegal drugs than from...say the authorities or the representatives from the drug cartel. I imagine a sting operation wouldn't be any better.

Dr. Anderson directed his fury at David peppering him with numerous questions. He, the captain of the ship, and the head of security all accompanied David to where he said the drugs were stashed. I was ordered to remain in Dr. Anderson's office. I complied. Didn't move a muscle. Didn't get out of the chair.

When it was confirmed that the heroin was indeed on board, Dr. Anderson allowed his disappointment to seep through his rage. His display of disappointment was the killing blow, more so than the anger. In a chilled but grim voice, Dr. Anderson and the head of security confined David to his cabin posting guards at his door. All his electronics were confiscated and his cabin thoroughly searched. Then they made the needed contacts with organizational and government agencies.

Within the hour, we had changed course and were headed to Miami. Agents from the FBI, DEA, and the Justice Department would be there waiting. Word spread rapidly throughout the ship. Not a surprise.

"And what is your involvement in this, Dr. Angel?" Dr. Anderson asked, once he was back in his office and was able to focus on me.

"I came as...moral support for David. He came to me with this...trouble. It was I who advised him to notify the authorities starting with you," I told him truthfully.

"I see you are no longer wearing your engagement ring." Pointedly looking at my hand.

"Correct." Twiddling my naked finger, rubbing on the whiter skin where the band once was. "I have ended my engagement with David. He knows my thoughts on his behavior and the situation he's gotten himself into. He needs to solve this before I can ever reconsider such a relationship with him. Ever. I can't marry a man that I don't trust. This David is a stranger."

Dr. Anderson grunts in response but I can see he agrees with my decision. I feel vindicated. It's so easy to feel guilty in such situations. In the end, it does nobody any good.

"You do realize that you could be...tainted by your association with David?" he asked carefully.

I heaved a sigh. "I understand that may be a possibility.

Guilty by association may be some people's attitudes, but I think I can stand proud and strong on my record. My fear is the damage that may befall Global Medicine and the good works that we do. Funding may dry up or become lean as a result."

Dr. Anderson also appeared concerned, nodding in agreement.

"Exactly. I've already contacted the head director of our organization. Maybe they can do some damage control or find a way to keep this from getting too public and too much coverage in the media spotlight."

The look he gave me had me worried. Was it pity? Regret? "Dr. Angel...Sera." He rubbed a hand over his face.

He had my full attention. I was hyper alert. This couldn't be good.

"It pains me to be the one to tell you... You have been such a wonderful addition to this team..."

"Just say it, Dr. Anderson," I told him softly. My stomach was clenching as tightly as my clasped hands I held in my lap. He sighed then nodded.

"Top brass wants you to take a leave of absence until all of this blows over." He couldn't quite meet my eyes before. Now he did.

I was stunned. I should've figured something like this would happen, but with everything else going on, frankly, it didn't even cross my mind. Doing what I did, working for Global Medicine, was my life's work, my life's purpose. I was doing what I had always dreamed of doing. Now it was in jeopardy. All I could do was look at him, not caring that the hurt and disbelief showed plainly on my face. Dammit! I was devastated. I could feel tears welling up in my eyes.

Dr. Anderson gave me a critical once over. He rose from his chair and came around his desk. Like a father, he drew me up from my chair by my arms and gave me a kind smile.

"I know this is sudden. I know this hurts and is horribly unfair. So far, you have done the right thing. You need to know that. Believe it." He gave me a wane smile.

"I'm going to be straight with you. Things will get a whole lot uglier before they get better. No doubt...no doubt, you will be questioned and re-questioned until you are ready to scream. At some point you might even want to think about getting a lawyer."

Oh my God, I never thought that I might be implicated and have to defend myself. This new shock took my breath away.

"A lawyer?" I gasped.

I collapsed into the chair. Hurriedly, Dr. Anderson dragged a chair up close and sat by me. He gently took my hands into his and patiently waited until I had regained control.

"Sera, listen to me," he said in his firm no-nonsense voice.

With a shuddering breath, I gave him my full attention. Even still I couldn't keep my lower lip from quivering.

"Sera, it was a good thing you did, advising David to turn himself in. He might not appreciate it now. Hell, he might never appreciate it. Truth is, you may have saved that boy's life. Now you need to think about yourself. You started doing that when you broke off your engagement. Nothing good ever comes out of sticking with a lowlife or weak-willed person like that," he said.

I flinched.

"I know that hurts," he acknowledged. "I'm sure you loved him, maybe still do," he murmured sympathetically.

I swallowed hard then shook my head. "I loved the old David. He's gone," I said, choking back a sob. "I don't know this person, this David. He's a stranger..."

"Put some distance between the two of you. Don't contact him and if he contacts you, don't engage him in conversation. Don't go see him. Hell, get a new cell number, get a new email address."

I nodded. Dr. Anderson was giving me sound advice. I would be an idiot not to heed it.

"Trust in the system. You have up to now. It won't fail you in the end. Keep your head on your shoulders and keep it raised high. You've done nothing wrong. Once the shit storm has died down, we can talk about you coming back as part of the team. I'll contact you when I hear things or need to let you know if anything changes."

I knew I was being dismissed. We rose together. Dr. Anderson stuck out his hand. Automatically, I did the same.

"It's been good working with you, Dr. Sera Angel. Hope to do so in the near future. I will always be honored to write you a letter of recommendation, if and when you desire it," he added.

"Thank you, Dr. Anderson. I have enjoyed being a part of the team and making a difference in the lives of others. I can't think of anything else I would rather do."

We moved to the door. Just as I was about to walk through I turned to him.

"You've taught me alot. I just want you to know, I will always be grateful for that. I pray this isn't a final farewell but a see you soon kind of moment."

He gave me a sad smile. "That is my fondest wish too."

Chapter 2

Sera

D r. Anderson called it right. As soon as we docked in Miami, a detail of federal agents boarded, more like swarmed, the ship. Everyone save for Dr. Anderson, the captain, and the head of security were required to remain in their cabins.

David was handcuffed and taken off the ship in record time. I'd not seen or spoken to him since the day he was ordered detained in his cabin. Strangely enough, I felt no remorse for my part, only sadness and no little amount of anger for the realization that his life was pretty much over and my work with Global Medicine was now at and. Where would life lead him? Me? No telling. At least, I still retained my liberty. Sincerely, I hoped the best for him. It wouldn't be easy.

Each member of the crew was questioned. Our cabins and luggage were thoroughly tossed and examined. Nothing was left unsearched or left unturned. Drug sniffing dogs were brought in to search the ship. They were looking for hidey holes. Couldn't say I blamed them. If there was one mule onboard, why not others?

And just like Dr. Anderson warned, I too was questioned onboard then taken into custody, though not in handcuffs, for additional questioning. When I was finally allowed to leave, my passport was seized and I gave them the address where I would be staying. I was told to keep myself available for the foreseeable future. They would be in touch.

In a daze, I went on my way. I booked a flight to Albany, New York and returned to the farmhouse I shared with my sisters, Precious, Grace, Faith, and Heavenleigh. Yeah, I know what you're thinking. How crazy were my parents when they picked the names out for their kids? Right?

Plenty of times, my sisters and I asked that same question. Sure, we knew our parents loved us, but people can be so cruel. Not all, but most of us got teased. Tormented. There were many days when we would come home from school in tears. Becoming adults hadn't stopped the taunts and off-hand remarks.

It taught us to grow a thick skin. We also learned the meaning of true friendship. My sisters and I grew closer and stronger for it. It was to them I turned to now.

We hugged each other enthusiastically when I walked through the door, surprising them by my unexpected arrival. It soothed me to see their gleeful expressions and when they leaped up and ran toward me with arms open wide.

"What are you doing home? We didn't expect to see you for months." Precious, the eldest, was the first to plunge in verbally and physically, helping me with my luggage.

"There was a change of plans. We docked in Miami three days ago," I told them.

"Three days..." Grace began then stopped, giving me a quizzical look. "Why didn't you come home sooner? Couldn't you get a flight?"

"Better yet, why didn't you call?" Pre asked, hands on her hips.

We sat down and I told them everything. As expected, they were stunned then they became angry. How wonderful to have people who love you so completely and have your back.

"Why that louse!" Grace seethed. "I'm glad you gave him back his ring. Asshole."

"What was he thinking?" Pre demanded, still stunned.

"Probably about his own damn self and his megalomaniac pleasures," Grace answered.

"How much of this shit is going to land on you?" Pre asked.

That's Pre, always zeroing on the point that many miss. Grace gasped, placing a hand over her mouth as her concerned eyes landed back on me.

"It's anybody's guess," I told them truthfully. "Could be nothing or more than I would ever suspect. I could lose my job with Global Medicine. I've been put on an indefinite leave pending the outcome," I said, getting choked up. That was the killer for me.

I loved what I was doing. To give that all up because of David... I didn't want to imagine it, couldn't. But I knew I had to face it. I don't think I could ever forgive him. How many more lives was he going to ruin before this is all over?

"Why would you lose your job over something awful that David did?" Grace asked.

"Tainted by association," Pre said. "People might think she was in on it but couldn't be nailed due to lack of evidence. Or that she knew but didn't speak up soon enough. She was his fiancée after all. Whistleblowers are rarely praised in public. Often they are made out to be worse than the villain."

"Global Medicine might get lots of negative media coverage. That could lead to a loss of funding donations needed to continue their work. They will want to distance themselves from David and anyone close to him," I said.

"Namely you," she surmised.

"Yep."

"What are you going to do until then?" Pre asked.

"Pick up a few modeling jobs if I can. See if they need help in one of the regional free clinics. Find another job." I shrugged.

"Well, not right away. You should take a week or two off and rest up. Then you can make plans," Pre advised.

"Yeah, I might take a couple days off, but I think if I keep busy I won't have time to think about stuff and indulge in self pity," I said.

"Well do what you think best, sis. Know we'll always support you. You aren't alone."

∞∞∞

Their words had been so comforting. The problem was that I didn't want any of my family to be harmed. I would do almost anything to prevent that. My gut clenches. If I were honest, it's more than the turbulence that is making my stomach twist and churn.

I had taken two days off. By the third, I found myself calling up my modeling agent and signing up for a series of photoshoots. I even agreed to take part in a runway show, something I normally don't do. In addition, I agreed to be on-call for private viewings.

Wealthier clients at times would rather view gowns on live models in a private showing than go to a runway show. It's a bit old fashioned, but not unheard of for an elite clientele with deep pockets who are willing to pay.

"Ah, *mon cher*," Henri greeted me upon entering his studio, kissing me on both cheeks. "How good it is to see you," he said, meaning it. When he picked up my left hand to kiss my knuckles, he took a step back. His startled eyes sought out mine in widening shock and dismay.

"You are not wearing your engagement ring," he exclaimed.

"No. The wedding is off. I broke up with David."

"How tragic for you," he exclaimed, clucking his tongue. "Was he naughty?"

"*Oui, très méchant*, very naughty," I replied. "Henri, *s'il-vous-plaît*, I would rather not talk about it, okay?"

"Poor, *mon petit*, you suffer from a broken heart." He tsked.

"Not really." Henri gave me a questioning look. "Let's just say, I saw a side of David that I've never seen before and it left me feeling dubious. I've learned that the man I thought I knew was not the real man," I said.

"The scoundrel played you false and now that he is revealed, he is not the man you desire," he summarized.

Close enough. I shrugged, not wishing to discuss it any longer. Thankfully, Henri took pity on me and moved on.

"You are here to work so let's be about it," he said.

I agreed wholeheartedly.

For me, it became a time to work and make money, a lot of money, by standing around in pretty garments. Three days a week, I donated time at a free clinic. It filled my days and helped me focus on other things besides David.

∞∞∞

Two weeks later I became convinced that I was being followed. I was not totally surprised. I had first suspected it when
I left the federal offices in Miami. Now I was certain of it. I'd
seen the same black car with darkened glass parked outside
my home along the country road. It reappeared outside the
clinic and when I was on location for photoshoots.

One day, as I walked toward a café where I was meeting
a friend for lunch, I noticed a car slowly following me. Just to
prove to myself that I wasn't imagining things, I got out my
cell phone and dialed my friend, told her that I had to cancel our lunch date and would explain later. I stopped walking
suddenly, then whirled around and went in the opposite direction.

Sure enough, the car quickly turned around and headed
back in an attempt to find me. I quickly darted into a shop and
watched from inside as the car drove by.

On another day, I noticed an odd man standing in the
free clinic. He just stood there. When I asked the receptionist
about him, she said that he had been there for quite awhile,
wasn't with anyone else, and hadn't asked for help. He always
seemed to become more alert when I made an appearance in
the waiting room or could be seen by the nurse's station.

Whoever they were, the whole thing was creeping me
out.

I was called back for questioning several more times.
Each time I had to go to New York City. I took the train instead
of driving, even then I thought I was being tailed. The last trip
in for questioning, I mentioned that I suspected I was being
followed and asked politely for them to confirm it. Of course
they didn't, but I suspected I was right by the silent communi-
cation I observed going on between agents. When one left the
room, just after I confronted them, I became less positive it
was them.

A photo of a very handsome dark-haired an dark-eyed man, flawless in features and form was placed in front of me. "Do you recognize this man?" I was asked.

"No. Should I?" I asked.

"Look again, Dr. Angel. Are you sure?"

"Positive. Who is he?" My question was ignored—or was it?

"Have you ever heard the name Peter Schlange?" I was asked.

"Schlange is German for serpent or snake," I murmured.

"That's right."

"Peter. I've heard the name Peter but not Peter Schlange. David said his contact person was a man named Peter. David was afraid of him. Afraid that Peter would kill him or have him killed. I got the impression that though Peter had some power, that he was not...how to say...the all powerful one," I told them.

"Dr. Angel, do you recognize this individual?" one of the agents asked, showing me a still picture of a tall and nicely muscular dark haired man. This man had a commanding appearance, one who was powerful and knew it. I studied the photo before giving them my answer.

"No. I've never seen this man before in my life. Does he have something to do with what David got involved in?" I asked. "Who is he? Is he someone important?" I pressed.

"His name is Luther Devlin. If he or anyone associated with him approaches you, you need to inform us immediately," the agent said, sliding me one of his cards.

"Okay," I said, taking the card and placing it in my pocket.

"So who is Luther Devlin?" I asked.

"Luther Devlin is an underworld leader of an organization known as Apocalypse Seven. They've been known to smuggle drugs and other illegal contraband and blackmarket items. We believe they are involved in money laundering, kidnappings, and assassinations. They have associates we suspect have infiltrated into governments and the military around the world, as well as international businesses," I am told.

"An organized international conglomerate focused on criminal activity of various sorts," I replied.

"Yes. Very organized. Very dangerous. With fingers in the pies of most of the illegal activity that has been a cancer on the civilized world. They have a huge network from which they operate."

"Why are you telling me all this?" I asked.

I was starting to get scared. My hunch had to be correct, but I wanted one of them to say it. I needed to hear it.

"This is the organization and the man with whom David became embroiled with," the agent confirms my fear.

It took me a few minutes to process what he said. Again, on some level, I wasn't surprised, yet hearing it was another matter. I closed my eyes. As if this nightmare couldn't get any worse. It has.

"Do I need to be worried? Am I in danger? Is my family in danger? Could this guy be having me followed?" I had so many questions.

"It's always best to be cautious. We never know how this guy thinks. I wouldn't be surprised if he has information on David and what's going down. He would be interested in learning what more you know that isn't already on file. The fact that you are no longer David's fiancée is to your advantage," the agent said.

Another agent pursed his lips and looked long and hard at me. It was making me nervous.

"Dr. Angel, I want you to be aware that David isn't very happy with you. He has been saying a lot of...harsh things about you..."

"He's blaming me for the predicament he placed himself in?" I was incensed. Strange how anger can dry up one's fear.

The agent nodded.

Placing both hands on my chest, I asked, "Did I do the right thing? Was it wrong advising David to turn himself in?" I asked. "I don't see myself as a hero, but I'm no coward. I couldn't be party to what David was doing. If he hadn't followed my advice, I would have turned him in myself. I was not going to get myself entangled in such activity. Now it seems that I am more caught up in it than ever."

"Dr. Angel, you did the right thing. The mess David is in is entirely his own doing. His behavior is typical of people with addiction issues who find themselves on the wrong side of the law as a result of poor choices. It's not uncommon for them to blame others for their plight. They usually blame those who had a hand in making them face their errors and taking the first steps toward a lawful or meaningful resolution. Currently, he's receiving counseling and being monitored by an array of specialists. Don't blame yourself for what David has done."

"Believe me I don't," I said with conviction. "But I am becoming frightened. Not only am I concerned for my own safety but for my sisters and others that I serve and work with," I told them passionately. "What do I do about that?" I asked, truly seeking guidance.

"Have patience. Live one day at a time. Soon, either David will take a plea deal or he won't. If there's a trial, a jury and judge will decide the matter and it will be over, for you, at least. Afterwards, you get your life back."

It all seemed so simple laid out like that. Even then, I had a sneaking suspicion that it was a bit more complex and daunting than that.

Chapter 3

Sera

"It's a very exclusive client, cher," Henri told me. "Our client wishes for a private viewing, but not just a simple viewing done in a private room in a boutique. Oh, no. Oolala, he wants to see his selections as they would appear in a real church."

"You're kidding," I exclaimed.

"It is the truth, I tell you. I swear to you. The client is paying for his wedding. His lucky fiancée shall only have the best. They say she is most similar to your coloring and size. The lucky bride to be has seen several of your photos and has asked that you be the one to show the gowns. And since she desires it, so too does our client. He demands it and therefore our boss says do it," Henri said with a dramatic swish of his hands.

"We shall make the event an opportunity to shoot candid shots for the magazine as well." Henri looked critically at me. "Why so dour?" He patted my cheek. "Cheer up. It will all go well. The client will pay. His little bride will spread herself wide in appreciation for his generosity. In turn our boss will receive a large payment for the exclusive service and so shall we be handsomely compensated. All are winners here," he declared.

If so, then why did I have an odd feeling in the pit of my

belly? I rubbed the spot hoping it would relieve the tension that's knotted within.

"Who is this gazillionaire?" I asked.

"That is part of the mystery. He shall not give his name though his credentials are impeccable. Our boss says it would be suicide to deny such a request as this."

Two days later, I found myself in a side room in the beautiful Cathedral of the Immaculate Conception getting readied for the private showing and photoshoot. Five dresses had been pre-selected and I was to model each one and sashay down the aisle, stand in front of the altar, kneel before rising and turning around, in a mock wedding ceremony before repeating the process with each dress or until the client was satisfied and the bride-to-be said yes to the dress or the client had enough. Whichever came first.

For this I would receive the handsome sum of two grand. I hadn't slept at all the night before. There was something about this showing and shoot that didn't sit well. It didn't help my nerves when I discovered that the client was to remain behind a screen. Evidently this guy was uber sensitive about revealing his identity.

The third dress I tried on was an elegant off the shoulder flounced organza ball gown with a veil or cape that attached at the shoulder. When the wind picked up the gauzy veil causing it to flutter to the side or behind the bride like wings, it made the bride look like an…

"Angel. You are a stunningly pure angel. All white and light. It's as if you truly have iridescent wings," Henri praised as he snapped photo after photo.

When I got to the altar, I heard someone calling me from the right. I turned toward the voice.

"David!" I exclaimed.

Surprise and bewilderment had to be evident on my face. I couldn't believe my eyes. There he was moving quickly and carefully from the shadows into the light that illuminated the altar.

"Wh-what are you doing here?" I asked, stunned.

"Some...associates helped me get here. They knew it was my wish to see you as I have always wanted you. As my bride." He gave me a smoldering smile. Somehow it seemed hollow, forced.

Yep, it really was David resplendent in a formal tux. What the...?

"Go to him, Angel. He is your lost love come back to life. He is here to wed you," Henri said, trying to stage the mood, to direct the photos he wanted.

I wasn't having any of it.

I took a step back. David's presence here was not a good thing.

Like a snake, he jetted out his arm, snagging my hand in a painful grip. Roughly, he pulled me to him.

"David," I gasped, "I don't understand." Desperately, I tried to pull away from him.

I sent Henri frantic looks hoping he would realize that this was no romantic fantasy come to life, but a horror story playing out. He needed to get out and call the police.

David grabbed hold of my arms, shaking me roughly.

"David, you're hurting me!"

"I'm hurting you? I'm causing *you* pain? This isn't anything like the hurt you caused me by turning your back on me, babe," he said, through his teeth.

I could see the tears of rage filling his eyes. A part of me thought that maybe he had gone mad.

"Can you imagine how it felt when you walked out? When you rejected me?" He roughly shook me again.

Still grasping my arms, he pulled me into him and leaned in until his mouth was near my ear. "Do you want to know what I kept thinking all the time I was locked up in that concrete cell? Huh? Do ya, babe? I kept thinking of other solutions, other ways out of the mess. And then I realized, I do have something that might satisfy the man I owe all that money. That I could make a deal and hand it over and everything will be put to right. I would be free."

"What are you talking about, David?" I frantically asked, struggling to be free of his painful hold. Whimpering when his hold tightened painfully.

I could see that Henri was finally realizing that something was wrong. He began to walk away, pretending he was taking photos but really trying to escape.

"Go!" I said in a raised voice. "Help, you need to get help." Attempting to remain calm, but speaking in a loud voice that would carry. Though I directed my words to David, they were meant for Henri, hoping he would realize that I was really speaking to him.

David looked at me as if he were momentarily confused.

"How did you get out?" I asked, trying to distract him.

"I traded my greatest treasure for my freedom. But I wanted to see you one last time in the way I had always dreamed. Here at what should be our wedding," he said.

"What was your greatest treasure?" I asked, confused.

I was really getting nervous as I was seeing men in black suits who were silently approaching, quickly moving into position around us. Who were these guys? What the heck was going on?

Quickly, he spun me around, pressing my back into his front. One of his hands went around my throat and the other around my waist. My breathing was rapid and shallow. My fear was escalating. He placed a moist kiss on my cheek.

"You were my greatest treasure," he said in my ear.

I blinked in confusion, picking up on the past tense.

"Now, you belong to him," he said, directing my gaze toward the man who emerged from behind the screen.

I'd seen that face before, but only in a photo. A photo shown to me by the FBI.

Luther Devlin.

"Hello, Seraphima," Luther Devlin said in a wickedly seductive voice. "For some time, I have wanted us to meet, and now we have," he said, spreading out his hands and giving me a brilliant killer smile.

The man was indeed handsome. Even more so in person. But I knew that his physical beauty masked an ugly soul. Did he realize that I knew a bit about him and his exploits? I remained silent.

"Oh, how precious. She's shy," he simpered.

I looked from Luther over my shoulder to David. Devlin must have figured that I was still a bit confused.

"I know this can be a bit overwhelming, my dearest. It really is all very simple. You see, David here had another idea than the one you advised him. He proposed a trade, you for his freedom," he said.

"How do you know about me?"

"Ah, David did not tell you? He and I have met before. In fact, I invited him to my home on more than one occasion. In repayment of some of his debt, he performed some plastic surgery on my mistress at the time. When he was there, he saw she was looking through a few of those bridal magazines women like," he explained.

"She was constantly hounding me to wed her. As if I had any desire to do that." He laughed darkly and shook his head. "Well, I let her indulge herself in her little fantasy until it no longer amused me. When David saw the magazines, he pointed you out. Told us how you, in addition to being a doctor, also modeled on the side." A faraway gleam entered his eyes.

Suddenly, I found myself captured by those dark eyes, unable to break their hold.

"When I saw that picture of you in that bridal gown, I knew I had found my mate. I simply had to have you. And to learn that you are yet unspoiled... I took it as a sign that you were destined to be mine. *Mine*." The possessiveness of the word left no doubt he meant what he said.

"When David proposed the deal, I had no choice but to say—yes. Yes to the dress, and yes to the woman wearing the dress. My own sweet angel," he said, pressing a manicured hand to his chest while giving me another dazzling smile.

I found myself being spun around to face David. "And I get the honor of bestowing the first kiss on the lucky woman. A farewell kiss," he said, before grinding his lips on mine.

I didn't respond but held myself stiff in his arms. A pop echoed throughout the cathedral seconds before I felt David jolt. Warm crimson liquid splashed over the white dress I wore. Blood. Then David was slumping heavily into me before crumbling at my feet.

David had been shot. Blood was pooling on the marble floor and being absorbed in the hem of my gown. Instinct had me kneeling beside him to check his pulse and his wound. No sooner had I begun to move, I was hauled back up and to the side. Peter.

"Why? We had a deal," David wheezed.

Very calmly, Luther Devlin sauntered over to David. Pulling a mint from his pocket, he carefully unwrapped it and plopped it in his mouth while examining David.

"The deal was the woman for your freedom. You got your freedom. The cost for kissing what is mine? That is your life."

Devlin placed a foot on David's body, pressing down to extend the pain David was feeling. David groaned, biting his lip before screaming in agony.

"Nobody touches what's mine and lives. Nobody betrays me. This is the cost," he said.

Devlin pulled out a gun, cocked it then aimed it directly at David's head. "Your debt is now paid in full," he said then pulled the trigger.

Before I could scream, Peter clamped a hand over my mouth. My arms were seized so I couldn't run away. Tears were running down my cheeks, I was shaking with fright. When the hand left my mouth I pressed my lips together.

A muffled pop, another gunshot, sounded from the direction of the vestibule I'd been using as a changing room. When another of Devlin's men joined us soon after, I closed my eyes, understanding what that meant. Poor Henri! No help would be coming. What would this wretchedly evil man do to my sisters if he could so callously murder David and have his henchmen do the same to Henri?

Luther Devlin turned his attention on me. "Make this a lesson," he said. "This is what results when one betrays me. What you need to understand is that you are now mine. You may not believe it nor want it. But this is the way it is and will be for some time."

Taking out his pocket handkerchief, he wiped my mouth clean. He held me still by placing his hands on either side of my face. Then he kissed me, passionately. Neither did I resist nor respond. When he pulled away, he carefully studied my face.

"I will delight in teaching you how to please me," he said before stepping back.

With a snap of his fingers, Peter stepped forward. "We go now. You know what to do. Make it so," Devil ordered.

Turning back to me, he said, "Peter will take you to your new home. Do not be naughty, pet. He shall not harm you for you are mine, but neither shall you misbehave. If it is reported you have done so, I shall see you punished. It may delight me, but it will not be so enjoyable for you. Or maybe it will. Hmmm. We shall see." He winged his brows before disappearing into the shadows of the cathedral.

Before I knew it, I was being ushered out by Peter accompanied by his men George and Frank.

"Where are you taking me?" I asked anxiously.

"You heard Mr. Devlin. We're seeing you home, your new home, Angel," Peter said.

Before I knew it, I was being ushered down the aisles and out of the cathedral. Frantically, I looked about trying to search for help, a means to get free. Nothing. No people. No help.

Peter pushed me into the back seat of a car. George slid in on the side while Frank got behind the wheel and Peter rode shotgun. I think I was in some sort of shock. Next thing I remember was a cloth being pressed over my nose and mouth. The smell of chemicals hit me before I felt dizzy.

Chloroform. Then it all went dark.

∞∞∞

How and where did I get onto the plane? I don't know. I don't remember. Where are we headed? That too is a mystery.

From what I can see through the small window, there are mountains. Only a very few lights are visible. I take that to mean that we're not near any major cities or towns. Must be farms or ranches, small rural communities. Lightning illuminates the clouds. Its flashes allow me to see more than what the night reveals.

I keep looking, hoping to identify any kind of marker that will tell me where we are, where we are headed, besides into the west.

A sudden loud bang causes me to yelp and the guys to curse. George grabs the arms of his seat in a death grip. The plane shudders and shakes ominously. The guys are instantly alarmed.

"What the fuck?" Peter exclaims as he baubles his phone at the same time reaching to grab hold of something to keep from being tossed about.

"We've been hit by lightning," Frank grits out. His face is grim when he tosses a glance at Peter.

From my position in the back seat, I can see weird flashing lights on the control panel before they all go out. It's as dark as pitch both inside and outside the plane.

"Damn, it fried the electrical systems." Frank curses.

Peter manages to turn on his cell. It's blue light eerily illuminates the interior.

A quick glance over at George shows that he has turned deathly white. Guess he isn't much of a flyer. I begin to laugh, which instantly creeps the guys out. That only serves to make me laugh all the harder.

George and Peter start yelling at me to stop. George belts me one. I switch to humming and singing. Frank is still testing the systems seeing what is operational and what is not. I have a feeling we're flying blind. I can feel we are dipping lower. Maybe Frank wants to fly under the storm.

"Here," Peter says to George, passing him a cloth. "Shut the bitch up."

Even Peter looks uneasy.

Before I know what's coming, George pins me down and presses the cloth over my nose and mouth. My survival instinct kicks in. I begin struggling, kicking, flailing my arms, scratching at George in my bid to be released.

"When you stop struggling is when I know you've had enough," he taunts maniacally.

Chloroform. Again.

Gradually, my body slackens. I feel the tension leave my body as the chemical takes over. I hear Frank calling mayday but getting no response. Paul is cursing and frantically trying to reach someone on his cell. Doesn't appear he's having much luck either.

In the near distance, a side of a mountain looms up ahead.

"Pull the damn plane up," Peter is screaming.

"What the fuck do you think I'm doing?" Frank replies. Panic laces his voice.

I feel my body going under.

"This is it boys," someone shouts.

Maybe this is a blessing. If I'm to die this way, maybe it's better to not feel it when it happens. That's my last coherent thought before everything goes dark.

Chapter 4

Sera

Now I know people have heard of the Bermuda Triangle. Who hasn't? But have people ever heard of the Nevada Triangle? Didn't think so. Not many have.

The Nevada Triangle is a 25,000 mile area in the Sierra Nevada Mountains located between Reno, Fresno, and Las Vegas, located in both Nevada and California. It's also where Area 51 is located. Who hasn't heard of *that*? Am I right?

Evidently, in the past six years roughly two thousand aircraft have gone missing when flying over the area. Most have never been found or recovered, including craft and crew. Some chalk it up to UFOs or the US Air Force's continual experimentation on aircraft and defense systems. Others say that the area is rife with air turbulence and when combined with the uneven terrain, can make flying over the area a hairy venture for even the most experienced pilot.

I've always wondered if our crash was bad luck, happened just by chance, or divine intervention. In hindsight, I can't help but wonder if miracles actually do happen. What really dictates our life's course, our life's journey?

So why am I telling you all this? Seems this is where the plane carrying me crashes.

∞ ∞ ∞

A coppery taste is in my mouth. The smell of burning wire, plastic, and fuel fill my nose. The sounds of someone moaning fill my ears muffling all other noise. It takes me awhile to discover that the noise is coming from me. Slowly, I open my eyes.

I'm alive.

I feel giddy. Abruptly, I come back into my head.

This isn't a time to lose it, I tell myself.

The sky is getting lighter. Must be morning. If I find the sun, I'll know the cardinal directions.

That's right, Sera, I tell myself. *Keep thinking. Use your head. Don't panic.*

Gingerly, I move my head. No extensive pain registers, though my head throbs. A slight touch to my temple and my fingers come away sticky. Blood. Must have been cut. There is more on my chin and neck. If this is the worst of my injuries, I'll take them and be glad.

Cocking my head, I listen, trying to determine if I'm the only one left alive. Though I don't hear any noise beyond the crackling of a still smoldering fire, I caution myself to be alert. Then begin the process of assessing the state I'm in.

I detach my brain from my body and slip into my doctor mode. I don't want to freak out. This should help as I try to figure out what to do next. I discover that I'm still strapped in my seat even though the plane looks like it has collapsed around me leaving me in some sort of a twisted metal and fiberglass bubble of sorts. The nose of the plane is completely gone, like it has disintegrated. Some of the smell isn't just wire. I can see the smoldering remains of a body. Must be Frank. Poor schmuck must have died on impact.

There are no signs of Peter or George. At this moment, I don't know if they survived the crash or are dead. One thing is for sure, they aren't here. I unfasten my seatbelt. Finding a piece of jagged metal, I use it cut through the zip ties that still bind my wrists. Now, to get out of here. When I move to boost myself out of the seat, I scream out suddenly overwhelmed by excruciating pain. It takes a few deep breaths before the pain subsides long enough for me to think clearly.

I pull up the skirting of the dress. That's when I look down and see my left leg. It's at a strange angle. My leg is broken. No, not only is it broken, I've suffered a compound fracture of the tibia. The bone is sticking out through a jagged puncture and tear in the skin. Even though I'm a doctor, the fact this is me and my leg, makes me sick. I have to catch myself to keep from gagging. Don't want to cover myself, or where I'm sitting, in vomit.

Think, I order myself. *What must be done?*

Methodically, I go through the steps. Stop any bleeding as such injuries may have punctured veins. Best thing is to immobilize the leg without setting it, but I am more afraid of infection setting in as I don't know how long it will take to find help or if someone finds me. Besides, looking at the piece of bone protruding from my skin is realllly off putting. It makes me want to hurl each time I see it. My mind is playing tricks. Whenever I see it, I instantly feel more pain.

I've got to get out of here. There's nothing around that I think can help me set the bone. However I will need to prepare a splint. Looking around, I see wire and seatbelt straps. Both could come in handy.

I go for the wire first as it seems easier to tug free and with a bit of stretching I can just get a hold of some without moving my leg too much. I can snag lengths of it. Now I need something to cut it. A piece of jagged metal might do the trick. It does. Next, I test it on the seatbelts. Yep, it might take a bit more time but it works too. I cut my own then bundle all my stuff in one portion of the voluminous skirt creating a bag of sorts and hold the hem with my teeth.

After several tries and false starters, along with a lot of grunting and screaming, I make it up on my right leg and wobble-hop my way from the plane. Looking back at the wreckage, I can't believe I've survived. There's still no sign of George or Peter. Wonder if they got out okay or if their bodies are littering the side of the mountain.

I don't have time to worry about them. My leg requires my attention and it's screaming. I locate some right-sized pieces of metal that have snapped off the plane. Grabbing these, I hop toward a nearby stand of trees and scrub plants.

Each hop is jarring and sets my leg to hurting. I grit my teeth, biting down harder on the fabric stuck in my mouth. Forget stopping the tears that flow. My breathing comes in gasps. Finally, I reach my destination. Carefully, I lower myself to the ground and drop the gown from my mouth.

Closing my eyes, I allow myself some time to rest. Must have passed out. Suddenly, I find myself waking up. Though stiff and sore, I feel a bit more rested. A quick look at the sun tells me several hours have passed. The sun is well above the horizon, not yet mid-day but fast approaching.

After a brief pep talk, I grit my teeth and place the heel of my foot in the near ground level fork of a sturdy scrub bush. Using my body weight, I slowly pull backwards while stretching forward to use my fingers to assist my bone in receding into my flesh. It takes a couple of tries and then a couple more before I am satisfied with the bone alignment. This will have to do until I can get proper medical attention.

Dots start forming in front of my eyes. The additional lightheadedness tells me I'm about to pass out. Not totally unexpected. I lay down in anticipation and let the inky waves take me under once again.

The sound of birds chirping brings me to wakefulness. I roll to my side and vomit. Again, not unexpected. Ripping a piece of my skirt, I use it to blow my nose and wipe my mouth. Water. I'm going to need water. I make a mental note to look inside the plane. As I recall, the guys had brought some bottled stuff and traveling mugs of coffee or some other liquid. From the red hue of George's face, I surmised his travel mug might have a bit more than just coffee. Hopefully some of it has been left undamaged.

As quickly as I can and with a few breaks in between, I manage to bind and immobilize my leg in a makeshift splint. Again, I allow myself to rest before pushing myself back up. My plan is to make my way back to the plane, scrounge for anything useful then move back into my evacuated seat and settle down for the night with my leg elevated.

Tomorrow will be soon enough to make further plans. Besides, maybe by then I'll be rescued.

Chapter 5

Sera

The Sierra Nevada Mountains are beau-ti-ful. Absolutely gorgeous. The scent of pine and juniper makes the air seem fresh and clean and the elevation gives one a lightness not felt on lower elevations. It's late spring . Snow lingers in spots and on the higher elevations. Colorful wildflowers bloom in the expansive chaparral.

Chirping birds, the sunshine, a gentle breeze, and what you have is the recipe for paradise. Not a gentle, tame, hothouse sort of paradise, but a rugged yet beautiful Eden. Not a tame garden but an Eden nonetheless. It's a wilderness that is meant to delight and challenge those who have settled here and call it home, those who are willing to work alongside it, not conquer it.

Waxing poetic as I am, I have a lucid moment to feel my brow. Yep, just as I suspected. I've got a fever brewing. Not surprising as I'm sure more than enough dirt is lodged in my leg. I didn't give it a proper cleaning. Another wrinkle. I can't help but laugh albeit a bit hysterically. Time's going to be a factor. Quickly, I need to decide what I'm going to do. Really, I have only two choices. Do I stay or should I go?

First, I need to relieve my bladder. Afterwards I pop a few ibus I discovered in the remains of a first aid kit that survived intact. My scavenger hunt resulted in a variety of goodies I thought I could use: pocket knife, blanket, backpack with a shirt, clean men's underclothing, energy bars, oxycodone (seems someone was sampling the merchandise or was being treated for something), porn magazine. Yeah, I flipped through it myself all the while snickering, blushing, and scoffing as I went.

I would have tossed it aside but ended up keeping it when I found the lighter. The little portion of the plane that remained intact is enough to give me a bit of shelter and protect me from rain and wind. All in all, I decide that if I ration the food and water, I'm better off staying where I am then venturing through unfamiliar rugged wilderness. Sure, my family spent many vacation days and weekends camping and trampling through the great outdoors, but the Sierra Nevada was not one of those areas.

Besides, Dad always cautioned his daughters that if we ever got separated or lost in the woods, to stay put. "Remain where you are. Eventually someone will find you. The best staying put scenario would include some sort of shelter, food, and water." Check, check, and check equals staying put. Big check.

It's the waiting that becomes the problem. Sort of like waiting for Godot. Is the rescue team ever going to show? In such times, your mind can become your greatest enemy. I spend my time singing, flipping through the porn magazine, and reading the articles. I watch the birds to see if there is a pattern in when and where they flew. I had heard that in arid climates, birds tended to fly toward water twice a day. If that's the case and I have to leave this spot I now know in which direction I will head. But that isn't the plan. Staying put is what I will do and I'm sticking to it.

∞∞∞

It's true what they say about the best laid plans... It is two days later that all my plans go up in smoke, sort of like the pages from that porn magazine I used for kindling to my perverse satisfaction.

Not sure what woke me, except that the ambient sounds was different. I had gotten used to the sounds of nature that surrounded me. It became my new clock, the way I measured the day. Now, the joyful chirping of the birds are not to be heard. Silence reigns where there should be noise.

Cocking my head, that's when I hear it again. The snapping of twigs. Something or someone is taking careful steps toward the plane. The footfalls sound hesitant, but they seem to be getting closer. Excitement fills me at first, thinking I've been discovered, rescued. Tears pool in my eyes. Just as I'm about to call out. I snap my mouth closed and shut it tight.

A rescue team would not creep up on a crash sight. There would be hollering. People would be calling out to survivors and to each other. There's none of that. My mind races. Is it an animal or is it Peter or George or both? The thought that those two guys might still be alive and out there, has me hunching down to better conceal myself.

Fool, I admonish myself. If I need to get out fast, I need to be prepared.

As quickly and as quietly as I can, I stuff everything that I think I need into the backpack. I had already put on the socks and the pair of tennis shoes I'd found. Though the shoes are too large, I stuffed the toes with seat cushion filling. They'll serve me better than walking around in fancy high heels. Sure, they won't match my gown and all...but I am not on a fashion shoot just now. I smile at my own humor, making we wonder if I'm losing my mind.

I've created a crutch out of a length of a tree limb. It might come in handy as a weapon if necessary.

Before I attempt to flee, I decide it's best to figure what is out there. The snuffling and chuffing is my answer. A quick peek verifies it. Bear. It must have smelled the scent of barbecued human—what was left of Frank.

Yep, the bear uses its paws and claws to turn over and move bits of the plane to uncover what remains of Frank, then drags him out. I hear the *chomp chomp chomp* of its jaws as it feeds. At some point, it stops. Coming alert, it rises up on its hind legs to scent and scan the area. Apparently, it doesn't like what it's discovered. Securing a chunk of Frank's remains in its jaws, it moves off back into the safety of the trees and scrub.

Air releases from my lungs in a heavy *whoosh*. I hadn't been aware of holding my breath. Closing my eyes, I lay my head back in relief. It doesn't seem like seconds pass before there are additional strange noises. All my instincts tell me that these are humans, not animals. Shit. The need to run is almost too much to handle. The need to know what I may encounter outweighs my desire to flee. Forget the adage about the curious cat. Normally I'm not a rubbernecker, but in this case, I figured that I am better off with as much information as possible.

This time, I rise to my feet. I shift the backpack into place, covering it with the blanket I've fashioned like a poncho. Crutch in hand, I am ready to either fight or flee. Granted I'll be no gazelle, but I will have a fighting chance.

"Fuck it, Peter! Put me down." I recognize George's pained voice.

Damn, the two have somehow survived, though it sounds like George has been injured. That's all I need to make up my mind. Staying is no longer an option. I'm out of here. I'll find a place to hide and watch and wait. Then I'll decide my next course of action.

With that plan firmly in place, I maneuver out of my

hiding spot, ducking behind a boulder. With the coast appearing clear, I make my way behind a stand of pine, blue oak, and scrub that I think will conceal me until I can move a bit further away. A vantage point is what I need. Somewhere I can watch the crash site without being revealed. Unfortunately, there aren't a lot of options.

From where I hide, I can see Peter limping about the crash site. From time to time he bends down as if getting a closer look at something. Then he stands up and studies the area. Finally, he walks back to where George sits leaning up against a boulder.

"Whaddya got?" George asks through clenched teeth.

"I'd bet my bottom dollar that Devlin's new whore is still alive," I hear him say, kicking at the dirt and rock around his feet.

"What's the tell?" George asks.

"To start with, where the bitch sat is pretty much intact. If you and I survived, she must have," Peter said. He squints and begins looking around again, scanning the trees and scrub looking for anything that might tell him where I've gone.

"It appears someone's been camping inside too. Smart to stay near the wreck just in case Frank's mayday signal was received. We've been missing close to a week. Someone's bound to figure we're not around and come looking."

George grunts his response to Peter's observations.

"Devlin will want his pretty pet recovered. He'll send someone to find us," George says with confidence.

"Agreed. He won't like losing her so soon." Peter squints at the sky, rubs the back of his neck before hunkering down on the ground near George. "Some select things are missing," he informs George. George cocks his head, listening. "Your backpack, first aid kit, straps from the seats have been cut. Food and water—gone."

I can clearly hear the stream of curses coming from George.

"What about Frank?" George asks, peering over at Peter. Peter shakes his head. "He didn't make it. Not much of him left." George grimaces.

"Impact?" he asks.

Peter nods. "Fire and from the looks of the tracks, a bear got what was left."

George leans over puking out his guts.

"Jezzus, George!" Peter scrambles up on his feet. "How did you ever get to be a hitman and bodyguard when you have such a weak stomach?"

George spat then gave Peter a grin. "Guess I'm a sensitive guy deep down inside."

Peter gives him an appreciative laugh. "I'm going to look around a bit more. Keep your eyes peeled in case she returns or you see her. Either way, we'll rest up and see what can be done to find her. Believe me, our lives depend upon it."

"Our lives?" George questions, looking up at Peter. "Shit man, we just survived one hell of a storm and a plane crash. Are we still accountable for the cunt?"

"Yeah, we survived. There isn't a body to prove to Devlin that his new slut isn't dead. He'll demand verification—if we make it out of here alive. If we don't have her, live or dead, we might as well dig our own graves," Peter says.

"Devlin doesn't tolerate failure or being disappointed," George reasons.

"He surely doesn't," Peter agrees, as he walks off to continue his search.

∞ ∞ ∞

"Well, well, well. Look what we've got here." Peter's menacing voice wakes me instantly. He kicks my bad leg sending shards of pain through it. Instantly, I scream as I grab at it.

Both Peter and George are looming over me. Peter reaches down and viciously yanks me to my feet. The pain in my leg is excruciating. A guttural scream rips from my throat. I wobble, struggling to gain my balance on one leg. As I reach for my crutch, George punches me in my stomach. I double over and collapse on the ground. Drawing breath is a struggle.

The punishment doesn't stop. George keeps kicking me. It doesn't seem to matter where his foot lands so long as it makes contact with my body. My legs, side, belly, and back absorb the blows until I am curled into a tight ball of agonizing pain.

Peter grabs me by my hair, hauling me up on my feet again, only to backhand me across the cheek. The blow sends me flying, landing me hard on the ground. I'm so disoriented by this time that I'm barely aware of being dragged back to the wreckage that has become a makeshift campsite.

I feel something poking into my back. "Are you awake yet? Bitch, I'm talking to you. Are you awake?"

I moan in response. My body hurts from head to toe. One of my eyes is swollen nearly shut. My cheeks and jaw feel puffy. Bruises most likely cover most of my body from the beating I took. And I think I may have a few cracked, if not busted, ribs.

Of course, there's constant pain in my leg. Only now it's more pronounced. If the heat coming from my cheeks is any indicator, I think I have an infection. If I don't get help soon, I may be in serious trouble. Speaking of being in trouble...

I look over and see George and Peter. Screw the infection. I'm already in trouble. I close my eyes before pushing myself up into a sitting position, praying for at least one more miracle. A small flock of birds catches my eyes as they fly overhead. That and the gentle touch of the breeze on my feverish skin is enough of a sign. I must fly away. Escape is my only chance to make it out of here alive.

"May I have some water, please?" I ask respectfully.

George motions to the fire. There in the blaze is what's left of the burning plastic bottle. I look at him with a mixture of anger and incredulousness on my face.

"Why did you do that? Are you stupid or just dumb?" I ask.

George growls and takes a menacing step in my direction.

"Here we are, out in the middle of the wilderness and you burn one of the only useful containers for carrying water?" I angrily gesture toward the pooling liquid plastic.

Peter turns toward us upon hearing my words.

"Please, tell me you didn't burn them all?" From his guilty look, I've got my answer. *Blast.*

"Did you eat up all the energy bars too?" I level an accusing glare on the man.

From the look on George's face, the answer is an obvious yes. It's hard to hide my glee when Peter rips into him.

"Three weeks, buddy," I tell him, holding up fingers. "That's all the time you have until you die without water and food. It gets really miserable near the end to go out that way." I give him the evil eye. "I should know. Remember? I'm a doctor."

When he begins to launch himself at me to deliver another punishing blow, I shout, "Stupid, yet again. Another stupid move." At least it has him stopping.

"Whaddya gonna do, leave me here while you and him go off to find water? How are you gonna bring it back? Oh, take me with you? I already have one fractured leg. If I'm too weak to walk, are you gonna carry me? The longer you go without food and water, the weaker you'll get. Ever stop and think about that?" I mock.

I don't let up.

"Oh, guess not. You're such a city boy. You might be city-smart but you sure are country-stupid. If you keep acting before thinking things through, you won't last long enough to be rescued."

"We'll let you die and be a feast for the bears," he snarls back.

"Okay. And what are you going to tell your big boss man Devlin? That you didn't have the sufficient wilderness survival skills to keep a itty-bitty female alive?" I taunt.

"Shut up!" he screams.

Peter steps in between us, physically pushing against George.

"Go walk it off, George. Can't be angry with her when she's right," he says, earning a scowl from George. "You are an idiot," he sneers.

Peter watches George walking off in a huff, mumbling and cursing up a storm.

"And you," Peter says, turning on me. "You shut the fuck up. I don't want to hear anything more from your lips," he orders, pressing me back onto the ground. His nose nearly touching mine, he's so close.

"At this point, I think all I need to do is bring back your body. It will be you who decides if you remain alive or dead. If I think I got to kill ya, I might be tempted to discover just what Devlin found so...alluring about his angel. He'll never know. It will be our little secret. I sure won't be telling. And you? You'll be dead," he grounds out.

Before I can stop him, he presses his lips to mine. I fight and struggle against his hold.

"Behave or I'll be the one to see you punished," he says, giving me an evil grin.

When he too walks away, I curl up into a ball, blinking my eyes rapidly to fight back the tears that threaten to fall. My mind races. *What do I do?*

Suddenly I freeze. I've been left alone.

Both of those idiots are gone. Now is my chance. I might never have another opportunity. Looking around me, I locate the backpack and the blanket. With renewed energy and strong determination, I rapidly get to my feet with the crutch in hand. Quickly enough, the backpack is secured and the poncho-blanket tossed over my head. Purpose behind every step, I head in the direction I believe the birds indicated I'll find water.

Though I hurry, I make sure I am not reckless. Stumbling and falling would only slow me down. Steady will win this race. I don't even bother to sneak and hide. Putting distance between the wreckage and myself is my objective. Where I once would not have pried myself away from the downed plane, now I want to be as far away as possible. It's as if the spirits or the graces have either given me a cloaking device or have given me wings. All I know is that if and when I am recaptured by those thugs, they will see me dead. And I really want to live.

How I wasn't caught, is still a mystery to me this day.

Once I start walking, I don't stop. On and on I go, only resting a little at a time. When I find a little stream, I stop and drink my fill. Only then do I permit myself to sit and eventually lay down. When I begin feeling pain raising its ugly head, I pop another oxycodone that is still in the backpack. Marking the spot of the sun, I know I only have a little time left before it becomes dark. Drinking my fill and then some of the cold mountain water, I urge myself on.

Downhill is now my way to go. If I keep moving, I'm sure to run into something or someone that will see me to safety. Even when it starts growing dark, I keep on moving using the light of the moon to make my way over the uneven terrain.

Not until I stumble for the third time, do I call it a halt until it grows light once more. Noting a thicket of scrub among large stones and trees, I make my way there. As a Highland warrior of old, I take my broadsword of a crutch and use the straps of the backpack as a sheath. Balancing on one leg, I hop over to a tree with low-hanging branches that are reachable.

Using what I consider to be my last spurt of adrenaline, I manage to haul myself up and find a place to perch safely until the morn. The night sounds: the hooting of an owl, the howling of a lone coyote, the rustling of animals on the ground, are my lullaby until exhaustion overcomes me and I fall into a fitful slumber.

As the sun rises in the east, I search from my high perched vantage point, scanning the landscape for a direction to head. Making sure that I have not been followed. Encountering those two jerks is the last thing I want.

Off to the side I could see a wisp of smoke rising from the ground. Hope blossoms. Maybe it's a campfire. With excitement building, I scramble down from my perch and head off in that direction.

I've not gone far when the hair on the back of my head stands up. Slowly I turn around. Whimpering inside. No matter how many steps I took or how fast I walked, it wasn't enough. With my leg a mess and the pain that shoots through me with each jarring step, it would take me three or four just to match a single step taken by George and Peter. I have not been able to outdistance them. The evidence is standing not too far away.

They've found me, again.

Even after they spot me, we just stand there looking at one another like we're mirages. The promise of pain and death are written on Peter's face. George has the look of anticipation. Sick bastard.

For some reason I'm not so much scared as angry. I've become numb to most of the pain I should be feeling. It has become routine, a new baseline from which to operate and function. Death, however, is something I'm not ready for. Determination is my shot of adrenaline to not go down quietly. I will fight, fight to live.

With that in the forefront of my mind, I unwind the cord and bit of cloth wrapped around my wrist. All the while, George and Peter are moving toward me. They think that I've given up. Well, they're wrong. I'll be giving them a demonstration on just how wrong.

Picking up a rock I place it in the Egyptian style slingshot I fashioned days earlier. I kept it wrapped around my wrist so it would be close at hand. I made it for the purpose of hunting birds and rabbits, small game that could be easily killed with such a weapon and used for food. It works great for defense as well.

My dad had shown my sisters and I how to make them out of almost anything. He also taught us how to use it. When camping or in our backyard, we would often practice. Outside of hitting targets, I've used it on an angry dog that chased one of my sisters threatening to bite her. After I hit it a couple of times, it yelped and had run off. They also worked well on childhood bullies. I'd done that a few times in middle school. It's really satisfying to see a boy run home crying for his mommy, telling her that the local Angel girl had just walloped him. Yeah, Angels can sprout horns, wearing them proudly along with our halos.

When working with Global Medicine, I spent many delightful hours with Ethiopian children playing with home-made slingshots. Those times, we killed cans propped up on a wall. It had been a way to gain their trust and make friends. That will not be my purpose today.

Make it count, I tell myself. *No use in wasting a shot.*

With this in mind, I aim and hit Peter square in the middle of his forehead. His reaction is almost comical. Taking a step backward, stunned by the blow, a quizzical look comes over his face that nearly has me in stitches. He blinks hard and fast, shakes his head, wobbles, then falls to his knees before keeling over.

George is equally shocked. People have asked me why I went for Peter first. I tell them it was better to take out the brains of the pair. George is the brawn, mean and brutal. But he does stupid things. Often, he acts without thought. I count on him doing so again.

Peter is down for the count. And I really believe that George thinks that Peter is dead. George rises from checking Peter where he lays on the ground, blood oozing from his forehead. George's face has turned nearly purple in his rage. A menacing snarl erupts from him as he bares his teeth. Then he launches himself in my direction.

Without delay, I hurl a stone in his direction. It makes contact, causing him to flinch and falter in his steps. Quickly recovering, he shakes off the pain and continues to run toward me. Again and again I fling stones at him, each hitting their mark. They don't stop him like they had Peter, but they do give me time to duck into the trees.

My pathetic skip-hop-runs are no match for the rampaging George. What I need is another method to slow him down or stop him completely, if I'm lucky.

"I'm going to find you, bitch. I'm going to catch you. Do you hear me? Your ass is mine. When I get a hold of you, I'm going to fuck every hole in your body. Then I'm going to break your other leg and each one of your fingers before I break your arms. Before I am through with you, you'll be begging me to kill you," George roars.

I wind my way through the trees hoping it will slow him down, getting in a few more hits with the slingshot. It's more like poking a bear. They sting him but don't make him back down. If anything, they've managed to further enrage him. Not the reaction I'm going for. I've seen some of the damage on his face. I know some of the stones made contact with his chest, arms, and legs. He stops or slows down for a spell but he always keeps coming. Maybe that's why he's kept on as a heavy for Devlin. George might not be the brightest bulb but he's hard to take down.

Something needs to change. Something has to happen. My strength is quickly becoming depleted. I am not sure how much more I have in me before I collapse in a puddle of pain and exhaustion. Something grabs a hold of my blanket poncho.

"Gotcha," George crows triumphantly.

Letting out a scream that scores my throat, I push my head through the opening of my poncho-blanket. George curses as the pulling momentum lands him on the ground. While he seeks to gain his feet, I swing the backpack hard into his face, releasing it as he falls once again. Deeper and deeper into the woods I go, hurrying as best I can with my leg and the crutch.

George is back on his feet chasing after me. Pulling back on a low hanging branch, I let it go, snapping George in his face and chest. Instead of running, I launch my own attack. While he is still on the ground dazed from the whack to the face, I use my crutch to beat him about the head.

George kicks out his legs, swiping my good one from under me. I fall down heavily. The impact jars my broken leg sending up new waves of blinding pain. As I writhe in agony, he lands bodily on me pummeling me with his fists as he curses and screams.

All I can do is put my arms up in an attempt to ward off the blows that keep raining down. Suddenly he stops and I find myself straddled by him. My chest is heaving, my heart is racing, and my muscles are quivering. He's gonna kill me. I see the feral gleam in his eyes.

Pinned as I am, my efforts to buck and fight him off are useless. With one hand, he grabs me by the throat. With the other, he places a gun to my head. With a maniacal gleam in his eyes, he cocks the gun. I go completely still.

"Ah, I see I've got your attention," he hisses breathlessly.

This is it. It's all over now. The flashing of my life before my eyes is interrupted by a large form looming over George. He must have seen my eyes widen in surprise, for he looks over his shoulder.

Bear.

We must have crossed paths with a momma bear and her two cubs. I can hear their woofing, chomping, and bawls of alarma as they scamper up a nearby tree. Momma bear is none too happy.

George lets out a yell as the bear swipes an angry paw across his back. Now that George is more focused on the bear than me, I seize upon his momentary distraction. I take hold of his wrist with both of my hands and turn my head to the side as I twist the gun away from my head.

Automatic reflex has him squeezing the trigger. The gun fires. Instead of hitting me in the head, it hits my left shoulder. All I feel is the instant fire that comes in its wake. To all other sensations, I am beyond feeling. Numb. Survival instincts have kicked in. If I recoil now, I'll surely die. This is the final showdown. We both know it. One of us will come out of this alive. The other dead. I count myself lucky. I have a bear on my side.

George is torn between struggling with me and protecting himself from the bear. Taking my cue from the bear, I add my teeth into the mix, biting down on his wrist with enough force to break the skin. I delight in the yelp it elicits. The two pronged attack from two furious females proves too much for George. He relaxes his gun hand enough that I am able to point the gun away from me.

When the gun fires again and keeps on firing, the bear takes off with her cubs and I collapse with the dead weight of George pressing down on me. I kick and wiggle wildly until it triggers in some part of my brain that George isn't moving.

Though it's very difficult, I force myself to lay still. All my instincts are poised for fight or flight. With nearly what is left of my strength, I shove against his body pulling and pushing frantically until I have extracted myself from beneath him.

Bright red blood is smeared over my dress. How many days has it been? I am still dressed like a bride. It's clear that George is dead. One of the bullets has taken off half his face. Another pierced his chest. Nobody can survive such injuries. Still, I do the doctor thing and check for a pulse. Yep. Two down and one left, maybe.

For the moment, I feel safer than before meeting Devlin back in Albany. How crazy is that?

Okay, Sera, what are the facts? What do we need to do and how do we do it? I ask myself. Can't stop now. Gotta keep going.

Fact is, I'm still in danger. That has not changed, though the danger may be different, I still wasn't, no pun intended, out of the woods. I need to move on and find help. Obviously, help is not coming to me.

This isn't some fairytale where the princess sits in the castle tower waiting for her prince to come, bust her out, carry her away on his white horse, and marry her so they can live happily ever after. This is the real world.

Which means, I am no princess and it will have to be me doing the saving, the rescuing of myself. First though, I'll give myself time to rest. I needed one. Not all my body heat and increased delirium is due to running and fighting for my life. I'm burning up with fever. My left leg is swollen and has begun to turn colors and smell. Not a good sign.

Resting is an option taken out of my hands. I can feel the telltale signs again. I'm going under. The peacefulness of the darkness is claiming me once again. I welcome it.

Chapter 6

Gabriel Slayer

The storm that came through last night has me up early this morning. Well before the rise of the sun, I'm dressed and sipping my first cup of coffee. I hear a faint knock on the kitchen door before it opens and in walks my ranch foreman, Zeke Scriber.

I take out another mug, filling it with steaming coffee before handing it over to him.

"Saw the light on," he says by way of greeting. "Gotta hand it to ya, boy," he says with a wink and an appreciative shake of his head, "ya called it. That storm sure blew in and out like a whore on a timer."

I chuckle at his colorful words.

Zeke has been working here at Paradise Ranch since before I was born. Even when I was a youngster he looked old. Looking at him now with his slim build, slightly slumped shoulders, bowed legs, and scruffy grey scratch on his jaw, he hasn't changed.

Even that peculiar light in his blue eyes is the same. He has a way of measuring a person. It unnerves quite a few, but I'm used to it, having been raised right here on the ranch.

"Figured ya be up earlier than usual to check the fence line," he says as he sips his coffee.

"Figured right," I reply, saluting him with my mug of coffee. "Just heading out when you showed up."

"Got the boys up. Divided them into teams. One will go do a general check of the herd and another will go check the northern and eastern fence lines. Got a third that will go with us to check the western and southern lines, unless ya got another idea." He peers at me expectantly.

"Sounds good to me. Seems you got everything in hand," I say with respect. I give him a curious look. "Why did you reserve the western tract for us?" It would have been my choice as well, but I want to hear his reasoning.

He scrubs a leathery callused hand across the nape of his neck. He returns my gaze with a puzzled look. "Don't rightly know. And that's the truth of it. But I got this peculiar feeling in my bones that that is where we're supposed to be. Since I can't shake the feeling..." He runs a hand over his whiskery chin and jowls before running it around his neck once more.

The old timers put a lot of stock behind their intuition. They have accumulated so much experience that it gives them their own sixth sense of a sort. Not like they're psychic, but they do have an uncanny ability to simply know things and be right without specifics.

"Me too," I acknowledge. It earns me another once over.

Any further discussion stalls when a bleary eyed Elizabeth comes shuffling into the kitchen. Zeke turns beat red when he sees that she's finishing tying her robe together. I hide my smile behind another sip of coffee. From the way Zeke acts, one would think Elizabeth is walking in with nothing on but her birthday suit.

Elizabeth is another longtime resident here at the ranch. I've known her since before the passing of my mother.

My dad hired her as a cook, housekeeper, and nanny for me and my siblings. When I had two kids of my own, Daniel and Lailah, she stayed on helping to raise them when my own wife, Mary, died six months after giving birth to Lailah. That was five years ago.

"Sam Hill, Gabe, you're up early this morning," she yawns, helping herself to coffee and pouring more for Zeke. I shake my head when she goes to refill my mug.

"Stormed last night. Need to check the fences," I tell her.

She starts pulling out pans and stuff from the fridge. "Well, let me fry you up some breakfast before you go. Seems you're going to need your strength for what's to come today."

"Already made breakfast." I indicate the dirty dishes and pan still in the sink.

"Landsack, how am I to earn my keep with you doing my work yourself?" she exclaims. "Next thing I know, you'll be demanding I step aside and retire." The smile she hides behind her mug takes some of the aggrieved huff out of her words.

I place a kiss on her cheek, amused at how Zeke blushes even more and turns away uncomfortably.

"Hush, you know I'd never do a thing like that. Why, this house and the entire ranch would go to rack and ruin if you weren't here to supervise. And what about Daniel and Lailah? They'd turn into demons, both of them," I soothe.

That earns me an appreciative chuckle and a swat on my arm as she moves away. "True, true," she says.

Speaking of demons, in comes my two children. Rubbing the sleep from their eyes. Still in their pajamas. Both have sleep tangled hair. To some, they may look a sight. To me, they're adorable.

"What's going on?" Daniel, my seven year old, manages to get out through his huge yawn.

Yawns being what they are, little Lailah follows suit. Then she rushes to my side grasping hold of my leg in a fierce grip that belies her delicate frame.

"Are you leaving us, Daddy?" she asks, tears welling in her eyes.

I crouch down, bring her into my arms. She lays her head on my shoulder as I lift her, holding her tightly.

"I'm not leaving you, cherub," I croon. "Zeke and I just need to go check the fence line," I explain my early rise.

"Cuz of the storm?" Daniel chirps.

"That's right," I acknowledge. "That's part of the work required if you want to run a successful ranch. Storms can be destructive."

"They aren't just des...destw..."

"Destructive," I supply Lailah with the word.

"Destwuctive," she repeats with a knowing nod.

"How's that?" I inquire.

"Zeke says that storms can bwing in good as it sweeps out the bad. It might bwing down fences. Those be the weak bits needing wepair. Now they have new pawts that make them stwonger than ever," she says with the confidence of youth.

I look over at Zeke. This morning he's awash with crimson. Though the high color stains much of his neck and face, I can see the pride sparkling in his eyes.

"Sat with them a bit last night to help them ease their worries. The lightning and thunder were a bit fierce at times," Zeke murmurs.

"If Zeke said it then it's right. Guess it's all in how you look at it."

"You'll have to fix the fence before long anyhow, now you know just where to do it and make it better," Daniel says, not wanting to be out done by his younger sister.

I place a kiss on Lailah's cheek before setting her down. "Well, your dad and Uncle Zeke need to get so we can do our work. Elizabeth, we might be out for more than a day."

She grunts. "Take your cell and call so I know when to expect you," she orders.

"Yes ma'am," I obediently reply, earning a swat with the dish towel as she walks behind my back. The kids giggle at seeing their dad spanked by Nana Elizabeth.

I reach for Daniel to deliver his kiss, but the little monkey scrambles up my legs and torso smack into my arms. He's still young enough where he eagerly permits my hugs and kisses. I know in a few years it may not be so. I want him to know every way I can tell and show him that I love him. He clings to me, hugging me tightly.

"Ooh, that is one heck of a bear hug, son," I praise.

He leans back in my arms and gives me a toothless grin. The tooth faerie has been making frequent visits of late.

"Can I come, Dad? Pleeease!" he weedles.

"Me too, me too!" Lailah insists jubilantly, jumping up and down.

Elizabeth steps in, placing her hands on Lailah's shoulders. "Now children, your father is needing to work. You mustn't bother him. He doesn't need to be worrying about the two of you when he's out looking over the range," she admonishes.

Daniel and Lailah lower their heads and stick out their

lower lips in a definite pout. I look over at Zeke, who shrugs.

"We might be gone more than one day," I tell them. "It might be muddy and wet."

"Cold," Zeke adds. "We ain't taking the landrover. It will be the wagon," he warns.

"Goodie." Lailah claps in excitement. "I like the wagon. Besides, I gotta go," she says, a bit pensively.

I furrow my brow. "Why do you *need* to go?"

"Cuz, the faewie said I must. I don't want to make the faewie mad at me, Daddy. But I weally, weally, weally wanna go. I need to find the angel," she pleads, lacing her fingers in fisted prayer.

Everyone stops and looks at Lailah. Zeke's eyes crinkle in delight. Elizabeth shakes her head. Daniel gives her a look that suggests she's plum crazy. I scratch my whiskered jaw and chin.

"Faerie? Angel?" I give her a searching look.

"Yeah, a faewie comes and speaks to me mostly at night. She tells me things. Last night she came telling me that an angel had come down fwom heaven. It's lost and hurt. Faewie said I would find it if I went closer to the mountains," she says, pointing.

"Were you planning on listening to the faerie?" I ask.

Zeke gives me and her a sharp look.

When she hems and haws, twisting her hair and shuffling her feet, I know I have my answer. Crouching down to her level I snag her hand and pull her closer to me.

"Look at me, Lailah," I command softly.

She peeks at me through her dark lashes so like her mother's. "Are ya mad at me, Daddy?" she asks in a slightly quivering voice.

"About the faerie?" I ask, seeing her nod.

"I'm not mad at you seeing or talking to your faerie. Your Uncle Luke used to talk to a bear that visited him most nights when he was your age," I say in a consirator's whisper, looking to Zeke for confirmation.

Zeke nods. "It was the darndest thing. Sometimes he weren't asleep when he was having his talks with the grizzly bear," he says with a shake of his head.

"And the angel, Daddy?"

"Nope, not angry about that either. It's a good thing that you want to find something or someone that might be lost and injured," I reassure her.

"Then what, Daddy? Why are you fwowning?" she asks anxiously.

"Cherub, tell me honestly. Would you have gone off today in search of the angel?"

She slowly nods. "I planned on getting up eawly and taking Beezlebub," she confesses.

Zeke seems more disturbed by this than I. I can hear his faint whispers as he curses or says a few choice words he doesn't want the kids to hear.

"And that, young lady, would have made me so mad that you might have gotten a paddling," I tell her sternly.

She gives me a wide-eyed look, covering her bottom with her hands. I give Daniel a stern look when he tries smothering his giggle.

Big fat tears pool then overflow her green eyes. I'm not going to comfort her, yet. She has to understand why I'm mad.

"Daughter, there is a reason you and Daniel are not to

leave the yard without telling someone. Can you tell me why that is a rule in this house?"

"Do you tell someone, Daddy?" she challenges.

I narrow my eyes at her. I don't like the sass mouth and she knows it.

"Of course he does." Zeke speaks up in my defense. "*Everyone* who lives and works on the ranch follows that rule."

Elizabeth nods when Lailah looks at her for the truth of his words.

"Why is it a rule for *everyone*?" I press. "Even little girls given quests by faeries?"

"I know, I know, " Daniel says when Lailah remains silent.

"Okay, Daniel, help your sister out," I invite.

"Cause she might get hurt and nobody would know where to find her," he supplies.

Zeke pats his shoulder in praise of his words.

"That's right, Daniel. Lailah, do you understand?" When she nods, I ask her to tell me with her words.

"Cuz you gots to know where I am if you need to find me." When she sees that I'm still waiting, she thinks some more then adds. "I might get hurt and need help, just like my angel," she finishes.

"Right. It's simply too dangerous to go out so far and alone without a word to anyone. There are so many things that could happen, too many to even think about. You might think you'd be careful and safe but you never know. And because the rest of us don't have faeries looking out for us or telling us what's up, we have to communicate to each other."

Her adorable cherub's face scrunches up in concern.

"Then what do I tell faewie when she asks me to do stuff like that?" she asks.

"You either tell her no or you come talk with me. If it's really urgent, then speak with Nana Elizabeth or Uncle Zeke," I tell her. "Can you do that?"

She nods.

"Okay, go get dressed. Hurry it up, if you still want to come along," I tell them.

Pandemonium breaks out as they whoop and holler with glee before charging up the stairs to their rooms to change.

"I'll get their gear and load it up," Zeke says, turning toward the store room where we keep all our camping gear. He knows that I need to have a few words with Elizabeth.

Elizabeth feverishly goes about packing sack breakfasts for the kids. "Elizabeth, how long has Lailah been visited by faeries?" I ask.

"You're a good father," she says with a sigh.

"Elizabeth!"

"Oh, for about six months, more or less," she says with a shrug. "Never really marked it on the calendar. Maybe longer…"

"I know that it isn't unusual for children to have imaginary friends…but these are my children. I need to know what's going on in their lives. This seems like something big, something I should have been aware of," I say, chastising myself, not Elizabeth.

Elizabeth halts in her food production and sidles over to squeeze and pats my arm. "I was going to tell you, but…you know how things get. I haven't been worried. It started kind of slow. At first, I thought she was dreaming about some of the stories we read just before bed. She always likes the ones with faeries. Then when she let it out that a real one often came to her at night and during the day...again, I didn't make a fuss," she says with an indulgent smile. "There are many cultures that believe in the wee folk and see them as a blessing if they're visited by them," she says with a chuckle.

I wait for her to continue.

"But things have recently become quite peculiar," she says curiously, scrunching her brow. "I mentioned that I lost one of my favorite earrings. Must've slipped off my ear. I looked high and low for the infernal thing then gave it up. Then Lailah told me that her faerie friend said to look in the Delft china cup in the display cabinet. Together we went and did just that. And there it was."

She squeezes my arm to get my attention. "Thing is, Gabriel, I hadn't been in the cabinet for over a month. Had no reason. How did it get there? Hmm? At first I thought maybe Lailah had found it and thought to play a trick and put it there herself." She shakes her head. "That mite is too small to reach the cup. There's been other things too," she says.

"Go on," I urge.

"Like how she knows who's calling before the phone rings. It's like the child's got a knowing that just isn't...natural."

"You don't think whatever this is is something harmful do you?" I ask.

"I've puzzled over that one myself. Of course, if I thought it was, I would've told you before now. I think it best to wait and watch. Time will tell us what we need to know," she says with a bob of her head.

I can hear the kids tromping down the stairs in their eagerness to come along.

"Okay, cherubs, go find Zeke and he'll mount you up or find you a spot on the wagon."

I can't help but smile to see their enthusiasm. Just like my own dad, I think it's important that my children know this land. That they appreciate it in all of its savage splendor and rugged beauty. There's fun to be had in hard work. Work is a requirement here where we live. Might learn that when they're young so it becomes routine, a habit, and not just an unwanted and unappreciated chore.

"Gabriel," Elizabeth's maternal voice calls me back before I'm out the door. I take the two sack breakfasts and slip on my cowboy hat. "There's much in this world that we don't understand. Only the pure of heart truly understand it and appreciate it. Lailah is one of those people, and your son," she says. "And so are you."

I give her a gentle smile. She isn't saying anything that I don't already know, except the part about myself. That's a bit hard to believe.

"Thanks, Elizabeth. I'll be in touch."

Chapter 7

Gabriel

T he rain created enough mud that it prevents us from going out as far as I intended. We end up spending one night out to humor the kids before returning. I have my hands full on the return.

When Lailah learns we're headed back, she bursts into tears. Nothing seems to console her. To her, she has failed. Failed to complete the task given her by her faerie. Fearing she would cry herself sick, I take her up in front of me on my horse and hold her across my lap. Finally having enough of it myself, I motion for the rest to keep going and stop my mount.

The front of my shirt is wet from her tears. She has gone from silent crying, weeping, loud sobbing, and now to hiccupping and sniffling.

"Lailah, please stop crying, cherub," I plead.

"But Daddy, you don't understand," she manages to blubber out.

"Yes I do, darling. I get it. You think you've let down your faerie. That she will be cross because you haven't found the angel as she said you would. Am I right?"

Lailah nods.

"Do you understand why we had to cut this short? Why

we have to turn back?" I ask, taking out my bandana and wiping her eyes and snotty nose.

She shakes her head.

I point to the ground. "See the mud and puddles?"

Again she nods.

"There's just too much of it. Trucks and land rovers would get stuck in it. Wheels of the wagons are getting stuck in it. We've already had to pull ourselves out twice. The horses may hurt themselves. We aren't going to risk our equipment, horses, and the men that way," I explain.

"But Daddy, I've got to find the angel. How am I gonna to do that?" she asks.

"Tell you what, the first thing you're going to do once we get home is explain it to your faerie. What's her name anyway?"

"Violet."

"Violet. Okay. Tell Violet what I told you about it being too muddy and dangerous just now. Can you do that?" I ask.

"Uh-huh," she hiccups, I have her attention. I have her tell me what she is going to explain to Violet.

"That's right. Then you're going to tell her that your daddy is going to help you with your quest."

"Weeeally?" she gasps. Her tears magically dry up.

"Yup. I'll send out riders over the next several days, when they say conditions are better, we'll head out again," I tell her, drawing pleasure from her squeal of delight.

"In the meantime, you have a big important job to do that I'm giving only to you," I tell her.

"Meee?" she exclaims, her eyes growing as large as moons.

"Uh-huh. When we get back, I want you to go straight up to your room." She gives me a suspicious look. I have to fight not to show my smile. "When you get there, I want you to do two things. I want you to draw a picture of Violet. Then draw me a picture of the angel we're looking for. Will you do that for me?"

"Why do you need a picture of Violet?" she asks. Clever girl.

"Well, just in case I see her in the house or around the ranch, I don't want to mistake her for an intruder. You know what happens to poachers and intruders," I remind her.

"They get in big trouble." Her eyes are as round as saucers.

"Yes, they do. Some even get hurt and we don't want that happening to Violet, do we?"

"Nuh-uh," she says with feeling. "Okay. But what about the one of the angel?" She gives me a suspicious look.

"Ever see those pictures of kids on the milk cartons?" She nods. "Those are people who have disappeared. Their loved ones are looking for them. The milk cartons go all over the country…"

"So people might see them and know they're missing?" she asks, understanding at last.

"Exactly. Me and the boys need to know if we come across the angel when we are out and about. When you've finished making your picture of her, you and I will run copies on the printer in my office…"

"And we can hang them up…"

"And hand them out," I continue over the interruption.

"That way evewyone knows what she looks like," she concludes.

Content, Lailah snuggles back against me and promptly falls asleep. When we rejoin the group, I give a nod to Zeke. His eyes crinkle with affection, giving an indulgent shake of his head when he sees the slumbering child. The rest of the way home is peaceful. Everyone down to the horses is glad of that.

∞∞∞

Four days later we head out once more. The ranch is plastered with copies of Lailah's drawing.

"Looks like an angel," Jeb, one of our long time hired hands, says, scratching his head as he examines the picture. "Pretty one too," he praises, earning an appreciative smile from Lailah.

"See, she has long blonde hair and blue eyes," Lailah points out each detail. "And this is her dwess and her wings."

Dutifully, Jeb studies them. "Mhm-huh. White and flowy like an angel. What's this?" he asks, pointing to some red areas.

Lailah gives him a sorrowful look that melts his heart twice over. "She's been in an accident. Violet says she's hurt. So I dwawed blood where Violet says she is most hurt."

"You don't say. What sort of accident?" he ventures.

"She fell all the way fwom Heaven," Lailah says, adding in hand movements to help explain. "Wight down fwom the sky. There be bad people after her. The Devil's evil doers. I think they want to hurt her some more. We gotta find her before they do," she says in all seriousness.

"Don't worry there, little lady. Your pretty angel…"

"Sawah…her name is Sawah," Lailah supplies.

Jeb clears his throat. "Your pretty angel, Sarah, came down in the best place possible." He bobs his head with firm conviction.

"Weally?"

"For certain. This here ranch is named Paradise. If an angel came down from heaven this would be the best place. There are many of us here that work for the archangel himself and he be a Slayer," Jeb tells her seriously.

"Huh?" She wrinkles her nose in confusion.

"There be all sorts of angels. Some are like your Sarah," he says, flicking the picture. "Others are what's called archangels. There are a total of seven, or so my granny told me. Your daddy's name is Gabriel." Arching a brow at her.

"Uh-huh," Lailah says.

"Gabriel is the name of one of the archangels."

Lailah's eyes grow large and round. "I didn't know daddy was an angel," she says with awe.

"He probably isn't supposed to tell most people. It's a secret," he says with a wink.

"What's an awchangel?" she asks in a loud whisper that has Jeb grinning.

"Well, the way my granny used to tell me, they're guardians of Paradise, warrior angels. Gabriel is tasked with defending chosen people from other evil doers or creatures. He's a protector."

"My daddy is a wawior angel?"

"What's your last name?" Jeb asks, thinking it would prove his point.

"Slayer. You know that, Mr. Jeb," she chides.

"Do you know what a slayer is?" Before she can open

her mouth he answers himself. "It's a person who kills others in order to protect his people. Have you heard of the story of David and Goliath?" he asks.

"David killed a giant with only a slingshot. He saved his people. The giant had killed many of his people already and was gweatly feared. Nobody wanted to fight him. David had the couwage to twy though most thought he would die."

"Exactly," Jeb replies. "Better yet, archangels will stand between the people they are helping and the bad guy."

"That's my daddy?" Lailah had to be sure.

"Your daddy doesn't go out looking for a fight, but he is darn good at protecting those that need it. If an angel were in trouble, there would be nobody better to get help from than the archangel, Gabriel Slayer, himself," Jeb proclaims, helping her hang the picture.

Together, they stand back and admire their handiwork.

"I think your Violet knew what she was doing telling you about your Sarah," he says.

"You do?"

"Mhm-hmm. By selecting you, you went to your daddy and told him what's up. Now he knows to be ready, to be alert. Tomorrow we head out. We'll find your Sarah and bring her back to the heart of Paradise and keep her safe. Your daddy will see to that. Good thing you told him," he praises, giving her a wink.

Lailah chews on her lip. She blushes. "Guess I should always tell Daddy when Violet tells me secwets or asks me to do things," she muses.

"I think that be a right smart thing to do. You just never know what powers people have and will gladly lend you until you go to them. There are all sorts of magical people living here in Paradise," he says, grinning when her eyes turn large and round.

He holds up a hand to ward of further questions. "We'll keep that for another time," he promises. "Right now, you and me got to get ready to go out in search of your lost angel."

Jeb pats her on her head and sends her skipping off toward the big house. When she's out of earshot, he lets out a chuckle in full force.

Zeke comes out from where he hid, listening to the exchange. "You did right by that girl, Jeb." Nodding in the direction Lailah had gone.

Jeb merely shrugs and grunts in response to the praise.

"That one's got a keen mind. She'll be back when she's finished with this angel business," Zeke says, chuckling. "Whatya gonna do then? Filling her head with thoughts of magical people living in these here ranch."

Jeb scratches his chest and chin as he thought. "I'll send her to Hunter," he finally says with a grunt and decisive nod.

"Hunter? Why that one?" Zeke asks, intrigued.

"It'll be good for him. I'll tell the little one that he can help her find unicorns. They live here in abundance, being Paradise and all," he says.

Zeke laughs and slaps his knee. "Uni-unicorns?" he can barely get the word out. "It takes a maiden with a pure heart to find such a thing," Zeke reminds Jeb.

"Yup, sure do. But the way I'm thinking, if that yung'n is able to talk to faeries, she'd be the one to catch a unicorn or two."

∞∞∞

Two days out and the kids are still excited. I like having them enthusiastic about the ranch and all the doings that are part and parcel of keeping a spread like ours operational and profitable. So many farms and ranches are disappearing. It's hard work. Hard work doesn't guarantee success. In many ways it's a gamble. The hours are lousy and the pay even lousier. It isn't an occupation one can break into easily.

We're one of the lucky ones. Paradise Ranch has been in my family since the middle of the nineteenth century when one of my ancestors came out when gold had been discovered near Sutter's Mill. Thankfully, that Slayer had a head on his shoulders. He'd followed the stampede of people coming to California and the adjacent parts in search of instant wealth. Most poor suckers rarely struck it rich.

Instead of investing his money and time digging and panning for gold dust and nuggets, he bought land, lots and lots of land. On that land he raised beef, sheep, and poultry. Over the years Slayers added orchards and vineyards. The crops grown are those that feed us and those that work the ranch. Meat, cheese and butter, and eggs became our stock in trade. Then we added olives and olive oil, and now, wine.

Before diversified farming and permaculture became an agricultural fad, we were practicing it here in around the Sierra Nevada Mountains. The climate is similar to what you'd find in the Mediterranean. So we can raise an interesting variety of plants and livestock, but we have to be careful stewards of the land.

The key is to not compete with the land but to work with it. Nothing wrong with challenging it but it will challenge you right back, returning the favor. The key is to know before you go too far. Mother Nature has her own way of rewarding or exacting her revenge. So far we've been on her good side. I intend to keep it that way.

Over the years, prime agricultural land has been lost to mega estates or one of the many housing developments needed by those who seek to cater to an elite clientele. Urbanites, now living in the country, still want their fast food, drug and grocery stores, shopping malls, and eateries. More land gets gobbled up in the process.

Hobby farms were the next to come. Now I don't want to disrespect those who have found such a life fulfilling. Some fill a niche market. Unfortunately, many of them haven't done their homework and fall into the fads of the time. I can count the number of emu, llama and alpaca, and peacock farms that have popped up then disappeared just as quickly.

I was born on this ranch and here I'll die. From the time I could crawl, I've been learning the trade. I've done every job that's to be found on the ranch. Dad required me to experience it all first hand and do it well. No job was too dirty, too lowly for a Slayer son. My education didn't end with on the job training. Dad insisted that I get a college degree. Mine's in finance and environmental engineering with a minor in agriculture.

I'm proud to say that Paradise operates totally off the grid. We produce all our own electricity and water. We're able to produce so much energy from the systems we have in place that we sell some to the local power company. Water conservation and filtration, composting, are some of the principles we have always been incorporating here at Paradise. No different from how those early pioneers lived. The only difference is that we have the technology to store, process, and recycle the resources and byproducts required for a comfortable modern lifestyle.

I guess what I'm saying is, I'm damn proud to be a Slayer. I'm proud and appreciative of the legacy that has been handed down to me and mine. I would do anything and everything within my power to keep what is mine, to protect what has been so graciously placed into my keeping. That goes for my family and those who work for me. All are mine, my responsibility. I protect what's mine.

So it pleases me to no end when my children express an interest in the land, in the ranch. They need to learn from the ground up what goes into maintaining our livelihood and our home. From a young age, I want them to respect the land and take delight in what it's willing to give us when we treat it with kindness and respect.

When we find downed or damaged fences, everyone pitches in to fix them. Everyone. That includes Daniel and Lailah. Of course we give them jobs they can handle, but they can proudly say they are part of the team.

For the next two days, we work hard, eat heartily, and sleep like the dead. After dinner, we sit around the campfire. One of the boys brought along his guitar, another his harmonica. Zeke tells stories that have the kids and several of the hands sitting on the edge of their camp stools. We gaze at the stars, counting the satellites that pass overhead.

Each night, everyone reassures Lailah that tomorrow will be the day she'll find her angel. To tell you the truth, though I think it's all part of her imagination, there's a little part of me that wants it to be true.

"Daddy?" Lailah calls out in a sleepy voice as I am tucking her in her sleeping bag. We placed her and Daniel in the wagon. It will keep them off the damp and cold ground and away from critters.

"Yes, cherub?" I softly reply, soothing away the hair from her forehead.

"What will I do if I don't find my angel?" she asks.

"We'll just have to keep on looking," I tell her.

"Do you mean it?"

"Sure do. Few things are more important than finding a

lost angel."

"She's not just lost. She's also hurt. You don't think that's what's keeping her fwom being found do you?" Worry is evident in her voice.

"Don't worry yourself over that. If Violet says you're meant to find her, then find her you will. You just gotta have patience," I counsel.

"Is that the same thing as when Nana Elizabeth says about watching a pot?" She stretches her toes and yawns.

I chuckle softly. "Yeah I guess it is. A watched pot never boils. If all you do is keep looking for the angel, you may not find her, might overlook her. So you live each day, each minute the way you should and before you know it you'll look up and there she'll be."

"Like magic." She smiles dreamily.

"Yeah, it's a kind of magic," I agree, leaning down to kiss her on the head. "Now sleep, faerie whisperer. We've got a big day ahead of us tomorrow."

"'Kay, cuz I'm gonna find my angel tomowrow." She yawns and closes her eyes.

"Whatya find?" I ask, strolling over to where Zeke was inspecting the ground.

He points. "Tracks. Horses. Some shod some not. I'd say about six of 'em." He stands up from where he's been crouching and inspecting the ground. In one fluid motion he takes off his hat and passes his shirt cuff over his brow before replacing his hat to sit atop his head. Together, we peer around the landscape.

"Ours?" We keep a number of horses. A few we set to roam the ranch instead of keeping them corralled for the winter. Sometimes they all come back, sometimes not.

Zeke shrugs.

"Keep an eye out. If they're some of our mares and their young, we'll send out a team and round 'em up," I order. I know he'd do it anyway without me saying so.

"Always do, always do," he mutters.

We're just wiping our lunch plates clean and sitting back for another cup of campfire coffee when Lailah comes running over.

"Daddy! Daddy, come quick!" She's grabbing my hand trying to haul me to my feet.

"Darling, let your old man rest a spell." I gently rebuff her.

"But Daddy, it's Sawah. It's my angel. I saw her. She's coming. She's coming, Daddy. She's here!" she exclaims in the hyper way only a child can move and sing their excitement.

Instantly, I and the rest of the crew are on our feet. This time, *I* grab a hold of her hand. I've learned that kids on a mission or one's as excited as Lailah often get by you quicker than lightning or an angel on the wing.

"Show me." My entire body has jumped to alert mode.

"That's what I've been twying to do, Daddy."

I follow her as she runs us around the wagon and points toward the bit of clearing that separates the trees from the fence line. It's still a fair distance but I can make out a figure dressed all in white with long blonde hair. Her hair is flowing out behind her as is the fluttering of what could be mistaken for wings. She isn't using those wings to fly. Nope, not this one. This angel was flying across the chaparral on the back of a white horse.

"Well, I'll be damned," Zeke says. He's the first to break the silence that has fallen over the stunned group.

It's enough to bring me to my senses. White isn't the only color I'm seeing. Once my eyes are believing the sight is real, I notice that red is covering a portion of the puffy flowing gown, just like in Lailah's drawing. That isn't all. One of her legs doesn't hang right as she sits astride the horse.

She's holding onto the mane. I can see no tack of any kind. I'm unable to make out the features on her face but she's riding that horse as if the hounds of hell are on her heels.

When Lailah lunges forward, I do what any father would do. I pick her up and place my overly excited and sqirming daughter in Cob's arms.

"Hold onto her. Don't let her go. I'm trusting you to keep my kids safe," I tell him.

Running to my own mount, I quickly gain my saddle and head in her direction, ignoring Lailah's frantic calls. Grateful hearing Zeke soothe her.

"Hush, child. Remember what Jeb told you about your dad? It was your quest to find the angel. Seems you've done that. Now it 's your dad's quest to see her safe."

"Uncle Zeke, Violet says she's hurt," Lailah wails.

"Then you and Cob had better go and prepare a bed for her in the wagon. She'll be needing to rest and where we can tend her wounds while seeing her back to the big house," he reasons.

"Daniel, stay close to Cob," Zeke directs. "Watch over yer sister."

"Yes sir." He scrambles onto the wagon to get a better look at what's happening.

"Jeff, Toby, stay close I'm going to see if I can lend Gabe a hand," he says.

Chapter 8

Sera

I don't remember much after my last encounter with George. Don't really recall when I woke up. At some point I must've wandered through the rest of the woods. When I came out on the other side, I was staring at a vast field beyond a fence.

Fences meant people. People meant help and safety. My heart skips a beat. I briefly close my eyes, taking several breaths, nearly breaking down and sobbing. Please, I pray to anything good that may be listening, that this will be the end of the hell I've been experiencing.

"It's so beautiful here," I say out loud, jumping upon hearing my voice.

"What do I do now?" I decide to keep up the verbal dialogue, hoping it will keep me more alert.

"Follow the fence or make a straight line keeping the fence at your back. You're bound to run into someone," I reason.

Easing through the barbed wire, pieces of toile from my underskirt snag on the sharp prongs. A quick tug, and I'm free. I hobble along the fence for a time, feeling my energy flagging. Then I hear the distinct sound of hooves hitting the ground.

Whickering and snorts follow, announcing a group of

horses that are running wild and free. Both the horses and I come up short, each surprised by the presence of the other. I've heard that horses can sense fear and anxiety. I do my best to project calm and my sincere excitement of seeing such a wondrous sight.

A white stallion rears, kicking up its front legs, and shaking its mane. It acts as if it's showing off. He's one handsome male and knows it. He shows no fear but genuine curiosity. I can detect no aggression on his part. After checking me out from a distance, he leaves the rest of the herd behind as he slowly moves toward me.

"Hi, there," I coo. "You're such a handsome fella."

Hoping my calm steady voice will not spook the horse or make it think I am a threat. I don't want or need any more trouble than I've already encountered. The horse tosses up its head as if it's answering.

"I'm looking for some humans. Do you know where I might find some?"

I'm not sure what possessed me to have a conversation with the animal, but unless it's a totally wild horse, there has to be someone looking out for it. There may be a farm or stables nearby. When I get a closer look. I notice it's wearing a loose fitting halter. So it had to come from somewhere. Maybe I'm going crazy. My fever is burning. This may be part of the hallucinations that are known to bombard people in such a state.

Then the horse does the strangest thing. It sidles up to me, presenting its side as if inviting me to climb on top. A ride would be welcome at this point. Tentatively, I place my hand on its withers. The beauty's muscles quiver under my fingers. I can't help but run my hand up its neck and caress its cheek. For some reason I'm compelled to wrap my arms around his neck.

It feels good to hold onto something solid, real, and

alive. Tears form in my eyes. When I pull back my head from where I buried it in the horse's mane, it tosses its head once more, encouraging me to mount. It leads me to an outcropping of rock. Carefully, I scramble up on the weather-worn stones, pull myself onto the horse's back, and straddle him. After steadying myself, I grab a handful of its mane.

"I'm ready," I tell the horse.

With a hop, it begins a steady pace. As I become more sure of my position, I encourage it to go faster. Soon I am flying across the pasture. This is heavenly, it's paradise. I never knew how exhilarating it was to gallop across a field on a horse with the wind blowing through my hair. For the first time in as many days, I feel—free.

The horse slows to a fast walk, giving a wicker, tossing its nose toward an area just to the right of us. There, in the distance, I can see two wagons, several saddled horses, along with...people. *People!*

I can hardly believe my eyes. Tears blind me as the horse heads in that direction. Words get stuck in my throat preventing me from calling out. It doesn't seem to matter. I hear a voice calling to their dad. Next thing I know, a man is galloping toward me on a painted mount. Another man, hot on the first one's heels, is racing toward me as well.

The first rider maneuvers his horse next to mine, pulling on the loose halter, until it stops. The second rider quickly dismounts. Both men soothingly talk to the horse, keeping it calm and still. The older man pries my fingers from where they've locked onto the horse's mane. When I am free, the first rider gently pulls me onto his lap.

"How is she?" the second rider asks.

"She's burning up. I think she has a fever," he says. "Seems pretty beat up too."

"In-infection," I weakly croak out. "Infection...in my... leg...broken."

"Take it easy now. You're safe. We're going to get you back to the big house and get you all the help that you need," says the man who holds me. "Rest easy. We'll take care of you."

I give him a weak smile. "Thank you," I breathe out on a sigh.

"What's your name, little lady?" he asks.

"Seraphima Angel, but people call me Sera," I tell them.

"Well don't that beat all," says the older man.

Chapter 9

Gabriel

Ghost Runner is one of our most cantankerous stallions. He does things his way and is willing to fight with most anyone who tells him no. We let him roam with a small herd of mares that we want him to breed.

He's a smart one. Learns and figures things out. There never has been a stall or trailer that can hold him for long. He always manages to get out. When he's kept closer to the big house, oftentimes we find him helping himself to the feed if his dinner comes late. We've learned that if we give him his freedom to run, he'll stay within the boundary of the ranch.

Ghost Rider's known to be a mean son-of-a-bitch, biting, bucking, and kicking whoever gets in his way or he takes exception to. Few can ride and sit long enough to lap the ring. I never would have thought to see him allowing a green rider and female, in a billowing white dress to boot, sit him long enough to ride across the expanse of wild sage and scrub. He was as gentle with her as a mother is to a babe.

Lailah's angel must have stumbled across him in her trek through the chaparral. How she convinced him to let her ride is a tale I'm wanting to hear. Ghost Rider seems to know where he was taking her and it looks like he was bringing her straight to us. He even followed us back to the wagon.

"Daddy, is it her? Is it my angel?" Lailah calls out excitedly.

I do not envy Cob. He has his hands full holding onto that wiggle-worm. But he has kept my kids safe. I'm grateful for that, though I expected no less.

"Well, cherub, I think this might be the angel Violet said you'd find," I say, still a bit stunned.

I dismount keeping the woman secure in my arms. Didn't want her to get too jostled moving from place to place. In addition to the fever, I can see that she has sustained many wounds. Blood on her shoulder, tells me it might be from a gunshot. Her face is swollen and I am sure there are more bruises under that fancy dress she's wearing.

Now I'm no expert on women's fashion, but her angel dress looks more like what a woman would wear to her wedding. It's ruined now. There seems to be more questions than answers. I want to get to the bottom of it as soon as possible.

"Toby, call Sheriff Dobbins. Tell him what we've got here. He'll want to meet us back at the big house," I order.

"Sure thing, boss," he says, stepping back and pulling out his cell.

"The rest of you start breaking down camp. Looks like we're heading back. We'll put together another fence fixing team later. Daniel, go help Cob."

I continue my inspection of the fallen angel. Her leg is wrapped in a makeshift splint. Between it and her shoulder, those might be the worst of her injuries. I sure hope so. But I've seen guys get kicked by a rogue horse or an angry steer with no visible injuries who drop dead a day or two later. Best to get a professional to check her out. With that in mind, I pull out my cell phone.

"Steve, I need you to transport Maggie to my location.

Yeah, out in the field. We found an injured woman. She's got what looks like a gunshot to the left shoulder and a broken leg, compound fracture that has been set in the field prior to us finding her. She's burning with fever and will need medical care beyond what I or the boys can give her," I tell him.

Steve is one of our chopper pilots. It comes in handy for emergencies or when we need to find lost herds of livestock or searching for poachers and such. I give my boys bonuses when they earn their pilot's license.

Maggie is our full time nurse-practitioner. She's married to one of our hands whose family has resided on the ranch since nearly the beginning. Her services come in handy, helping me see to the welfare of those that I consider part of the Paradise family.

After I give Steve our location, it's a matter of making Sera comfortable until they arrive. Maggie says to keep her awake and talking until she can better assess her injuries. I place Sera Angel on the bed that has been prepared for her.

Lailah hasn't taken her eyes off the woman since I brought her into camp.

"What can I do, Daddy?" she asks.

I heft her into the wagon to sit next to her angel. "I need you to sit here and keep her company. Hold her hand and talk to her. Nurse Maggie says we need to keep her awake and you're going to help do that. Think you can?"

"I can do it, Daddy." She scoots closer to Sera.

Lifting Sera's head, I help her sip some water. Her lips are cracked and her voice sounds parched. I bathe her forehead to help cool her down. She fades in and out of consciousness. The cool cloths we apply to her face and neck seem to bring her back.

"Hi, Angel Sewa," Lailah says when the woman's eyes

latch on to her. "I'm glad I found you. Violet, my faewie fwiend, said I would, but I was getting really worwied that I wouldn't. We had to put off coming out here cuz of the rain. Guess it worked out okay," my little girl babbles.

Sera first looks at my daughter as if she's confused. Slowly, a bemused expression comes over her face as she listens to Lailah. Suddenly, Sera seems overcome with fear. Her face stricken with panic.

"Oh my, oh my," she gasps. "Children, people..." she begins to ramble as she struggles to sit up and look about her.

"Settle down now," I urge, pressing her gently back to help her lay down.

Yet she struggles. Clearly, she's exhausted and weak from her ordeal. When she realizes that getting up is a fruitless endeavor, she looks at me imploringly.

"Forgive me," she whispers in anguish.

"For what, darling?" I soothe. "There isn't anything to forgive. You've done nothing wrong. We want to help you and are happy to do so," I tell her.

"No! You don't understand," she says in a rush. Tears fill her eyes. "I've put you all in danger, the children too. I couldn't live with myself if you all were harmed because of me," she says.

My eyes sharpen, my mind and body come to fully alert. "What do you mean in danger?" I demand.

"I was taken against my will. Kidnapped," she says in a low voice. "Mmm...my ex-fiancé was shot, killed in front of me," she says fighting back tears. "I was supposed to be modeling bridal dresses for a private showing. But it was all a ploy. A trick. A set up. The man responsible is a very powerful bad man," she says.

"What man? Do you know who he is?"

"Yes. His name is Luther Devlin. I was being taken to him."

Luther Devlin. I've heard of him. He owns a number of casinos in Reno and Tahoe. Seems to have his fingers in a number of different pies. He and I don't operate within the same circles, but anyone who lives in these parts has heard of him.

"How were you being taken to him?" I ask.

"By plane. I started out in Albany, New York."

I raise my eyebrows at that.

"You've traveled clear across the continent. You're in eastern California, in the Sierra Nevada Mountains," I tell her. "Reno and Tahoe are not too far away. Was that where you were headed?"

"I don't know where they were taking me. I was drugged and unconscious until I woke on the plane when it encountered turbulence. A storm. I think we were hit by lightning. There were three men with me. We crashed. The pilot died. Another, George…he died too. I'm not sure about Peter. I think he may be hurt, but I don't know if he made it or not. He was the one in charge and in contact with Devlin before the crash," she says.

I ask her questions as she continues to reveal what the last few days has been for her. Frankly, I'm impressed by her ability to survive as she has. What she went through and the courage…

"The local sheriff has been notified and will meet us at the big house," I tell her.

Zeke and I'll see about posting guards for a while until this is all settled.

I watch as her right hand disappears into the slit on the side of her skirt. Must have been a pocket inside. Clever. She pulls something out, handing it to me.

"Here," she says. "This is the name and number of the FBI agent who I've been working with. I've carried it with me since this whole mess began. Call him. Please, please call him."

I do just that.

After speaking with the agent, he assures me that others will be waiting at Mercy General Hospital in Sacramento. Could have taken her to one of the hospitals in Reno, but if her story is true, that would be like placing a lamb near the entrance of a den of wolves.

Once our copter arrives, there's a change of plans. My children, under heavy guard, are taken back to the big house. I give orders to Elizabeth that they're not to leave the house until she receives word personally from me. Gave the order that guards are to remain at the gates onto the property and each entrance of the house.

Zeke takes some of our best trackers and heads back to see if he can locate the downed plane or any of the three men that Sera says had a hand in kidnapping her. Sheriff sends some of his own men with them. If there's a crash site or bodies, they'll be the ones to find them. In the meantime, I've got a family and people to protect. And now I've got this angel.

How does one protect an angel from the Devil himself?

Hospitals. Never understood how so much chaos is actually a coordinated synchronized dance of healing and help. The thing is to not get run over in the meantime. I stand out of the way as Sera is placed on a gurney and wheeled to a triage room.

People in scrubs and white coats keep running in and

out. Machines are brought in. For some reason, I don't want her to be out of my sight. The need to protect her is strong. I rub a hand over the nape of my neck. Damn, I'm tired. But I can't ignore the fire that seems to be smoldering deep within. I haven't felt that sort of heat since…Mary.

Sweet Mary. *My* Mary. We met while students at USC. I'd taken to sitting by her in one of my lecture courses. She had the sweetest smile I'd ever seen and a way of making me feel calm. I liked the me I was when I was around her. I took to following her one day so I'd learn what dorm she stayed in, then made it my habit of running into her each day out of class so she'd notice me. Took me nearly the entire semester to build up the nerve to talk to her. Asked her if she wanted to study together over coffee. It was all downhill from there.

I had never been happier in my life the day she became my wife except maybe the day I became a father. My life was perfect. Then that all ended when she died. It wasn't an accident or anything sudden. No, it was a long farewell, but all too short just the same. Mary went in for a regular check up with her doctor. Went back when routine tests showed a strange anomaly. Turned out to be cancer of the cervix. She died in my arms less than a year later.

It rained on the day we laid her in the ground. The weather matched my mood that horrible day. All I could think was that the love of my life was gone. I was left alone to raise our two children who would never know their mother. I became angry and bitter until I ran across a letter that Mary had written and placed in my desk.

She told me that I still had a life to live. That if I truly loved her I would find a way to heal my heart and love again. She might be dead, but I was not. As long as I continued to love she would still reside within my heart. I had a duty to live, and to live and love well so our children would experience it, see it, and do the same. Love would be the only memorial she wanted left in her name besides happy and healthy children who would grow into awesome adults.

For the first time, I allowed myself to weep. When I finally wiped my cheeks dry, I felt refreshed, cleansed, and reborn. Over the weeks, months, and years that passed, I discovered that I have become a better father, a better friend. I did everything a bit better. I owed it to Mary, to my kids, my people, and myself.

Now here I was back in the hospital outside a bustling room while doctors work frantically to save the life of a woman who my daughter says is an angel brought from heaven for her to find. This woman has fought to live, to survive, and has done what most would not, could not. For the first time since I lost my Mary, I feel my heart zing as if it's awakening from a long dormant sleep. Pain and hope tug on it, stretching it, making it ache.

I can't keep from rubbing my hand over that area, as if pressing on that organ will relieve the ache within. Helplessly, I watch the doctors work on Sera. All the while, I wonder if this fallen angel, fleeing from a sort of hell, was brought here to torment me or as an answer to a prayer.

∞∞∞

Wasn't surprised to find two FBI agents joining me in the waiting room I'd been ushered into while another agent stayed in the room with Sera, and still yet another remained at her door. I don't know the full story but am determined to learn all I can. What is this woman involved in that has her so heavily guarded?

We move to a private office where I fill the agents in on what has transpired.

"How much of a threat is Devlin?" I ask the agents. I need to know what I'm up against and what I need to do to keep mine protected.

"I'm not going to lie," Agent Johnson says. "I wouldn't want him sniffing around my business or my home and family."

"If the man is such a threat, why is he still out and about? Why isn't he locked up or dead?"

"Devlin's smart. The man's ruthless, there's no doubt. He's a cold-blooded killer. It's getting enough evidence to convict him of a crime in a court of law that's been difficult, until now," is the reply I get.

"How is Sera mixed up with Devlin?" Wondering just how much Agent Johnson will tell me.

I sit in silence as the agent carefully tells me what he can. It's enough to see the bigger picture, even if a few pieces are missing. Any idiot can figure those out.

"So, good citizen, Sera Angel, does the right thing, exposing criminal activity. Now she's the one victimized. She's in surgery, injured because some of your agents were inept in their duties. How was her ex-fiancé...David, able to get out from where he'd been locked up? Have you investigated your own people? Maybe someone within your organization is dirty." I'm fuming from all that I've learned.

"We've been looking into that possibility," is what I get.

To me that's code meaning they know they have a mole, but ferreting him or her out has not happened as of yet. They're more worried about the PR nightmare then justice. How did they plan to keep my daughter's angel safe if they can't trust their own people? Is Sera's safety my responsibility? Damn right it is. I'm making it mine. The same way I now know I'll be taking extra measures to keep my family and people safe.

There's a part of me that wants to claim her. The moment she stepped foot on Paradise ranch, she became mine. I can't in good conscience let her fend for herself. The FBI, DEA, and the Justice Department aren't able to protect her. They've proved that already. I know I can't do any worse, in fact I'll bet I can do a whole lot better.

"Mr. Slayer," Agent Johnson calls to get my attention, "I would like to extend to you the FBI's gratitude in assisting us in finding Sera Angel. Agents have been brought in and more are on their way. We can handle things from here. You can go home now. There is no longer any reason for you to stay," he says, trying to hurry me along.

I know when I was being dismissed. Ain't happening. I'll leave when I am good and ready and not before because some suit says I should.

"Well, Agent Johnson, that's where you're wrong," I tell him, receiving a look of surprise.

"I have men out looking for that crash site. That little lady was found on my property. I expect you do intend to send out your own investigating team." I hold his gaze, seeking acknowledgement and verification of all that I've said.

"Yes, in fact we're already organizing a team," he replies.

"I assume you'll be needing access to my property. That means I'm not yet out of the picture, nor will I be brushed aside while your men are on my land," I tell him. "Now, I'm more than willing to be cooperative and accommodating, but I expect the same courtesy and respect in exchange." I give him a pointed look.

"Just so you know, I'm making Sera my business until she says otherwise. Seems not too many people have had her back, though she's been an upstanding citizen trying to do what's right. I think that should come with some sort of protection. Well, I'm going to see that all changes, starting now," I tell him.

"Mr. Slayer, Dr. Angel," *A doctor?* That catches me by surprise. Something I try to conceal, "is a material witness in an active homicide. She may well be the only witness we have that actually saw Luther Devlin shoot and kill another man," the agent went on.

Ah, now it's coming out. This has nothing or little to do with drug smuggling.

"I gather that. But that doesn't make her your prisoner," I retort sharply. "That makes her a person *needing* protection. That doesn't make her the bad guy, but a victim with a high chance of being re-victimized either by Devlin or by your agency."

Johnson doesn't like hearing that.

"Do you think Devlin will really allow a witness to a murder he committed to roam free? He'll come after her first chance he gets once he knows she's alive. And what about my family and those in my employ? Their lives are in danger as well. You can't expect me to tip my hat and saunter home as if all is fine and dandy." If he thinks I'll do just that, he's the one smoking something funny.

Johnson gives a sideways glance to the other agents.

"So what's going to happen to her?" I ask.

"I can't discuss that with you, Mr. Slayer," Johnson says in a tight voice. Oh, so now he's going to clam up. There is something about the man that doesn't set right. I vow to keep a watch on the guy.

"Will you put her in protective custody? Will she be able to go and do as she pleases?" I press.

Any further dialogue is interrupted by a doctor coming in. He is dressed in surgical scrubs. Agent Johnson and myself stand up to meet the man.

"Are you Agent Johnson?" the doctor asks. Receiving an affirmative reply, he turns to me, "And you must be the man who found and brought in Dr. Angel."

"What sort of doctor? Are we talking about a PhD...?"

"Dr. Seraphima Angel is a family doctor and an OBGYN. She works, or at least she did, with Global Medicine providing medical care in places around the world or at free clinics when she's in the United States," he tells me. There is great respect this doctor has for Lailah's angel.

Though it might have broken with patient privacy protocol, he does not make me leave when updating Johnson on her condition. I don't excuse myself as I probably should have. I'm staying and hearing it all. The way I see it, the more I know, the more I've got to work with.

"She will need time to recover. It may take up to three months, maybe longer before she is fully healed. She will need physical therapy. We will watch her carefully to make sure that she doesn't get an infection and that the rod and screws put in her leg to help fuse her bone are not rejected," he tells us.

Relief fills me to learn that she wasn't shot in the shoulder as I'd feared. The bullet just grazed her skin. She's got a few cracked ribs and enough bruises and scrapes to make her tender and sore for a while. These will all heal. All she needs is time and a safe place to stay and rest. Paradise is the perfect place. Of this, I'm convinced.

"She's awake and in recovery. She's asking to see you, Mr. Slayer, if you were still here."

A slow smile spreads over my face. Inwardly, I'm delighted by the look on Agent Johnson's mug when he hears

Sera's request.

"When can I see her? I'll need to question her," Johnson says, catching the doctor as he's escorting me to where Sera waits.

"Not until tomorrow. She needs her rest. I'll let her know you're here. If she has enough energy to see you, we'll send a nurse out to let you know."

Johnson frowns but nods.

∞∞∞∞

"Hi, Angel," I say softly. Her eyes are closed and I don't want to scare her.

I stand by the side of her bed. Her eyes open when she hears my voice. She looks so peaceful lying there.

"Hey." Her voice sounds drowsy and her eyes are a bit heavy. It's to be expected.

"The doctor said you wanted to see me," I prompt.

"Yeah, thanks for sticking around. I wasn't sure if you would stay or head back to your ranch."

"Just seeing things through. I got a daughter who will want a full report on the angel she found riding a white horse as soon as I step through the front door. Besides, I wanted to make sure you'd be okay." I keep my voice low and calm.

Her smile is breathtaking. Though she has been cleaned up considerably, she remains a bit pale. She sports more than enough visible signs of her ordeal: an array of bruises, cuts, and scrapes. They stand out sharply against her creamy-white flesh. In spite of all that, one can see the rare beauty she is. I don't think all that beauty is just physical. There is a...purity, a deep down goodness that shines through. Angelic is another word that comes to mind.

"I'm glad you stayed," she says a bit breathlessly. "I just wanted to thank you for what you and everyone did. You saved my life." Tears pool in her eyes. A few overflow to run down her cheek. I wipe them away.

I see her try to reach out weakly with her fingers. Gently, I take her hand in mine, giving it a tender but firm squeeze. Nobody wants to be alone when they're hurting. Sometimes the touch of a hand does more to ease the pain and affect healing than all the medicine and painkillers in the world.

"We're all really happy we happened to be there. It was your smarts, courage, and bravery that got you to safety. Now you need to save your energy for getting well," I tell her.

"Doctor tells me I'll be laid up for quite some time," she says. I don't like the shadow that comes over her face.

I clear my throat. "Do you have a family, someone that you might want to get in contact with?" I suggest. "They might be worried about you, being gone so long as you have without hearing from you or knowing where you are..." I let that hang.

"I have sisters, family, but..."

"But you're afraid of placing them in danger," I finish her thought.

I'm right. She nods weakly. Tears fill her eyes once more, making her blue irises look fractured. I swallow heavily. It's hard to not be affected.

"I've got my cell on me. Want to use it to give them a call?" I offer.

When she nods, I hand it to her then step out into the hall to give her privacy. I listen to the tenor of her voice until I'm certain that she's finished with her calls before stepping back inside the room.

Tears remain in her eyes, when I reach for the phone.

"They were happy to hear from me. I called my sisters that I share a house with when back in the states. They will notify the rest of my family," she says.

"Mind telling me what you told them?" I ask. "I know it isn't any of my business..."

"Of course not," she rushes out. "I didn't want to worry them. I told them that I needed some time away and when I was ready to come back home I would. Promised to keep in touch so they didn't worry. I don't think they quite believed me, but they will accept what I've said until this all clears up and I can tell them the full truth."

Gingerly, she touches her fingers to her head. A far off look enters her eyes before looking point blank back at me.

"I don't like lying to them, but I want to keep them safe. The best way, right now, is to not tell them anything. The less they know the better, I think." She searches my face for confirmation that what she did was the right thing. I nod in understanding. "I told them that it might be some time before I can contact them again," she says wistfully.

She turns her head to the side. I can see her blinking rapidly. Again I am struck by the strength of this woman. Here she is, injured, lying in a hospital bed, still in danger, and her only concern is for her sisters thousands of miles away.

"I know it can't be easy being away from family, especially at a time like this," I sympathize.

A small sob escapes her throat. Sera presses her lips together to suppress others that threaten. I can't stand to see her cry. Lowering the guardrail on the bed, I gingerly gather her up in my arms and hold her close. Soothing her as I would one of my kids who's woken up from a bad dream.

"Go right ahead and cry. Get it out. Tears can be a healing balm," I soothe.

That was all the invitation she needed. Her poor battered body convulses with deep racking sobs. I just hold her and let her cry until all her tears are spent. When she is done, I lay her back against her pillows. With a cloth I retrieved from the bathroom, I wipe away her tears and bathe her face.

"I'm so alone," she hiccups.

"Now what nonsense is this?" I demand. "When an angel falls from heaven and lands in Paradise, she has an entire army at her disposal, a whole host of angels." She looks at me inquisitively. "As far as I'm concerned Sera, you're one of mine now, one of us that calls Paradise home. We take care of our own and we'll take care of you, if you'll let us," I qualify.

"What's or where's this paradise?" she asks.

"Why, darling, Paradise is the name of my ranch. It's where the storm brought you. Kind of like Dorothy, and no, this isn't Kansas."

I delight in hearing her appreciative giggle.

"Whatcha say? Gonna let us take care of you? You'd be welcome for as long as you wish."

"Aren't you worried about the safety of your people and your children?" she asks worriedly.

"I figure, as long as Devlin is out there, they're in danger. You being here or out at the ranch won't change that. Might as well have everyone under one roof. When you're feeling better and even after the danger has passed, you're welcome to stay. Stay as long as you need. Take your time deciding what you want to do and where you want to go," I sketch out the plan.

I can see her hesitation. "My daughter, Lailah, would be overjoyed to have you stay," I tell her, giving her a wink. "Both my cherubs would welcome you into our home."

"Lailah! The name means night angel," she murmurs. "Cherubs." She gives me a sideways look. "What's your name?"

"Gabriel. My name is Gabriel Slayer."

Her eyes open wide. "An archangel. A warrior angel," she gasps.

"Yes, ma'am. Seems Paradise is home to a whole host of angels."

Chapter 10

Sera

I stayed in the hospital for a week. Gabriel came to see me practically every day. He even brought Lailah and Daniel on one occasion. Lailah gave me a copy of the picture she had drawn of me. I could see why the endearment Gabriel gave his kids was cherub. They're adorable little angels.

"See, and these are your wings. I got the color of your hair and eyes wight," she proudly points out. It's adorable the way she struggles pronouncing her rs.

"Wow, I've never had a picture drawn of me before," I tell her.

"You can have it. Daddy let me pwint off lots of them. I taped them all over the ranch so evewyone would know what you looked like," she says.

"Thank you. I shall treasure it always. First chance I get I'm going to find the perfect frame for this," I tell her, delighting in seeing her puff up with pride and pleasure.

"How are you feeling?" Gabriel asks, coming to stand behind his exuberant daughter.

"Better. Each day is a bit better," I admit. "Getting lots of rest."

My cuts and bruises are fading. The only lingering injuries are my shoulder and my leg. Both are healing. Had a bit of a scare with the leg thinking that infection had set in, but that was treated and on the mend. Time is all that is required, now.

"Doctor says they're ready to release you. You'll just need to have periodic check ups," he says, eyeing me in a peculiar way.

"It will be nice to be in new surroundings. Hospital beds can get a bit...monotonous," I say, after searching for the right word.

"Where do you think you will go to convalesce?" Gabriel asks. "You thinking of staying here, going into protective custody? Or have you decided to go back to Albany?"

"Well, I like sticking with the doctor I have now, so staying local is more along the lines of that. Being placed in protective custody isn't any guarantee that I'll be safe. I mean, Devlin was able to go around them all, get David out of the prison where he was being held, and even managed to get him to Albany," I reason.

Gabriel sneers at my words, making plain his feelings about the FBI agents involved in David's case.

"Yeah, if they have a mole in their agency, no telling who it is or what additional trouble they can cause. There's no way they can guarantee your safety." He agrees with my reasoning.

"Sera, my earlier offer still stands. You're always welcome to come back to Paradise with me. I've got a nice size house. You'd get a room of your own. There's lots to do. You could rest or work in our clinic or help around the place, whatever suits your fancy," he says. His eyes never waver as he lays out this option. He offered earlier, but I wasn't sure if he was just being courteous, displaying some sort of mountain or ranching etiquette.

I have to admit, of all my options, that's the one I like the best. My only real concern is the safety of his children and all those innocent people who live on the ranch and work for him. When I bring up my concerns, he waves them aside.

"Life is full of risks, some more apparent than others. If we refuse to act and do because of what we perceive may happen, then where does that leave us? I can take measures to protect my children. I can see that all those at Paradise are extra attentive and alert. There are things that are being done and will be done to ensure that all are kept as safe as possible. In the end, there is no guarantee," he says.

At least he's honest. He makes me feel more secure with him than I do with any of the federal agents that have been in and out of my room around the clock since my arrival. But he is right. There is no guarantee, whatever my choice, that I will remain safe.

"I accept your very generous offer," I tell him with a grateful smile. "When can we get out of here?"

To my utter delight, he tosses back his head and belts out a hearty laugh.

∞∞∞

"This is all yours?" I'm amazed, simply overwhelmed by the scope of it as I continue looking out of the truck window.

"Yup. All the land you see, all thirteen thousand acres is Paradise Ranch. It has been in my family for many generations," he says proudly.

"It truly looks like a paradise. Not a Garden of Eden, mind , but something more...oh, wild and untamed. Instead of placing humans at the top of the food chain as you would expect in Eden, it places them on equal footing with all the other living creatures that call this place home." I blush when he gives me an intense look.

"Sorry." I dip my head in embarrassment. "I hope I didn't insult you."

"None taken. In fact, I agree with what you said. I'm just impressed that a person who's never been here before can understand such a thing in just a short while." He tries giving me a reassuring smile. "I'm rather impressed." His voice has gone husky with silkily undertones.

The smoothness of his voice combined with the glint in his eyes only makes me blush even more. I'm drawn to this man. To amuse myself and satisfy my curiosity, I continue to watch him as he keeps two hands on the wheel and drives us to his home.

Gabriel is tall and broad of shoulder as one would expect of an archangel. His well muscled arms are a testament to his ethics of being a hands-on ranch owner. Lean muscles filled with strength from hard work. When he sees my gaze lingering on his large rugged hands, he grips the wheel that much harder. A secret smile emerges on my lips. You know what's said about the size of a man's hands... Gabriel's are some of the largest I have ever seen.

I clear my throat and hum a bit to cover my nervousness and my growing arousal. The looks he casts in my direction makes me blush even more. I think he knows the effect he's having on me. I like it.

I flicker a peek at his face. A faint blush has emerged under that tan. My own eyes twinkle in amusement.

A full head of short cropped, blond hair sits under that cowboy hat he likes to wear and is well paired with his hazel eyes. Both help to slightly soften his rugged handsomeness. I find it very appealing. It isn't just his looks that I'm drawn to, it's his aura. Gabriel seems able to emote, without any effort, a sense of calm confidence. It makes me feel safe. I haven't felt safe in the longest time.

Now that I've had my momentary fill of manly beauty, I go back to looking out the window. Such a difference in scenery from what I was raised in in upstate New York. I find I like it too.

"Do you raise only cattle?" I ask, not just to be conversational. I want to hear more of his voice.

"We raise a small herd of sheep and goats that are used in the making of cheese. Some are raised for meat and fiber. We also have orchards and vineyards. We've been diversifying what we raise, grow, and produce here at Paradise. Sustainable agriculture may be coming back into style, but it's something that has always been an overarching philosophy on how we do things here," he tells me.

"My sister, Precious, would love this. She's a chef that specializes in farm-to-table dishes. Most of what she serves comes directly from our family farm," I tell him. "She lives in what was once our great grandparents farm house just outside of Albany, New York. When my parents retired, they sold off most of the acreage. Precious and Grace—along with my other sisters and myself—pooled our funds to buy two hundred of those acres including the farmhouse and barns. Grace is a botanist by training. She operates the farm along with Precious who then serves up what they grow and raise in her restaurant. I help out some when I am stateside."

I saw the smirk when he heard her name.

"Precious, as in Precious Angel?" he asks.

I laugh along with him. It took many years to get to this point.

"Yeah, my parents named all their daughters names that

go along with Angel." I ran down the list of them. Afterwards, I notice that he's quiet for a spell.

"Bet that was rough at times," he says.

"We all know my parents didn't do it out of spite but of love, but yeah, it was rough growing up. We learned who our friends were and that sisters always had each other's back."

"Which must make all this...even harder for both you and them," he says with understanding. "Tell me about your family."

Since he truly sounded sincere, I do.

It's nice to boast about my sisters. I'm proud of each and everyone of them. Each of us has our own calling in life and attacks it with zeal and passion. We believe that if you take on anything, you do it to the fullest or not at all. We are either all in or all out. No in between.

"What about your parents?" he asks.

"Still alive. Retired to an ex-pat community in the south of Spain. We email more than we call or see them. It's like they're kids again. We were raised on our family farm. When Dad decided he didn't want to farm any more, he sold a good chunk of the land to a developer. My parents retired on the money that sale brought."

"What about you? Got any family? I know you have two children."

"My parents passed a few years ago. Dad died of a heart attack. Mom didn't want to live without him so she followed a few months later. Got one sister. She's married and lives with her husband on another ranch," he tells me. "Have one brother too, but he is in the military. Currently, he's stationed at Kadena, Okinawa. I'm hoping he joins me here when he's done with military life."

"Your wife?" I prompt. He has two children. Just because

he isn't wearing a ring and hasn't talked about a wife doesn't mean there isn't one. I'd rather know upfront and not be surprised…or disappointed.

I can see dark clouds move over his eyes before they quickly recede. "Mary died nearly five years ago. Cancer. I'm a widower. My dad's old housekeeper, who's been like a second mother to me, Nana Elizabeth, helps with the kids," he says with a bit of a shrug.

The simple movement doesn't mask that this man has battled loss and death. Though he has others on which to depend, he has stood alone for quite some time. He shoulders a lot. Yet the burden hasn't seemed to erode his strength or his goodness. It has only made him better.

Soon we're pulling off the main road. We follow a well worn trail that takes us up to a formal gate and entrance way. Two men are there who quickly open the gate allowing us to pass through. Once on the other side, Gabriel lowers his window to speak to the men.

"How's it going?"

"Been pretty quiet all and all, boss," is the reply.

The other one speaks up, "Did have some suits here flashing FBI badges wanting entry. Told them they would have to come back when you were here or with the sheriff. That we didn't have authorization to let anyone on the property without your say so."

"You did right. Don't know who is authorized to be here by the Feds or pretending. Best not take any chances." He raises a hand in silent goodbye. "Remain on alert. I'll send some boys to relieve you soon."

"Is this necessary?" I ask worriedly. "I feel that I'm putting everyone out and bringing danger where it should not be." I drop my head and moan into my hands. "What was I thinking?"

Gabriel glances my way.

"When we get to the house, I'll call Agent Johnson and tell him I've changed my mind and will go into protective custody," I tell Gabriel with conviction.

Chapter 11

Gabriel

I would have slammed on the breaks after hearing those hideous words. Instead, I slow the truck to stop, placing it in park, then turn a scowl on her full force.

"What the hell does that mean? Why would you go and do something like that?" I bark.

She blinks. Obviously I have surprised and confused her.

Good going, hotshot, I scold myself. *Let's just give her another reason to leave and go elsewhere.*

"Mr. Slayer..."

Oh, so now she's back to being exceedingly polite. I know a brush of when it's coming. "Call me Gabriel or Gabe," I snap.

"Alright," she says calmly as one would to a cougar getting ready to pounce.

"Gabriel, I'm one person. You have *children* and a large number of people who look to you for their livelihood. I don't want to be a disruption, nor do I want to place everyone in danger. You've had to take measures that disrupt the natural flow of things. I'm already an inconvenience and a potential lightning rod of danger," she reasons.

Her hands are beginning to shake. Either she's in pain or she's scared. My bet's on a bit of both.

I place the truck back into drive. "Soon as we get to the house, I'll see you to your room so you can rest. You'll want to take another of those pain pills." Happy to see her nod of agreement. I smile. "And I'll be the judge of what is and isn't an inconvenience. Trust me, I am doing as I please. It pleases me and my children to have you with us for the foreseeable future. If I thought your being here would place them in an unacceptable amount of danger, I'd tell you so. Truth is, when you crashed near my land and wandered onto Paradise, you became mine," my words have her looking sharply at me, "...to worry over, to protect."

I don't want to say problem. As far as I am concerned Sera is no problem. Devlin maybe but not her. She's a puzzle that I fully intend to figure out.

"You agreed to stay. I'm holding you to that agreement," I tell her firmly.

Sera listens to me all the while a quizzical smile blooms across her face. When I'm finished she simply sits back in the truck seat looking out the window as serenely as ever.

"Okay," she says compliantly.

Now, I'm the one puzzled. I keep looking over at her then back at the road for the rest of the ride to the house.

There are several other manned gates we travel through. I'm not taking any chances. The place is starting to look more like a military complex or western fort. I touch my hat to each of the guys who let us pass. With the last gate, my man leans in close to the window.

"Zeke says he's waiting for you and to tell you so when you came in, boss."

I nod, acknowledging the message.

"Whose Zeke?" Sera asks.

"He's my general foreman. He's the older chap that helped you down from the horse," I say. "Been with Paradise since before I was born. He was born on the ranch like many of those who work here. He's more like family."

"This is a complete community," Sera remarks, looking keenly at the number of buildings that surround the main complex.

"You're right about that. There are several people whose families have been here for several generations, nearly as long as the Slayers. Kind of like one of those Highland clans of old." I smile to myself at the thought.

"We do have homes and trailers out at other locations around the ranch. This is the main hub. We've got horse and livestock barns," I say, pointing them out. "Bunkhouse for the bachelors and a few cottages for couples. We've a clinic for humans and a vet clinic." That gets her attention.

"A clinic?"

"Don't have a regular doctor. Maggie is a nurse by training. She does what she can when it's needed. Would be nice to have a regular doctor here full time, one that was willing to make home visits to the stations further afield," I tell her, planting a few seeds.

"Cheese shed, winery, and olive processing over there." I continue to point out buildings as we slowly make our way up toward the big house that stands on top of a rise.

As soon as I park the truck, the kitchen door flies open and out runs Daniel with Lailah hot on his heels.

"Daddy, daddy," they squeal their jubilation.

I hoist both up into my arms hugging them close and giving them noisy kisses. Before putting them down, I twirl them around, delighting in their shrieks of joy.

Elizabeth has come out to see after the children. She stands to the side wiping her hands on a dish towel as she observes the greeting and arrival of our guest. Motioning her over, I make the introductions.

"I have heard so much about you. It's good to finally meet you and put a face to the woman who's like a mother to Gabriel," Sera says, with a friendly smile.

Elizabeth blinks in return. Then a warm smile erupts on her stern face.

"The children have been excited all day knowing that you'd be arriving. Each helped in preparing your room for your stay," she replies.

"Sewa Angel, you're here at last," Lailah exclaims, as she bounds over.

She would have jumped into Sera's arms if I hadn't spoken sharply.

"Lailah! You must be careful. Sera isn't fully healed. She isn't strong enough to hoist you up in her arms as if you're a spider monkey," I tell her.

Lailah places her hands behind her back, lowering her head, sticking out her lip in a pout. "Sorry, Daddy. Sorry, Sewa," she sniffles.

Sera's heart obviously melts. "Oh, darling. I may not be strong enough to hold you, yet, but I sure would welcome a hug and kiss. In fact, the doctor says I require at least three or more a day. It will help me heal all that much faster." She smiles in welcome. A twinkle glitters in her eyes.

Joy radiates from Lailah who bounces over to Sera giving her a hug before kissing her cheek. She giggles when Sera exclaims, "Oh my, I do believe I am feeling better. It was just what the doctor ordered."

"We've given you a room on the main floor," Daniel says. "That way you don't have to go up and down the stairs."

"Why, isn't that nice. How thoughtful you have been." Sera praises.

Daniel preens under the praise.

I scoop her up in my arms and take her into the house.

"This is the kitchen," Lailah says, following behind.

Daniel grabs her meager bag of belongings. I make a mental note to make sure we get her more of everything.

"So warm and cozy, just like a kitchen ought to be and filled with such tantalizing aromas. Bet someone here knows how to cook. Can't remember how long it's been since I've had a real home cooked meal. Can't wait! I best pay attention so my sister, who's a chef, can add some new recipes to her repertoire."

I'm amazed to see Elizabeth blush.

We give Sera a whirlwind tour of the main level before taking her to the room selected for her.

"See, Sera?" Daniel exclaims. "It has its own patio doors that go out to the garden. Daddy says that Momma loved sitting out there when she was sick. It made her feel better. Do you think you will want to sit outside?"

"Oh, most certainly. In addition to hugs and kisses, I think the fresh air and sunshine will do me wonders," she tells him, earning a smile. "My, look at the beautiful flowers someone has picked from the garden. They are so beautiful and fragrant. Umm." She sniffs the colorful blooms. "I wonder who was so thoughtful?"

"It was us. We did it, Sewa. We were careful with the garden shears and picked ever so many. Elizabeth said it would be okay and didn't scold us for the number we cut. She even found pwetty vases to put them in," Lailah tells her. Daniel nods.

"Everything looks perfect," Sera says, pressing her hands together.

I sit her on the side of the bed then help her take off her hospital slippers. Gently, I help her arrange herself in the bed, placing the walker nearby so she can use it to get in and out of the bathroom at will. The children in their excitement and desire to be helpful run around showing her how to operate everything, the lights, the room intercom system, the wall mounted television. I can see her shoulders beginning to droop. She's tiring.

"Okay, cherubs. That's enough for now. Sera's tired and needs her rest. Run along and help Nana Elizabeth. I'll be right out," I order gently.

Though I expect a bit of reluctance, none is given as each hurries from the room but not before giving Sera another kiss and hug. Elizabeth and I exchange knowing looks.

"I'm sorry if their energy was a bit taxing." I'm so used to their zeal that I forget others might not be used to the boisterousness and exuberance of children. "They're good kids and mean well..."

"There's nothing to be sorry about," she laughs away my concerns. "They are both wonderful children. I like them immensely. It's nice to be so warmly welcomed. Everyone has been so kind and accepting. I love their energy, their goodness." She gives me a genuine smile.

I soothe back her hair as she sinks down into the pillows with a weary sigh. "You're fully wanted and accepted here. You're one of the family. Slayers of Paradise take care of our own," I reaffirm the simple truth.

There is wonder in her gaze.

"Rest now. I or Elizabeth will check on you later. If you need something, just call out." I can't resist giving her a healing kiss of my own.

At first, I kiss her brow, then her cheek. Her lips are so enticing that I can't resist placing another there. When those velvety lips of hers tremble then part, I'm lost. My mouth sink into hers, delighting when she responds in kind. This is no simple welcome home kiss or gentle healing smooch from a friend. No, this is a "where have you been all my life?" sort of kiss. A lover's kiss. I never want it to end.

We both come back to our senses simultaneously amidst fluttering eyes and tremulous exhales and deep inhales of desperately needed oxygen.

"I'm not apologizing for that," I warn her as I back toward the door.

"Good," she retorts, licking her now swollen lips with her pink tongue. I groan.

"I can guarantee that it won't be the last," I warn, daring her to say otherwise.

She holds my smoldering gaze, saying, "Now I'll have something more to look forward to."

I laugh then groan again.

"Get some rest."

I smile when I hear her murmuring, "Yeah, like that's going to happen now."

"Zeke," I call out to my foreman as I approach where he's grooming his horse in the stables. "Just got Sera settled. She's resting," I tell him. "Boys told me you just got back. Find anything of interest?"

"Good to have you back on Paradise soil, boss," he says. "Yeah, you could say I found several things of interest. Glad I got my grandkids to show me how to use this darned cell phone. I took pictures of what we came across." He holds out his phone, offering it to me.

Quickly I swipe through the images while I listen to his verbal report.

"Found where Sera crossed over into Paradise. Left bits of her dress on the wire. From there it was easy to track backwards. Clearly, she wasn't interested in hiding her tracks. That made it easier. But it became evident that she was running, escaping from something..."

"Or someone," I amend.

Zeke nods.

"Found a body in the woods. Looks like what didn't get blown away by a bullet got messed up by a bear."

I grimace as I examine the pictures of the gruesome sight.

"Matches what she told me and Agent Johnson." Not that I doubt her word, but it goes a long way when statements match the evidence. "Got more?"

Zeke nods, wrinkling his brow. "She must've run into the woods to escape this guy." Tapping on the image of the dead man. "On the other side, there's a place where someone else got injured. Plenty of blood. No body. So at least one is still alive."

Hmm. My mind is racing with what we'll need to do. I keep listening, Zeke's got more.

"Was able to trace her movements back to the crash

site. Pilot didn't make it. He must have died on impact, burned a bit too. What was left was scavenged." He grimaces. It's known to happen.

From what I'm seeing scrolling through his phone, Zeke is becoming an accomplished photographer. His images speak a thousand words, displaying a clear and gruesome picture of what happened and what Sera has gone through and survived.

"Put out a warning to everyone to be wary of hitch-hikers and strangers in the area. This third guy, the leader of the, calls himself Peter. He appears to be alive and possibly injured. No telling what he'll do if someone stops and gives him aid. The man should be considered armed and dangerous. Anyone comes across such a person, they're to not engage but to alert one or both of us." I make that clear.

"Nobody goes out from the ranch by themselves. That includes you, Zeke." He wants to protest so I raise a hand to stave off his objections. "I'll be taking my own advice on this too." That mollifies him somewhat.

"Look," I reason. "We know this mobster guy Devlin is behind this entire mess. He won't have a problem going through us to get to what he wants. He went through a lot of effort to get to Sera when she wasn't even involved with his criminal plans. That tells me he wants her for himself. I'm not going to allow him or any of his goons to hurt one of mine. And that goes for you." I punctuate my words with a thrust of a finger toward him.

"The suits will need to get back to those sites. Sheriff's boys stayed behind making sure it didn't get messed up. Not going to be easy getting equipment in and out. It's not like it's close to a highway, not even a logging road or hiking trail," Zeke tells me.

"Another reason to be careful until that third person is found. We'll be having a mess of people wanting access," I say.

Zeke cocks his head, then looks over at me. "Appears we've got company." I look around to see three large dark SUVs coming through the entrance. All the vehicles sport government license plates. Took them long enough.

"Come on," I say to Zeke. "Let's head them off and get some sort of control going on. I'm going to insist on names of those that need to work the site. I want some sort of way to know just *who* is on our land, where, and why. They will need to check in and out each time." Zeke is in full agreement.

"Agent Johnson." I greet the man when he gets out of the lead vehicle. "What brings you to Paradise?" I ask him, as if I don't already suspect.

"We need to get a team out to investigate and process the areas containing evidence and the crash site," he says.

"A little late to the party aren't, ya? I expected you here long before today," I tell him. "Sheriff's boys have already been out at the sites. Some of his boys accompanied some of my men. They were able to re-trace the route Sera took from where we found her back to the crash site. They found the remains of two bodies..."

"I've read the reports," he says, taking off his dark sunglasses.

"Well then, how can I help you?" I ask.

"Interesting. I thought maybe you would be less than cooperative," he muses.

I give him a puzzled look. "Why's that? Have I given you any reason to doubt my willingness to be accommodating and cooperative?" I press, lifting my chin in silent challenge.

"You seem to have undue influence over Dr. Angel," he replies.

"Ah. Well, I wouldn't call it influence. I just gave her another option that she happened to prefer over those you presented her," I remind him.

"How is Dr. Angel?" he finally asks.

"She's resting. My children are overjoyed with their guest and making her feel at home. I assume you'll be wanting to speak with her later, once you've organized your operation."

"At her convenience," he affirms.

"I'll be sure to let her know. Now, if you want to get started with your investigation, you'll need to speak with my foreman, Zeke. Let him know what you need and we'll try and accommodate you," I tell him, silently chuckling at his widened eyes of surprise, before heading back to the big house. And he thought I'd supervise? I trust Zeke, besides, I've got a ranch to run.

∞∞∞∞

I ease the door open to Sera's room as quietly as possible. I want to reassure myself that she's really here and peacefully resting. Just a quick peek is all I intend. When I see her stretch languidly under the covers then yelp from the pain it causes, I move further into the room.

"Need some more of your medicine?" My voice causes her to jolt in surprise. I can't hide my chuckle. "Sorry to startle you."

She waves away my concern. "I didn't hear you come in."

"I didn't want to disturb you. Just peeked in to check on you is all." Couldn't help myself, but I don't tell her that.

"Have I slept long?" she asks.

I point to the bedside clock. "Most of the day. You needed it." I excuse it when I see her sudden jolt of surprise and frown.

"We're getting ready to sit down to supper. You hungry?" I ask. "Thought maybe you'd like to join us. If you're still feeling too tired or poorly, we can bring you a tray and you can eat here."

"Company sounds wonderful," she breathes.

How long has it been since she's been surrounded by the chattering of children and the warmth of genuinely kind people? Sure, the nurses and staff at the hospital were nice, but the place was sterile and cold.

Sera needs help tending to her needs. I'm more than willing to play nurse. It's not like I haven't done this before. After helping her in the bathroom, next I help her put on a thick robe before placing her in a wheelchair and wheeling her into the main part of the house. Lailah and Daniel wait like an honor guard expecting a visiting dignitary. Leading the way like Sierra reindeer, they gallop down the hallway whooping it up, announcing her arrival with all the exuberance of town criers of old. Sera laughs while I shake my head.

"You'd think my children have never had a guest to dinner before," I say with a bit of embarrassment.

"Ah, I've missed this," Sera reveals. "I've longed for the rich deep warmth of home and family. My sisters don't have kids, but when we're together en masse, there tends to be lots of verbal excitement and chatter along with a few heated debates."

It's Elizabeth that finally puts her foot down. "What has gotten into you two?" she says, a bit crossly, shaking a finger at them. "You're acting like hooligans," she admonishes.

"Oh, they're just excited." Sera laughs away the kids' behavior. "The cheerful sound of children's voices is as welcome as an angel's chorus to my ears."

"I helped set the table," Lailah boasts to Sera.

"And what a fine job you did too," she praises.

Lailah beams as she takes to her seat.

"I took out the trash for Nana Elizabeth and helped fold the napkins," Daniel says, not to be outdone.

"What a wonderful helper you are, Daniel. I'm not sure what Nana Elizabeth would do without either of her helpers. It's so good of you to help in such ways. I bet you even keep your rooms all nice and tidy," she says, grinning when she sees their telltale blushes.

She ignores their embarrassment. "Bedroom cleaning can be very difficult," she sympathizes after giving it a thought. "I was never particularly good at it myself when I was your age and even older. Why, my parents had to remind me many times to see it done. Once I even missed going to the zoo because I hadn't cleaned my room to my mother's satisfaction," she confesses.

"Did you cry?" Lailah asks.

"Worse. I pouted. That got me a smack on the bottom and a disapproving scowl from my dad."

Lailah's mouth drops open. "I didn't know that angels got spanked," she says.

"Oh yes. When we Angels were very naughty, we even got a paddling," Sera assures her. "When my dad asked me why I didn't clean my room like I had been instructed, I told him it was because I didn't know how. So, guess what he did?" she asks. "He helped me. My father showed me just how to get it done. After that, it never was a problem again." Sera gives Lailah a big smile, turning it on Daviel when he snags her attention.

"Never?" Daniel asks a bit suspiciously. "How's it work?" he asks, curious on what she would say.

"Want me to show you?" she offers. "I'll show you too if you'd like, faerie whisperer. Would you both like that?"

They nod eagerly.

"Good then it's a date," she says, passing the peas and helping herself to a helping of mashed potatoes.

"Gabriel, if you would like, I'd be willing to check over your clinic. I could see what equipment and supplies you have on hand and suggest what else you might want to stock. I'd even be willing to see a few patients if there's a need. I know you said Maggie..."

"That would be wonderful," Elizabeth gushes, pausing in loading up her plate. "You'd really do that?"

"Of course. And just so you know, I'm a board certified doctor and can boast of being one of handful of doctors licensed in all fifty states. My last employer helped me obtain those beyond what I originally had. I assure you, I can legally practice medicine in California."

"I imagine that was helpful being a traveling doctor of a sort, visiting different places as you did." Elizabeth and I exchange looks.

"Being a doctor is what I'm trained to do and the work I love. I would be honored to be of service to the people here." Sera gives me an expectant look.

"I'd say that would be great. I know Maggie would be relieved." That's the truth. "If you're up to it, I'll show you the clinic tomorrow morning," I offer, happy that she wants to find a way to be part of the Paradise community. Her services will be greatly welcomed.

Sera beams and nods. She turns back to the kids. "That

leaves the afternoon for us to see about your rooms."

"Tomorrow is Saturday," Daniel reminds her.

"Really? I've lost all concept of time and days of the week. Is there something you do special on Saturdays?" Sera asks.

"It's our play day," he tells her.

"Okay. Is that a reason why we can't straighten your rooms?" Sera asks him without blinking. I have to swallow my chuckle and steal my face to remain neutral.

Daniel turns away avoiding her gaze, ducking his head. "No," he mumbles before shoving another fork full of food in his mouth.

"Golly," Sera gasps. Her exclamation gets everyone's attention, particularly the kids'. Leaning toward the kids as if she were a co-conspirator, she whispers. "Don't tell me, you've never played the *I Got It Done* game."

When they shake their heads, she gives them a look of surprise that it has them demanding what it is. Sera purses her lips and shakes her head. Heaving a dramatic sigh, Sera looks at Elizabeth and then at me.

"Do I dare?" she asks us.

Thoroughly enjoying the show, Elizabeth plays along. "Well I don't know..." She shakes her head then *tsks*. That has the kids nearly coming out of their chairs.

"Tell us! Tell us Nana Elizabeth. Sera?" Daniel urges.

"Mr. Slayer? They're your children after all." There will be no staying on the sidelines for me it seems. "Do we dare? Are they ready for something as...as..."

"Magical as the *I Got It Done* challenge?" I reply with a straight face. "Hmmm." I make a big show of considering the matter.

"Oh please, Daddy, can we twy it?" Lailah pleads anxiously, holding her hands gripped as if she were praying or begging.

"Come on, Daddy," Daniel adds his voice to the plea. "Let us a try. We've never tried it before. We can do it if you would give us a chance. You said a Slayer can do anything if they put their mind to it and gave it their all."

"Did I say that?" I ask, scratching my head as if trying to remember.

"You did, Daddy. I remember," Lailah says, backing up her brother.

I look over at Sera. "They're soooo young..."

"But there are homemade cookies at the end if they succeed," Sera whispers. "Maybe you're right. Your kids probably wouldn't like homemade cookies." She shrugs as if the conversation is over.

"Oh, but we doooo!" Lailah singsongs. "We like oatmeal, chocolate chip, and peanut butter."

"And snickerdoodles," Daniel adds.

"Yeah, them too," Lailah agrees.

"We'll do whatever you tell us to do," Daniel promises.

"Pwomise," Lailah says, crossing her heart.

Sera gives them a sideways look. "Well if you don't mind interrupting your play day schedule... Okay, it's a deal. I'll teach you the game tomorrow afternoon," she says, holding out her hand to shake with each of the kids.

I halt the shake. "Now, cherubs, when you shake hands you're making a contract, agreeing to a deal. There isn't any going back. Once a Slayer makes a powerful promise that he or she is willing to shake on, they can't go back on their word.

You understand?" I instruct.

"Yes, sir. We understand," Daniel hurriedly says, obviously afraid that the deal won't be made.

"Yes, sir," Lailah echoes.

They each shake Sera's hand.

"Okay contestants, the game will officially begin after we have finished lunch tomorrow," she promises.

"Yeah!" they cry out in unison.

Elizabeth presses her napkin to her lips suppressing her laugh, making it sound more like a cough. I simply raise a brow when Sera gives me a triumphant smile. I swear, little horns protrude from just beneath her halo.

Chapter 12

Agent Johnson

"Johnson, I want a full report, now!" Luther Devlin orders. "How can such a simple task of bringing me my new pet and ridding me of that damned traitor be so complicated? Incompetent fools! I pay people to be good at what they do, to do what I order and what do I get?" he growls like the dog from hell he is.

I just listen, allowing Devlin to bitch and moan to his heart's content. Glad that I'm not in the room with him. No telling who the sonofabitch will take his anger out once he hangs up. The how of it is even more scary. At least it will not be me. I've been around him when he was angry. Not pretty and neither was the guy on the receiving end of Devlin's wrath.

When there is only silence, I realize I've spaced out for a bit, allowing my mind to wander. I blow out a breath. Mentally I scramble for a way to save face as well as my ass.

"I'm waiting," Devlin bites out.

"Sir, I have people scouring the area as we speak. If there is anything that connects to you, I'll take care of it," I try to assure him.

"Make sure you do." To many, this would be a threat. From Devlin, it's a promise. "And?" The man is becoming increasingly impatient. Never a good thing.

"It's as Dr. Angel said, Frank and George are dead. Haven't found Peter. The woman said she might have wounded him. Says she saw him go down with blood on his forehead where she struck him with a rock."

"A rock?" Devlin half laughs. There's a note of respect in his voice.

"Some slingshot she made," I explain. That got the man laughing. It makes shivers crawl up my spine.

"Bring her to me," he demands. "Alive and well and in one piece." The panting of his breaths suggests he's aroused.

"That might be harder than I once figured," I confess. The silence is creepier than listening to him fume.

"Explain," comes the dark order.

"I planned to bring her to you when she agreed to go into protective custody," I tell him.

"Brilliant," he praises. "Why isn't that happening?"

"That rancher who found her gave her another option."

Again, Devlin waits silently for me to continue.

"Seems he has a kid who helped discover her. The kid thinks Dr. Angel is a real angel sent down from heaven. Well, anyway, Mr. Slayer's offered Dr. Angel to stay with him and his family at his ranch," I explain hurriedly.

"Hmmm, angels from heaven. That's rich." Devlin snarks a laugh. "Who's this rancher and what's the name of the ranch?"

I tell him. The silence seems to stretch out for some time.

"Sir, I've done a background check. The ranch is large. It has been in the family for over a hundred years. There are no financial problems, no criminal activity, no run-ins with the law. Everything seems to be above board. This rancher, Slayer, thinks she's his responsibility and doesn't seem to mind taking care of her and seeing her protected. There isn't anything I or the agency can ding him on."

"You. Have. Access," he reminds me.

"Yes, Slayer has been very cooperative on that score. He does require that we supply him with the number of agents to be on his land each day along with their names and photo IDs. For him, it's one of the precautions he's taking to keep his staff and family safe."

"You have access," he repeats. The silence hangs between us.

"I'll take care of it," finally saying what he expects.

"That you will, my boy. Don't fuck up. Let me know when I can expect your arrival. Oh, and if you see Peter, tell him he's fired. See that he's properly terminated."

"Yes, sir," I reply. The line goes dead.

I curse up a blue streak, causing several of my fellow agents to swivel and look in my direction. Oh yeah, I'll terminate the SOB Peter. That asswipe has left a mess that I now have to clean up. His failure is now putting me in jeopardy on multiple fronts. I won't allow that. This mess, *his* mess, could potentially reveal what has been hidden for nearly five years.

After ending the call, I place my phone in my pocket. Scrubbing my hands through my hair, I make my way to the other agents who've assembled in the paddock that contains our transport. Thank God, for helicopters. Wasn't looking to spend any amount of time on the back of a horse or being jostling for hours in an old truck traveling over rough terrain.

"Boss not happy?" one of the agents asks, startling me from my thoughts.

"You can say that again," I grouse, admonishing myself to be more careful. Messes have the ability to morph and spread, getting into places and infecting things you once thought out of reach and safe.

There's a reason we're called moles. We don't like coming out into the light. Instead, we burrow through all the layers of an organization, creating tunnels for our true masters to use behind us.

I'm not stupid like David. I knew what I was doing when I said yes to Devlin's offer. Get paid by Uncle Sam *and* by Devlin. In this world, if you don't look after yourself nobody else will. You gotta get all you can while the getting is good. I plan to live a rich full life.

I'm no fool. I know how to stay under the radar. If I have to snuff out an agent who's getting wise, hey, it was their mistake sniffing my way. Gotta have balls in this world or you'll be run over by someone who does.

Like I said, I'm not stupid. If Devlin thinks others will take the fall for him, or he points the finger at me, I'll return the favor. I've saved up enough dirt on the man that he would shit bricks if he only knew the half of it. He'll be spending several lifetimes behind bars or even on death row with what I've put together on the schmuck.

So, I play along. Sure, he can have me hurt, even killed. But it would take time to gain another man with my rank within the FBI. For the time being, I'm safe. Now I've got a job to do and if I don't get it done, I know that I'll have to make alternative plans.

"Everything alright?" another agent asks as I walk over to where the rest are waiting.

"Yeah, you know how it is with higher ups and all," I mutter.

I get the knowing looks, huffs, and laughs.

Surveying the assortment of government agents working the case wearing crisp new jeans and unscuffed L.L. Bean hiking boots, I swear, most have never been out of a city, let alone been out in a country terrain such as this. This is one investigation and cleanup I'm not relishing. It isn't like we have easy access to where the plane came down. It's a true wonder how Dr. Angel managed to find help and come out of this alive after battling two able-bodied men.

"Takes forever to get out here," I complain.

"Mr. Slayer has let us move trailers out there so some can stay on site and process all that shit. He's even letting us take out a copter," he says, pointing to where it stands waiting for us in one of the paddocks.

"Well alright then. What are we waiting for? Let's load up. We don't have much to comb through, but I want to be thorough," I tell them.

"No stone unturned," one jokes.

"Yeah, but there are a lot of stones and logs and nature shit to go through," another adds. We laugh appreciatively.

"Any word on Dr. Angel?" I inquire.

"Nothing new. She's been given a room on the main floor so she doesn't have to manage the stairs to the upper floors. We've got people posted keeping an extra eye on her in case Devlin or one of his goons get any bright ideas," I'm told.

"Hmmm, you don't say. Sounds good, sounds real good," I murmur softly to myself.

"What?" they ask, not catching my words. "Oh, I just said, good, nice of them." Waving it off.

I turn away not wanting them to notice that the wheels in my brain are turning. This news is something I can work with. Just need to come up with a plan that won't get me caught.

"Any word on this missing Peter guy?"

"The blood sample that Dr. Angel says came from the wound he suffered to the head isn't the same as the other two guys or Dr. Angel's. So it's proof that there is another man unaccounted for. We've put out alerts. There hasn't been any report of a hitchhiker being picked up or an injured or lost man found in these parts."

"Maybe he's dead or just good at hiding," I venture.

"If he's hiding, he would need food and water and a dry place to stay. We're looking into any hunting or logging cabins that may be in the area known to the locals. We might even consider bringing up some sniffer dogs before the weather turns rainy again and wipes away any traces."

"Yeah, get that going," I order.

Gotta make it look good to the brass that we are trying everything we can. Now with Devlin wanting this guy eliminated, I've got more incentive to find the dick.

Gabriel

"That's the last of it," the NTSB lead agent tells me.

I've never heard so many alphabet names since I studied the Great Depression and FDR's New Deal in high school. We've had people from the NTSB, FAA, and FBI out here on a regular basis. Not sure why so many from various agencies have to be working on the same site. Guess that's one place our tax dollars end up. Overlap on top of overlap.

"So what's the process from here on out?" I ask, a bit curious. The ranch will be much quieter with all these outsiders gone. Maybe we can get back to our normal routine.

"We've moved all the material into a hangar where we'll reassemble as much of the plane as possible. The collected material will be gone over to see what we can learn. Then we will issue our findings in a formal report," the agent explains.

"What about Dr. Angel?" I ask.

"Not our jurisdiction," he says with a shrug. "Agent Johnson will be the one to ask." He points out the agent I'm familiar with.

I scratch my chin as I watch him observing the last of the evidence bags being loaded up in the van they've brought with them. The larger pieces had to be airlifted with the use of the chopper. They were brought back to the main ranch compound then loaded onto trucks brought in for the cleanup and removal. The kids thought it was interesting and really got a kick out of watching.

"Yeah, I know Agent Johnson," I tell the guy, not quite able to hide my dislike.

I watch as the mini convoy rumbles through the gate toward the main road. I'm more than glad to see them go. For some reason the crash and investigation has gone under the radar of the media. There has been no mention of it in the paper or on television. Curious.

I even did a search on my computer for Dr. Angel and the trouble her ex-fiancé had gotten into. Again, it's strange how such a sensational story has gone unnoticed by the media. Then again, there are few real journalists left. Most are talking heads, people who regurgitate headlines from one or two news sources. Few really do investigative stuff any more. Sad for a democracy when you think about it. When the general public receives very little of what is happening because of the over flagellating of non-breaking 'Breaking News' or twenty-four hours of the same issue, it's as bad as yellow journalism in its day.

I catch up with Agent Johnson who is making his way toward the big house.

"Can I help you, Agent Johnson?"

The man stops then slowly turns around to face me. His entire demeanor seems odd. My instincts tell me that the man is not happy to see me. Evidently, he was trying to see Sera without my knowing. Now, it isn't like I see myself as her boss or parent, her keeper, however, I do feel protective of the woman. Still not sure exactly why, but this man always seems…off.

"Just thought I'd go see Dr. Angel before heading out. We're wrapping things up. Needed to settle a few things," he says a bit defensively.

"Then you won't mind me coming with you," I say nonchalantly, noticing that he stiffens with my words. Interesting.

"Mr. Slayer, I resent your interference," he says testily.

Coming up short, I scowl at the man. "Interference? Why, Agent Johnson, I think I've been very cooperative and hospitable considering the circumstances. What evidence are you drawing on that suggests I've been less than amiable and obliging?"

Agent Johnson huffs. Clearly agitated and vexed. His display of irritation and anger confuses me. There is something else here as well. He seems a bit anxious and impatient. I shake my head, perplexed.

"Come along," I invite. "I'm headed to the big house myself."

Now that's a lie. I have lots of work to see to in and around the ranch, work that has been left unattended due to all the interruptions of late. I am not going to tell him that. There's no way I'm letting him into my home without me, whether it's to see Sera or not.

One of my men is guarding the door though it appears he is simply lounging. "Jeb," I acknowledge as I escort Agent Johnson through the door.

Elizabeth—no surprise—pops out as soon as we enter. It's like a sixth sense. She always knows when the door opens and closes or is left ajar too long.

"Gabriel, Agent Johnson," she greets us. I can hear the question in her voice and it's clearly stated in her body language and eyes.

"Where's Sera? Agent Johnson is getting ready to leave and needs to see her before he departs."

"Ah, she and the children are out in the garden just off her patio," Elizabeth tells us.

She silently follows us, watching as I show Agent Johnson the way. I take him through the den, not through Sera's room. For some reason, I don't want him anywhere near her personal quarters.

I hear the giggling chatter of my cherubs before I see them. Their voices serve as the perfect homing signal, allowing me to locate them and Sera. We follow the walkway that leads to the private garden.

"Weed or plant?" Lailah asks Sera.

"Hmmm. Weed."

With a yank, Lailah pulls the weed from the soil. She holds it up for Sera to inspect with a mile-wide grin.

"I did it," Lailah crows.

"Roots and all. That was a good pull. Now what do we do with pulled weeds?" Sera asks.

"We put it into the bucket and then we will put them in the compost pile so they will become soil," Lailah promptly tells her.

"That's right. Good job," Sera praises. "Shall we keep going?" She rewards Lailah with another smile when Lailah nods.

"How are you doing Daniel?" Sera calls out to him.

"I got half a bucket of weeds now," he announces proudly.

"That's fantastic, Daniel. Oh, look how much better that bed looks because of your hard work," she exclaims.

Daniel shrugs his shoulders, but I can see his faint blush.

My ears must be deceiving me as well as my eyes. I come up short. "Okay, Dr. Angel, who are these garden gnomes and what have you done with my cherub children?" I ask her in a gruff voice, placing my hands on hips.

Sera bats her eyes in exaggerated innocence. "Why, Mr. Slayer, whatever do you mean?"

"Rooms cleaned, homework done without complaint, and now pulling weeds in the spring garden? Are you sure these are my cherubs?" I squint my eyes and lean down to inspect my two giggling children.

"It's us, Daddy. We're your children. We're your vewy own chewubs," Lailah says, tugging on my hand and giggling. "Don't you know us?" she asks.

Daniel is giggling behind his hand and has come running.

I squat down and look deep into her eyes then over to Daniel. "Give us a hug." I hold my arms wide to receive them.

Lailah and Daniel both give me a bear hug. "Hmmm,

feels like my cherubs' hugs." Screwing up my face, I give them the once over. "But it could be a trick."

"Quick, give him a kiss," Sera instructs.

The kids comply. "Hmm, could be could be, but I need a little more proof," I tell Sera. From the corner of my eye, I can see this play has served to further irritate Agent Johnson. Good. Let him wait. He's taken his time, a few more minutes won't hurt a thing.

The way Sera's eyes twinkle with mischievous delight is adorable. Sera's simply blown me away with how she interacts with my kids and how they so readily respond to her.

"Tell me a secret only my cherubs would know?" I challenge them, my arms crossed in front of my chest.

I squat back down as Lailah whispers into my ear.

"That's my girl." I breathe a dramatic sigh of relief. She giggles and leans into me as we wait for Daniel's turn.

He does the same. I am touched by what he says. Placing my hand around the nape of his neck, I draw him to me and hug him tight and kiss his brow.

"Yup, these are my cherubs alright," I tell Sera and wipe my brow in relief.

She claps her hands in response.

"Tell you what," I say to my kids. "Why don't you two show me what you've been up to and let Sera talk to Agent Johnson." They eagerly nod their heads, each one taking one of my hands as they draw me into the garden to show me.

I give a nod of encouragement to Sera. She understands that I'll still be here, and ensure she isn't left alone with this guy.

"Dr. Angel, can I have a moment of your time?" I hear the man ask in a polite respectful voice.

"Would you like to sit down?" Sera invites him.

As the man drags a patio chair closer to hers, I move into close proximity with the kids.

Chapter 13

Sera

"Dr. Angel, I just want to let you know that the cleanup and site investigation is now complete. The debris from the plane and other evidence retrieved will be analyzed and then an official report will be issued and filed," Agent Johnson tells me.

"We're looking to connect the three men who you say had a hand in murdering David and who abducted you with Devlin. We've found the remains of two men, but not the third. Are you sure there was a third?" he asks.

I narrow my eyes. Not particularly liking his question.

"Of course, I know there were three. Peter is the third one. Frank was the pilot and George just muscle, a thug. Peter was in charge of the other two. Peter was the one who was David's contact." All this rehashing of the same information is infuriating. Makes me wonder if they truly believe me or if something else is going on. It sure doesn't instill confidence.

"Do you think you could work with a crime artist and give them a description detailed enough to make a composite sketch?" he asks.

"I'm open to that, anything to help catch the guy," I try to reassure him. Not sure why that hasn't been done by now.

"Look, I know I wounded him." I'm more than a little irritated and it reflects in my voice. "I saw his bloody forehead when I hit him with a rock from my slingshot. He collapsed. If he wasn't dead the blow knocked him unconscious. The blow was hard enough to at least give him a concussion. George went over to check him. Even *he* thought I killed Peter."

By this point, I'm very frustrated. I glance over at Gabriel, the one person who has always believed me. His scowl tells me he's heard my words. Gabriel, himself, told me that Zeke found the place where I hit Peter. Blood was found. Any analysis will show that that blood is not the same as the other two guys or mine. Why is this agent lying to me?

My spidey senses are tingling, warning me to be wary of this man. As if I wasn't already. The guy has always seemed a bit off from the moment I saw him. His eyes always seem to be calculating.

"I'm not doubting what you say happened." Johnson speaks in a voice normally reserved for an idiot or person he suspects is a liar.

"Then why are you acting as if I'm lying, stupid, or confused?" I challenge, letting out a frustrated groan. "You know, I'm really tired of people treating me like I'm a suspect in some hideous crime. You want to know why people don't report crimes they witness to the cops? Take a good look in the mirror. There's your answer," I heatedly tell him.

Johnson holds up his hands in a placating manner. "I'm not accusing you of anything. All I'm trying to do is give you an update on what's happening." Liar. His lack of insincerity is reflected in his eyes. It's making me wonder what his true motive is in seeking me out.

"Then maybe you should work on your bedside manner or your people skills," I snap back.

Johnson narrows his eyes. There definitely is something in here that makes me uneasy. I wish he would just leave. But I have a few questions of my own.

"Did you recover David's body? What of Henri?" I ask.

"Yes, the murder was phoned in by a priest who discovered David," he tells me.

I couldn't help but frown. He didn't mention Henri. Was I wrong about him getting shot and killed? Had Henri managed to get out undetected? Was he alive?

"There wasn't anyone else there?" I ask.

"Nobody," he says, looking at me intently.

"Just why were you there, Dr. Angel?" he asks.

"What do you mean? What are you implying, Agent Johnson?" I demand, incensed.

"David was found wearing formal wedding attire. A tux. You were wearing a wedding gown. The two of you had been engaged." His implication is clear.

"I was there on a job. I was modeling bridal gowns for a client. Unfortunately, it was all a set up. It was really Luther Devlin. David showed up before I saw Devlin or his thugs. David told me that he had made another bargain... Hey, I told you all this already. Why must I go through this again?" I demand. "Just check with the modeling agency I work for and they will tell you," I insist. "I can't even believe that you haven't already done that."

This was all very peculiar. It was as if the FBI, or more to the point, Agent Johnson, was dragging his feet, not doing his job, delaying in putting all the pieces together until the evidence had gone cold or became useless.

"What of David's case?" I persist.

"The case is closed. Oh, we'll keep searching for this Peter and look into Devlin being behind it all, but as for David...the case is shut down now that he's dead. His parents claimed his body. They had his remains cremated," he tells me.

I bow my head readying to brace myself against the flood of feelings that may descend upon me. Strangely, all I feel is a momentary ping of sorrow. The sorrow is for the person I thought I knew. That David is now gone for good. What a shame. He was so talented. What a waste. But there are no tears.

Anger is what remains the most. Anger at the person David had chosen to become. Anger at myself for not noticing earlier he had a problem, for trusting him so implicitly as I had. In a way, I'm glad. Glad that we didn't marry. I want to always trust fully the one I give my heart and my hand to. It's surprising that I also feel relief. Relief that at least that part is over.

Blinking my dry eyes, I look over at Johnson who is still studying my reaction to the news he's just delivered.

"I'm sorry," I murmur. "I don't feel what I thought I would. The David that died that day was a stranger to me. I didn't know him. The David I loved was gone by then. Pity." I sigh.

"There have been no threats made against you by anyone, including Devlin," he tells me. "We've had no reports of anyone trying to sneak onto the ranch. I think it may be safe to say that you're safe."

That should be reassuring. It isn't. It leaves me confused.

"Why would Devlin give up so easily?" I ask, more to myself than him. "Devlin went through a lot of effort and considerable expense to break David out of prison, transport him up to Albany and himself as well. It isn't cheap to request a private showing of bridal gowns and to do it on location." My brow crinkles in confusion.

"Maybe Devlin has moved on," Johnson tells me.

"I hope that's the truth of it." Really hoping this is the case. Devlin can have anyone. Why me? Surely, Devlin would have found someone more to his liking—and willing.

I make to push myself up to my feet. When Agent Johnson sees me make the move, he waves me back. "There is no reason for you to get up."

He hands me another one of his business cards. "I'll be in touch, but just in case…feel free to get a hold of me. If you think you see Peter or Devlin, don't hesitate to contact the authorities."

"Thank you, Agent Johnson. I'll remember to do just that."

"Just how should I get a hold of you…" he begins.

"I still haven't replaced my phone, but you can always call Mr. Slayer. I'll be staying on for a while longer yet. He can pass on any messages you leave with him."

I can tell Johnson doesn't like hearing this. Oh well, what I do is none of his business. I'm enjoying my time here at Paradise and really don't want to leave any time soon. As long as I'm not a burden, I don't see any need to go just yet.

I watch in silence as Agent Johnson walks away. After a short while, I feel a presence and look over to discover that Gabriel has joined me. I give him a half-hearted smile. He tilts his head, giving me a speculative look.

"Anything the matter?" he asks.

I shake my head. "No, just a strange feeling that I can't

seem to shake." Giving a bit of a shudder.

He follows where my eyes linger on the retreating form of the FBI agent then purses his lips. "I think I know what you mean."

I'm surprised and heartened to hear his words. "Yeah? At least I know it just isn't me," I murmur.

Chapter 14

Gabriel

Spring is a crazy time at the ranch. There always seems too much that needs attention. Though it's the tail end of calving and lambing season, it's also planting season. We work from sunup past sundown and sometimes all night long. We try to bring in the ewes and cows we know are getting ready to drop so we can keep a close watch on them.

Even with all the work, I like spring. Spring is the time of year of new beginnings. Many think that about the first of the year. They're wrong. January may be the start of a new calendar year but for a rancher or one that works the land, it's the arrival of calves and lambs and the sowing of the seeds that marks a new year. New life. And new life is the promise of a future filled with possibilities and so it is with each spring.

Since Sera has been with us at the ranch, I feel a new energy buzzing about that was absent before. Sera has brought new life to my world, to Paradise. My children seem happier. Even Elizabeth wears a smile more often. More frequently, I catch her humming as she goes about her work.

"Morning, Zeke," I say when he walks into the kitchen.

I grab another mug and fill it with coffee for the old man. He takes it, nodding by way of thanks.

"Got three more ewes that dropped in the wee hours,"

he tells me. "All twins. We've got enough new ones to fill orders and increase the size of our herd. Just two more waiting to drop. Got two heifers left to go and we'll be done with this season's birthing, of the livestock at least," he says with a short laugh. "Some of the women folk are due any time too," Zeke reminds me. "Our family here at Paradise sure is growing," he says off handedly.

"That reminds me," I say, looking over at Zeke. "You know the developer that bought out the Peterson spread?"

Zeke nods. "Who could forget. The land sits right across the main road from us," he says with a sneer.

"Well seems this developer is in way over his head and needs to let go some of the land in order to pay off his creditors." I delight in seeing Zeke's eyebrows nearly reach his receding hairline. "I'm going to meet with him over there later on today. Want to tag along?"

"You interested in buying?"

"The man made a mess of that land, building those new homes. All of them are vacant as is the old homestead. There are barns and plenty of out-buildings still intact. The guy built a community clubhouse and pool. Thought if the price is reasonable I'd see about purchasing it all and opening up the homes for those with growing families. We could convert one of the buildings into a school..."

Pride shines from Zeke's eyes. "Seems you've been giving this some thought."

I give him a crooked smile. We already have an elementary school of sorts. A couple of the wives originally began a homeschooling program that's grown to include most of the kids living in Paradise. As the kids age, it seems only natural to continue offering schooling for them.

One of the reasons so many family ranches and farms

fail is that people move away when they start having kids. Many think urban living brings with it more opportunities and comforts. One of those being schooling. Another is medical care. People who work and live at Paradise get free housing and meals that are offered communally. I plan to expand the medical facilities with the help of Sera. in addition to educational services. The new modern homes combined with recreational places like a pool and clubhouse will help keep those tempted to leave or attract others with skills needed on the ranch.

There is more to be done on a ranch than working with livestock. Which is why I want to attract more skilled workers. We have the freshest milk and make quality butter and cheese. Eggs and a variety of protein is raised and processed here on site. We grow an array of vegetables, flowers, and herbs. There are our orchards, expanding vineyard and winery business as well as our olives. Bees are kept on the grounds. Might be worth considering opening up a convenience store or farmer's market, maybe even a café.

All of this and more is part of the sustainable operation under which we operate. Most of our food is raised or grown right here on the ranch. I'm looking forward to the day when everything we serve up here on the ranch comes from Paradise.

Both of us turn as we hear a noise from the hallway. Sera. There she is already dressed and bright eyed. My brow furrows.

"What are you doing up so early?" Finding myself going to her instantly. She waves away my assistance.

"Thanks, I got this." She uses crutches to maneuver into the kitchen. Her leg is still in a boot cast. The thing is gangly and heavy. "You can pour me a cup of that coffee though," she says. "I'm still not as graceful as I'd like to be." In answer to my earlier question, she says, "Got a few things I want to get done at the clinic. Thought I'd get an early start."

At my raised brow she continues, "Maggie and I are going through everyone's medical records. We want to make sure everyone is up-to-date on their vaccinations. We are also going to box up the files that aren't active. Maggie and I have a few thoughts about how to possibly expand the clinic. Then, of course, there are a few patient appointments scheduled…"

When she sees my questioning look, she rushes to add, "We aren't going to do anything without your say so, but we wanted to see what our options are before approaching you. You know, get all the facts before we pitch the plan to the boss man." She half laughs.

"Want to give me a taste of what's to come?" I'm intrigued. Seems their plans may be playing into my own.

She bites her lower lip in that sexy way she has that makes me want to do it for her.

"Well, we thought about seeing if we couldn't make room for an x-ray machine. Depending on the one we get and where it's located it could be used for both people and animals from the vet clinic. An ultrasound machine would be nice to have around too. A birthing room and a recovery room for in-house surgeries would be nice. Maybe even a small surgical room and at least one more patient room. That way Maggie can see the cases she can handle and so can I at the same time," she reveals.

"That's about it, for now." She gives a decisive nod.

"Sounds interesting." I glance over at Zeke who is considering what he's heard, nodding while Sera laid out the basic concept.

"Make your proposal and what costs you think may be involved with construction and equipment. Then you and Maggie can pitch it," I tell her.

"All right." She smiles.

Sera finishes her coffee then heads out the door on her crutches. She's almost out when one of my boys rushes in, giving Sera an apologetic expression for nearly running her over in his haste.

"Boss, Zeke, come quick," Toby says breathlessly. His flaring nostrils and his grim expression alert us that something's wrong.

"What's up?" I demand, setting my mug on the counter.

"Me and the morning crew went into the lambing shed making the rounds like we normally do. That was when we... found..." He stops, looking over where Sera has come to a dead stop and stands listening.

"Found what?" Zeke urges.

"Don't think it be right saying with a lady present," he murmurs apologetically, rotating his hat in his hands.

"It's okay. Say what needs saying," Sera encourages.

Toby gives her a grimace and a look of apology. "Some of the new lambs have been slaughtered, hacked to pieces, boss."

"Stay inside and lock the door behind us," I order Sera. She would have objected, but I quickly stop that. "The children, Sera..."

Her eyes flare then she nods.

Zeke and I run with Toby to check out what he's reported.

"Shit," Zeke mutters. Several of the crew are loitering around, waiting for us to arrive and inspect the damage.

"Did anybody see anything?" I demand. "What about the cameras?"

We usually have remote viewing cameras set up allowing those on watch or supervisors the ability to check out the lambing shed at any time. It records everything just in case we have questions that need answering, like we do now.

"That's the funny part," I'm told. "The cameras blinked off. All we get is snow for about thirty minutes then when they're suddenly back on, this is what we find."

"Whoever did this knows about the cameras and how to operate them," Zeke puts in.

"Why? Why would someone do this?" Toby asks, dragging a hand through his hair after he surveys the carnage.

"Sacrificing the lamb. Sheep's blood... Could be symbolic," Zeke says, thinking out loud.

"Nothing symbolic in slaughtering an innocent ewe and her twin lambs," someone says.

"Not necessarily." I look over at Zeke. "You thinking what I am?" My anger is beginning to grow.

"I expected something would happen when there were so many outsiders around. Maybe one of those outsiders figured out how to access the ranch and the place. Our guard is down now that the site investigation and cleanup are finished," he reasons.

"Exactly. The third guy is still unaccounted for. And I'm convinced there's a mole within the FBI's investigative team," I tell him grimly.

"What do you want to do about this?" Zeke gestures to the carnage.

"This isn't the work of some screwed up kid or a rival rancher. This wasn't done by some drunk or person bent on pulling pranks. This was deliberate, thought out. There's a purpose behind it," I vocalize my thoughts.

I look squarely at Zeke.

"Document it. Call the sheriff. Have him or one of his deputies check it out and log it in. Take pictures, talk to our own. Something tells me this won't be the last. Tell everyone to be alert. No more solo jobs or riding out alone. Everybody has a partner and needs to check in and out," I tell him and those around me.

I receive nods, murmurs, and watch as Zeke pulls out his phone.

"Okay, Toby, keep a watch over this mess until the sheriff gets here. Take a few pictures while you wait. Let's keep the women and the kids out of here. Toby, you were right," I meet his eyes with a look of respect in my own. "They don't need to be seeing this. Let me know when the sheriff or his deputies arrive."

I move away, confident that my crew can handle the rest. I knock on the kitchen door. Sera has done as ordered. She's locked the doors. Rarely do we do that. Few doors are locked and barred. Same thing with cars. Most of us kept the keys in them. Ranch owned vehicles are also kept this way so they can be used when needed without any hassle. We have no crime here. Sure, a fight might break out from time to time, but that's usually the worst of it.

Elizabeth is the one to open the door and let me in. She purses her lips when she sees my face.

"Where's Sera?" I ask.

She motions with her head toward the dining area. Sera is sitting with my kids eating breakfast. It looks so...Norman Rockwellian. I feel my stomach clench and my heart thud heavily in my chest. Is it selfish to want that, always?

I must have made a sound because Lailah hollers. "Daddy!"

"Morning, cherub." I give her a kiss and do the same to

Daniel.

"Are the two of you finished with breakfast?" When I get nods, I encourage them to run up and brush their teeth.

"I'll be seeing them to school this morning," I tell Elizabeth. "I would appreciate it if you walk them home. We'll need to keep them close for a while yet."

Sera and Elizabeth both look expectantly at me. Both are waiting for an explanation. With the kids out of the room and ear shot, I tell them what was found and what's being done.

"Do you think it's connected to Devlin?" Sera asks.

I nod.

Her eyes cloud and I hear a pained sound coming from her throat.

"Now, I don't have any proof but my own instincts," I warn her, trying to not upset her too much.

I watch as she blinks rapidly and looks away. She's clearly projecting worry.

"Maybe I should leave," she whispers. Her eyes seek out Elizabeth before landing on me. Earnestly, she says, "I couldn't live with myself knowing that I've brought danger to your midst. If it's me they're after, they'll follow me and leave you all alone. If anyone was harmed..." She chews her lip. "Those poor lambs and that sheep." She sobs, cupping her face in her hands. Like a flick of a switch, her face screws up with anger. "How diabolical!"

Fear and worry, I expect. I never expected to see her rage. Yet here it is. I stand here watching it bloom and grow. This is no longer a peaceful quiet angel. This is a raging, avenging angel, hell-bent on striking down those who threaten Paradise and those that call it home.

That she's willing to sacrifice herself and leave the only place she feels safe has me drawing myself up wanting to battle all the demons from hell just to keep her here, where she belongs.

"Don't go getting any foolish notions about leaving. I don't want you scared off," I tell her with a point of my finger in her direction. I run my hand through my hair, trying to calm down. My frustration is building. I've got too much on my plate. Don't need to add worrying about her gearing up to run, slipping off, and trying to leave just now.

"Look, if you want to leave...I guess I have to accept that. If it were my decision to make, I'd be keeping you here," I tell her honestly.

Elizabeth gives a nod to emphasize my words.

"None of us want you to leave. And if my kids were asked, they would say the same thing. I know things are getting scary. Believe me when I say, you're safer staying here then leaving and fending for yourself." Of that I am convinced.

∞∞∞

Sera

"It's true, outside of my family, there isn't anything out there for me. I have no job. Global Medicine probably won't want me back. Even though I wasn't involved with David's stupidity, I will always be associated with it. I do like being a doctor. I guess I could set up shop anywhere." I'll have to give it some thought.

"Then stay," he says, drawing back my attention.

"Maggie has nothing but good things to say about your work at the clinic. Truth is, we need a full-time doctor close at hand. Expanding the clinic was something Maggie has always pushed for, but I never thought it possible as it has not been easy to find someone who wants a small country practice," he tells me.

"That's crazy," I reply in disbelief. "Who wouldn't want to work and live in Paradise?" I add with a chuckle. "I've always thought that I was born a century too late. I would love being a doctor making house calls. I want to live in a community where everyone knows each other. I don't understand the draw people have toward urban living where they live in too similar houses on postage stamp sized yards. Never speaking to one another or knowing their neighbors' names," I tell him with a shake of my head. "Sure, that life is great for those who like it, but not for me."

"You're still on the mend. You've got three or four months until your leg is fully healed. Take the time to heal," Elizabeth urges.

"In the meantime, you'll live here. Work as much or as little as you want in the clinic," Gabriel tells me.

"Okay," I whisper my agreement.

Gabriel's face lights up with a bright smile. He pulls me into his arms and holds on tight. Being held this way makes me feel safe. I feel myself melting into him. When I look up into his pleased face, his smile suddenly disappears. His head lowers. His lips touch mine and then I forget everything.

David and I have kissed. David wasn't my first. But never, ever have I been kissed like Gabriel kisses me. I'm positive my toes are curling. If I wore hair ribbons, they'd be on fire right about now.

My arms encircle his neck. I pull him closer. A moan escapes his throat before his questing tongue finds mine as I open my lips in welcome. Too quickly, I'm lost in the moment, in the kiss. Magical—heavenly.

I only come back to reality when I hear Elizabeth clearing her throat. Slowly, our lips disentangle. Then before we're totally free, we feverishly press them to the other once more. Gabriel gives me little nips as we begin to pull apart once more.

"Daddy!" squeals Lailah.

"Eeew," screeches Daniel who then quickly covers his sister's eyes and his own.

"Now you're gonna have to marwy her," Lailah sing-songs, dancing around the room.

"Huh?" I query. My tongue is still too tied to speak clearly.

"Nancy says that her mother said that when a boy and a giwl a kiss, then they have to get marwied. It's some kinda wule," she says seriously.

"Sewa and Daddy sitting in a twee, k i s s i n g. First comes love. Then comes marwiage. Then comes a new mommy with a big fat tummy, then she's pushing a baby in a baby carwiage," Lailah chirps over and over again.

"Lailah," Elizabeth warns with a giggle of her own.

It doesn't help when Daniel joins in with his sister.

"Okay, you two. Come on. I'm walking you to school today. Nana Elizabeth will come get you when it's time to come home for lunch and at the end of the day," he tells them.

"I'll tag along then head off to the clinic," I say.

As we make our way from the house, it feels like we're indeed a family. When Gabriel doesn't chastise Lailah and Daniel for their modified children's rhyme, I get all warm inside. I love being from a large family. I've always wanted one of my own.

I blush as I catch Gabriel looking at me. Does he know my thoughts? I'm already excited that I get to stay here in Paradise. To be able to stay here forever seems like a dream come true.

∞∞∞∞

Sera

It was something out of a gory horror movie. I've walked into a bloody nightmare. I stand in the doorway of the clinic, broken glass scattered and laying under my feet. All I can do is stand in utter dismay and disbelief.

Why? Who would do such a thing?

Since yesterday, someone has broken into the clinic. The place has been ransacked. Nothing has been left upright or whole. Everything appears destroyed or toppled over. I would have plunged in to see what else has been destroyed, but something holds me back. It's as if two firm hands have grasped a hold onto the back of my shirt and are tugging, refusing to allow me to enter farther. Have the few drugs kept on hand been taken? Usually those are kept under lock and key.

The knowledge of what has happened in the lambing shed helps prevent me from plunging in. With that in mind, I step back out. Gathering myself in order to think straight, I'm unaware that someone approaches me.

"Dr. Angel?" I hear the voice at the same time a hand touches my shoulder.

I yelp, nearly jumping out of my skin.

"Oh, Zeke," I breathe out in relief. "You nearly scared me to death," I exclaim, placing a hand on my racing heart.

"You alright?" he asks, crinkling his eyes the way he

does when inspecting something intently.

"Zeke, ss...someone's broken into the clinic. Looks like they've destroyed most of everything," I tell him in a rush.

"Stay here," he orders.

He hurries in a bow-legged run to look for himself. Quickly, he comes back out muttering and shaking his head. An angry look on his face. Swiftly, he goes to a pole with a bell hanging on it. He rings the bell three times, making it peel, disturbing the morning quiet.

Instantly, I hear shouts and the running of feet. Men and a few women come charging over. They come to a sudden stop when they look for the reason for the alarm, finding nothing. Cutting through the growing crowd, I see Gabriel quickly making his way toward us. When he sees me, he speeds up his pace.

"What's up?" Worry is clearly written on his face.

"Take a look inside the clinic, boss." Zeke motions him with his head.

I nod when Gabriel looks my way. "I'm okay." He lets his hand skim my arm before moving off.

I follow behind him as he hurries to the clinic. I can hear his cursing as I approach. Zeke remains with me along with a few others who came at the sounding of the alarm bell.

Zeke looks at me. My cue to speak.

"It was this way when I arrived this morning. I didn't go any further. I'm not sure how much is destroyed, but if reception and the waiting room is like this..." I can't finish.

Gabriel looks over my shoulder at one of his men. "Is the sheriff still here?" He receives an affirming reply. "Tell him we need him over here too."

The man runs off.

Taking me by the shoulders, Gabriel asks quietly, "Are you sure you're okay?"

"Just a bit rattled," I breathe, nervously pushing a stray bit of hair away from my face. When I see my hands are shaking, I clench my fingers into a tight fist.

"This is twice in one day," Gabriel says to Zeke.

Zeke simply nods then tosses me a glance.

"It's because of me, isn't it?" I say in an anguished voice. "Please don't sugar coat this. I know it is. I'm bringing harm and danger to you all. It's destroying you from the inside out. This can't continue." I begin to tremble and shake.

Gabriel takes me into his arms, holding me while we wait for the sheriff to arrive.

"I'm frightened," I whisper into his chest.

"I know, angel mine. I know. But I promise I will do all within my power to protect you," he replies in a fierce whisper.

"Whatcha got?" The sheriff approaches, tipping back his hat and scratching the top of his brow.

"Looks like someone broke in and trashed our clinic overnight too," Gabriel informs him as they walk into the clinic.

The sheriff pops his head out and whistles getting the attention of one of the deputies.

"We're going to have to process this, Mike," he calls out.

"Well, Gabe, seems you're having yourself a bit of trouble of late," he comments.

"You know how it is in Paradise, Sheriff. From time to time, demons try to break in. Angels must battle the evil brought to their door. In the end, the angels always win. Good always triumphs over evil." He gives me a poignant stare.

The sheriff gives Gabriel an appreciative laugh then disappears into the clinic, motioning Gabriel to join him. It's a while before they come back out.

"Dr. Angel, I need you to come in, careful now, and tell me if you see anything that might be missing," the sheriff requests.

Mindful of the glass and debris littering the floor I make my way back to the examination room and then the supply room.

"We don't keep any money in here. There isn't any reason as healthcare is free for all employees and residents," I tell him. "We keep the drugs and much of the equipment locked up in the cabinet safe back in the supply room." I head that way, aware the guys are following.

I breathe a sigh of relief. The drug safe hasn't been broken into. I open it anyway to check. Yep, all there. One less thing to worry about. The smile on my face disappears when I turn around and freeze.

"What?" Gabriel demands. Then he sees what's caught my attention.

On the mirror by the door someone had written with a sharpie that now lays on the floor: *It is mine to avenge; I will repay. In due time your foot will slip; your day of disaster is near and your doom rushes upon them. I am the devil's servant and he is my master. His will is mine and shall be done in accordance with His laws.*

"It's a play on the verse from Deuteronomy," the sheriff says softly.

"A warning," Gabriel states. "Just like the slaughtering of the lambs."

"The question is who did this? Was it Peter? Or is it

someone else?" I ask.

I can't help but shiver. It's a warning alright. The message is clear. Devlin's thugs are coming for me. They will kill all who harbor me, destroying anything they can that is good and innocent to get to me. Do they intend to kill me or simply take me to Devlin? Why does this man want me so? Am I the lamb being led to the slaughter or am I the ewe and Lailah and Daniel the lambs? I close my eyes. I don't want to think about it.

In a flash, my eyes are open and target on Gabriel. "I can't stay here," I say desperately. "What's to prevent them from coming after the children? You? Elizabeth, or anyone else associated with Paradise?"

"No! That isn't the answer." Gabriel's voice is firm.

"Devlin nor his henchmen, not even Satan himself has power here. They are only trying to scare you into fleeing. Here you're safest. Outside of Paradise you are not. They know this. They count on you being the noble angel you are and leaving. Once you're gone, then they will either kill you or worse. They may even take you to him, to Luther Devlin," Gabriel bites out.

I cover my face with my hands. No longer able to control them, I begin to sob. They rack my body as tears flow.

I hear Gabriel curse seconds before he pulls me into his arms. He places his chin on top of my head, then kisses that very spot. When he croons to me, I break down even more, crying harder. My tears have stained his shirt by the time I am able to calm myself enough to pull away. I sniffle, wiping tears from my cheeks.

"Sorry," I hiccup.

"Ma'am, you don't have anything to be sorry about." The sheriff looks at me with kind eyes. They crinkle at the corners.

But there is also a frank and steady focus in them.

"What Mr. Slayer said to you just now, you can take it to the bank. You're more in danger the moment you step foot off Paradise. I know you feel you're putting others in harm's way. No matter where you go, other people will be there too. Now, everyone here knows to be wary and alert, but not out there. So you see, you and everyone else are safer if you stay put. That's my official recommendation," he says with a definitive nod.

"Okay, but what's to be done to catch whoever is doing this? What measures can I take or others take to put this to rest? Can you use me as bait and draw the creep out?" I ask.

"Now that there is an interesting suggestion. I'll have to think on that a bit more. For the time being, you can't be going off on your own. There needs to be someone else with you always. Doors need to be secured so people can't enter every building and home at will. We'll bring in a few sniffer dogs and see if they can find a scent and see where that leads."

Gabriel takes hold of my hand. "There are other things we can do. We'll post round-the-clock guards. We have cameras we can use and alarms, motion detector lights. The kids will have to be monitored more closely."

"Okay," I say. "Why is it I can never seem to be able to say no to you?" I'm a bit bewildered.

"It's one of those mysteries you never overcome, for I have other questions and proposals to put to you and don't wish to be denied," he says in such a suggestively husky voice that I blush.

"Come," he gently orders, swinging me up into his arms. "I'm taking you back to the house. There isn't anything here more for you to do here. I'll get some people out here to clean it up when the sheriff is done with his inspection," he tells me.

"Meaning, you'll call Maggie," I translate. "I want to help," I tell him firmly.

"When you're rested," he replies.

"I'm serious, Gabriel. I'm not some weak hot-house flower that needs to be coddled and kept behind protective glass. I need to be out doing things, making myself useful. If you truly value me, you will let me become strong on the inside and the outside," I argue.

That gets his attention.

"I'm not a coward. Nor am I some dainty porcelain doll too fragile to face danger and hard work. I like to get my hands dirty and work alongside others. I may be an Angel but I'm not a queen."

A slow smile emerges on his face making his already handsome face all the more striking.

"And one more thing. If you don't let me do my fair share, I'll get Violet, Lailah's faerie to give you what for," I warn.

"You'll send the wrath of an interfering faerie down on my head for not letting you have your way?" he scoffs.

Patting his cheek, I tease, "You're so smart. You got it on the first try."

His growl makes me laugh. Gabriel doesn't put me down until I'm in my bedroom.

"Take a nap. Get some rest then when you get up you can go back out and help if that is what your heart desires," Gabriel tells me.

I reward him with a smile.

"Perfect. A true compromise. Then that is what I shall do."

Our silliness dissolves until we're left looking at each other in wonder. Slowly he lowers his head until his lips are a whisper above mine.

"I've wanted to do this since I saw you riding bareback across the chaparral. When I discovered my daughter's angel was flesh and blood, I burned with a desire, a need, that I hadn't felt for the longest time," he murmurs against my lips.

"Kiss me," I invite.

The kiss he gives me now is no less dramatic than the one he gave me earlier. He begins by gently plucking my lips with his. The swipe of his tongue along the seam of my mouth is all it takes for me to part my lips, allowing him to delve in. Our tongues touch, entangling in that ancient dance of seduction and passion.

I moan. I want, *need*, more. Giving it, Gabriel holds nothing back. Gasping from what we have shared, I stand unstable, panting as I gaze up at him. A quick glance in the bureau mirror reveals a woman, me, with passion glazed eyes.

"Stay." My need, passion has me acting boldly.

"Sera…" He says my name as if it's a blessing. "You don't know what you are asking."

"Oh, yes I do," I reassure him. "Help me. Help me take these things off. I'll rest better."

"Minx," he says with feeling.

He doesn't turn away. Nor does he deny me.

I let him undress me. When he is done, I stand naked before him. Unashamed. Unafraid. I have never wanted anything more in my life then how I want this man, right now. It's then that I know in the deepest depths of my soul that if everything I have gone through in my life was preparing me for this moment, I would do it all over again, and gladly.

As a virginal bride, Gabriel lifts me up in his arms after divesting himself of his own clothing. Ever so gently, he lays me upon the sheets. When he pulled back the spread, I do not recall. It's as if time stood still.

Following me down, Gabriel lays by my side. Reaching up I caress his face, cupping his cheek. I delight in the feel of his lips pressing into my palm. With fingers and lips, we take our time exploring each other.

Gabriel's muscles were earned through years of hard work and toil, not hours spent in a gym pumping iron. No. Gabriel pumps life. He lives a purposeful life, using everything he has been born with to make a life of worth, not just for himself but for others. How can I not be moved that such a man can be so gentle?

I lay beneath him relishing the feel of his calloused hands as they course over my skin exploring my body.

"So warm. So responsive," he croons, his lips grazing the shell of my ear.

I moan my delight at his praise.

"How sweetly you surrender to me." His voice is laced with amazement.

Ever so slowly, his lips and mouth move down my body. From neck to breasts where he feasts. I arch my back, giving him fuller access to each of my breasts as he sucks and teases my nipples until they harden into rose-pink pearls. Each draw sends jolts of electric current down to the juncture of my legs where I feel myself heating and moistening.

My body wants him. My heart aches for him. My soul seeks his. My mind is lost in him. I am his. That sudden understanding sends further shockwaves through my entire being.

"What is it?" he says, his lips pressing against my breast. He must have felt the moment I was hit by the sudden epiphany.

"Gabriel," I say his name like a prayer. "My very own guardian angel. Protector of Paradise. Warrior sent from heaven to fight demons sent from hell, my hell. You are mine and I am yours for all time," I whisper.

He pauses, eyes flying to mine. The light of the day lights him from behind, making him glow as if he is surrounded by a brilliant golden halo, heavenly armor. I have never seen such joy radiating from a man, jubilation that is centered on me.

"As it is and always shall be, amen," he reverently says.

We hold each other's gaze as he penetrates my core with his sword, filling me completely. Our breaths still as we revel in how it feels to have our bodies join as one. I arch my hips in silent command to move. Slowly and gently at first, he rotates and moves his hips in that age old thrusting rhythm.

"Yeeesss," I breathe. "Aaahhh."

"So, angels do sing," Gabriel says through pants of passion as he continues to pound into me. Faster, slower, harder, pausing then circling his hips. Gabriel is a master conductor and it is he who commands all the instruments to this symphony playing through my body. Any moment, this lady will be singing her hallelujahs.

"Gabriel," I gasp, throwing my head back, arching my hips.

He kisses my exposed throat. "Let it out. Let me hear you, oh seraphim. Announce your coming. You bliss. Your rapture."

Normally, I would be doubled over in laughter at the corny word play, but under the circumstances they're just what I need to push over the edge. A most powerful orgasm hits me. It rocks my body sending wave after wave of energy and light coursing through my body. All my nerves tingle, becoming instantly overly sensitive to the slightest touch and sensation.

I shout Gabriel's name at the same time he throws back his head, letting loose with a trumpeting of his own. His hot seed releases in waves deep inside my womb. He shudders then collapses upon my now still form.

Our heaving breaths sound more like a chorus as we lay in stunned silence. Finally, Gabriel rolls off me. Passion warmed and moistened skin glues our bodies together. Goosebumps rise over my suddenly chilled flesh. Gabriel gathers me into his side and pulls up the covers to keep us warm.

"I loved Mary, my wife," he whispers quietly. I hear him swallowing.

"You still do," I reply, feeling him startle at my words. "It's as it should be, Gabriel. Just because someone has passed doesn't mean you stop loving them. The love goes on long after the body is gone. The heart and soul remain along with the memories and the love," I whisper, my lips grazing his chest.

Placing a finger and thumb under my chin, Gabriel raises my face toward his. "Such wise words from one so young," he praises, placing a kiss on my smiling lips.

"Not my wisdom. It's something my granny always said," I tell him.

"Was she an Angel?" he asked with a grin.

"No. She was my mother's mother. She was a Flower." I chuckle at his wide eyes. "How did you think my mom came up with such names for her Angel babies? She comes by her creative lunacy naturally."

"Huh? You mean your grandmother named all her kids after flowers?" I could hear the chuckle in his voice.

"Uhm-hmm. Daisy, Lily, Rose, Hyacinth, and Jasmine. My granny's name was Violet."

He bolts upright. "Violet? As in Lailah's faerie?" He searches my face for the answer.

"Yeah, now that you mention it. It's the same name. Wow what a coincidence."

"Hmmm," is the response I get.

He stretches. "As much as I would love to stay here and linger, I've got lots to do today and now even more since this morning's events," he says with regret.

I stay in bed watching him dress. When he's ready to go, he leans down, kissing me. "I loved Mary. Still do. I will always treasure the relationship I had with her. But I want you to know, what I feel for you is not the same I felt for her." He blows out a breath in irritation, raking his hands through his hair. "I'm not saying this right. I have feelings for you, deep feelings. These are new to me, something pure and good like I had with Mary but different. You are a first for me," he says, shocking me to my core.

I reach out, cupping his cheeks and pluck a few kisses off his lips. "You are my first. That makes us even. We both are starting out new and fresh with one another."

Gabriel stands stunned. "But you were engaged, had a fiancé. How…I don't understand," he says.

"Yes, I knew David for several years. We dated, got engaged. We kissed, petted, but never were…intimate that way. It wasn't that I was opposed to it. Just…it didn't feel right when there was the opportunity or the invitation." I shrug. "I take it as a sign that he was never fated to be mine. That honor was reserved for another." I give him what I hope is a coy smile.

Before I can even blink, he's back in my arms. We're

rolling around the bed. Lips and arms are entwined. I'm giddy with joy. My heart is pounding like a drum as I lose myself in his passionate kisses. Some are feral in their wildness. Others are gentle and sweet. I enjoy them all. All I know is that I will never be able to get enough.

With a groan, he pulls himself away and out of my arms. "Rest. I'll check on you throughout the day," he promises.

The door closes quietly behind him. I let out a blissful sigh as I snuggle down deep into the warm soft bedding. Right this very moment, there are no worries, no fears. All's right with the world. I'm the happiest I've ever been.

Chapter 15

Gabriel

There is a lightness in my core I haven't felt for many years. The day seems fresher, my burdens seem not as insurmountable as they did this morning. I feel I could conquer the world and still have enough energy to enter and win an iron man contest.

Zeke meets me almost immediately upon leaving the big house. It's as if he has been waiting for me.

"Took ya some time seeing Sera back to the house, boss," he comments with a sideways grin.

"Took as long as it required," I quip back. "Everyone was satisfied in the end, for now." I give Zeke a cheeky grin.

Zeke chuckles, shaking his head then slaps me on the shoulder.

"About time, boy," he mutters.

As we walk away from the house, Zeke gets me caught up. "Sheriff can't say definitively that it's the same person, but he thinks along the same lines as us. Says he'll be stepping up patrols along the country roads and asking around with those who live a bit back off the main roads. They'll be checking camping spots. Who knows, maybe this Peter guy found a place to hole up."

"All those are good ideas, Zeke, but this guy has done damage twice right here. He's been here, just outside my home, your home. It isn't like he's stolen food or tools. He's brought death and destruction and violence to Paradise. That alone makes me want to rip him apart if I ever get my hands on him," I say through gritted teeth.

"You got a plan?" Zeke asks.

I pull out my cell phone. "Yeah, I got a plan. Not sure why I didn't do this earlier." I admonish myself.

I search my contacts, find the one I want and hit Dial.

"Isaac, Isaac Cavallero you old son of a gun," I chortle out my greeting when a voice sounds on the other end. "This is Gabriel Slayer." I laugh when he replies with a colorful nickname of his own.

As I listen to Isaac, Zeke gives me an understanding look. He knows what I am up to. My eyes follow him as he mozies his way back to one of the barns. He'll give me privacy to have this call, knowing I'll catch him up later.

"You're right. It has been way too long. We need to fix that right away," I tell him. "Hey, the reason for my call... I'm just going to come out and ask it. Are you still with the FBI? You are? Great. Here's why I asked..."

Isaac Cavallero and I go way back. His family owns land that joins with ours. They've been in the area, working the land long before my own. His ancestor who originally settled here was a Spanish Conquistador. Instead of remaining a soldier, he volunteered to raise cattle to feed the Spanish army. In exchange, he received over two hundred thousand acres of land. Over the years, they sold portions of it off. Today they still retain a hefty chunk, just like my family.

As kids, we became close friends. I stayed with the land while he went into law enforcement. His other brothers took over the ranching business. We've kept in touch as our lives allowed, which was not frequent enough in my opinion. That's one of the sad parts of growing up, drift happens between friends due to life's passions and choices.

I fill him in on recent events. By the time I finished the call, I'd given him Agent Johnson's information and received assurance from Isaac that he would personally take a look into the case and get back with me ASAP.

∞∞∞

"So, what do you think?" I ask Zeke.

We've just finished looking at the property that needs to be unloaded. The developer purchased a ranch that the children of the deceased former owner no longer wanted. So typical any more of the younger generations. Very few young people nowadays want to commit their lives to one of hard physical and mental labor. Mother Nature, erratic futures markets, government regulations can take their toll on those deciding a life on the land or not.

"Hmm, what we're talking about is twenty completed new homes, a clubhouse and pool, paved roads throughout the community and site preparations for another ten homes. The old homestead, complete with house and outbuildings and fencing all still in relatively good condition. All that plus an additional five hundred acres," Zeke summarizes.

"For a cash sale, I get it all for less than market value. Substantially below market value." I tell him the figures.

He whistles. "So, what did you tell him?" he asks.

"Shook hands on it. Said that pending there aren't any liens or prior claims and such, we should be able to sign contracts by the end of the month."

"So, when many ranches are going bust or selling off bits and pieces, Paradise is going in the opposite direction. We're expanding," he says with pride.

"I see this as our attempt at adding an intentional community for our people. We want to keep the best and the brightest. I want to attract those whose services are needed. This acquisition is part of that. Gives us more land to expand our operations. I want to expand our poultry business. I see us raising heirloom turkey and chickens to start. Maybe adding ducks and geese. We would be feeding ourselves and having more to offer our clients."

"You've been really thinking on this haven't you, boy?" Pride wrinkles the corner of his eyes and is reflected on his face. "Your daddy would be proud, real proud."

I feel a lump forming in my throat. Such praise isn't always given by Zeke, only when it truly has merited

"I've been doing my homework, listening to the trends and what may be coming down the pike. Researching what others have done and how it all fits into our philosophy and values," I tell him.

Paradise operates under high standards. Any new venture must mesh with those as well as be profitable. This purchase will be in keeping with those principles that so often can be at odds.

"You'll increase the size of Paradise, stop or slow development of the land, provide housing for many of our families, and a place in which to grow our operation. Not bad for one day's work." A second round of praise from Zeke Scriber. I may have to write this on the calendar.

"Guess going to all those community and government functions paid off," he says.

"Yeah, don't like going to all those functions but it is

part of the world we live in. Information is vital. The more we have, the more options result, not to mention the connections. Unfortunately, they're as vital as never before."

Zeke squeezes my shoulder. Another show of affection.

"Want me to send over Bill and have him do a cursory inspection of the buildings," he offers.

"Reading my mind, Zeke."

"Ever think about getting into raising heritage hogs?" Zeke asks, scratching his chin.

"You interested?" Somewhat amazed. "Get me some research and we'll talk more on it," I promise. "I like pork."

Never in my life have I felt that my future was brighter and full of exciting possibilities. I can't wait to share everything with Sera and hear her thoughts.

∞∞∞∞

"Boss, Zeke," Cody yells as we near the big house.

I roll down the window to better hear as I slow down the truck to a stop.

"What's up?" Giving him my full attention. Clearly he is agitated.

"I was just getting ready to call…shots have been fired over at the school room…"

That's all I need to hear. "Jump in," I order.

Once Cody was in the back, I hit the gas and sped toward the building that was used as our school house. Cody updates us on the facts as we tear through the ranch.

"Katie called, all frantic. Someone's been taking shots

at the school building. Most of the bullets hit the outside but a few got through the glass windows. When Katie and the other adults figured out what the pops and noises were, they had the kids take cover, then when it quieted, ushered the kids into the inner rooms for protection. It's close to dismissal, but nobody has left for home yet," Cody informs us. "Others not in the building hearing the shots went to check it out. All know the rule that it's off limits in homestead grounds to discharge firearms, unless there's a reason."

Yeah, that has long been a standing rule. On occasion, a rattlesnake or rabid animal wanders in and we put it down, but beyond that, guns and rifles are not tools that need to be used in such close proximity to the buildings where people work and live.

I look over at Zeke. Our thoughts are running along the same line.

"You think this is connected to the other two incidents?" he inquires.

"Let's keep our minds open. But my gut thinks so. I can't think of any who live and work here at Paradise who would do such a foolish thing as shoot off a gun in the main compound let alone shoot at a building full of kids and their teachers."

Soon, we're pulling up in front of the building. We pass others who are hurrying toward the building. A few have rifles in their hands.

"Stay alert," I order when we come to a stop.

Even before getting out of the truck, I can see the damage done to the building. Bullet holes pockmark the walls. A few have lodged in the wooden siding. At least three have gone through the windows. I turn in the direction from which they had to have been fired.

"Cody, go see that everyone is okay inside. Take thers

and stay there until you hear from either me or Zeke." I don't wait for a response, but notice that Cody has called over a few rifle toting friends. They all run toward the school building.

"Zeke, round up a few of the boys and let's check out where the shots have been fired from." I hear him whistle and motion for a few of the boys to join us.

"Teams of two. Let's fan out and go in these directions," I say, pointing around. Check every door, cupboard, any place this joker can hide. Remember he is dangerous and most likely still armed."

It was easy to find where the guy stood. He was well concealed behind a truck parked across the way. Simple but efficient. We followed the tracks until they disappeared into one of the buildings.

"Get one of the hounds to sniff out the spot this guy was standing and let's see if it can track him," I order.

It doesn't take long to get old Horace to pick up on the scent. He takes us right through the building and out another door. The trail ends where motorcycle treads are left in the dirt.

"Anyone see a motorcycle enter or leave?" I demand.

"Heard one when some of us went toward the school building after hearing the gun shots," I'm told.

Apparently nobody took notice of it, thinking it was one of the crew going out or coming in to help. Damn. Letting loose with a few more expletives, I pull out my cell phone and call the sheriff.

"You're gonna get tired of hearing from me," I tell him. I report the incident and after he huffs out a breath, he tells me he'll be sending out someone to take care of the scene and take statements.

After I hang up with the sheriff, I clap my hands to get

everyone's attention.

"People, as you know, we've been experiencing a few... unusual events around here that can be a bit disturbing by themselves and frightening when taken as a whole. Got the sheriff and a few of his boys coming out again. They're gonna want statements, so I would appreciate it if you saw or heard or did something that is centered around this most recent event, please go now and try to put it down on paper while it's fresh in your mind," I instruct them.

As I watch the people shuffle back to where they came from, a few moms and dads push through toward the school. I go along with them. My own kids are within.

"Zeke." He turns to me upon hearing my voice. "Anyone hurt?" I didn't think there was or I would have been told by now. But all the same, it's always wise to check.

He shakes his head. "Nah, just a bit shook up is all. A few are excited as some kids get at times, most want their parents."

"Can't say I blame them. I wouldn't mind my own pop and mom here right now," I tell him.

He narrows his brow, considering my words.

"Daddy!" I hear the chorus of my cherubs. I shut my eyes tight for a second, only opening them when the two come barreling into my legs, grabbing hold as if there is no tomorrow.

I put an arm around each of them, haul them up to sit on a hip, and lavish them with hugs and kisses to reassure all three of us. I need this as much as they.

"Hey, cherubs, you okay?"

"Yeah, we're okay, Daddy," Daniel says.

"Lailah?" I prod, turning to look at her.

Fat tears hang on her lower lids. Her lower lip is nearly hitting her chin. She nods slowly.

"Lailah, that won't do. Tell me, faerie whisperer, why the long face? Why the tears?"

"She's scared, Daddy," Daniel tells me. Worry for his sister is clearly sitting on his shoulders. I give him an appreciative nod.

Her face crumbles just before she flings her arms around my neck and tightly holds on while burying her head in my neck and shoulder. I can feel her tiny body begin to quake.

"Daaadddy!" she cries. "Daddy, I was sooo scared." The tears let loose and all I can do is hold her and croon into her ear.

"Her chair is close to the window where one of the bullets crashed in," Daniel tells me.

I swivel around to look around the room once again. I can see several overturned desks and chairs, glass that is scattered everywhere. Books and school supplies litter the floor. I also see blood.

"The first shot scared everyone. We didn't know what it was at first. Some of the big kids seemed to and so did Mrs. Parker. She yelled at us to get under the desks and to hurry. Before we could, a second bullet came in, breaking more of the window. Lailah was too scared to move so I helped her," he says.

"When I was pulling her under the window, a third bullet came in. It would have hit her if she hadn't moved," he says, pointing to where one of the school desks had a clear bullet hole that had ripped right through it. It took all my effort to remain calm. I did it for my kids. I did it to set an example for the other parents that were arriving.

"You did the right thing, Daniel." My voice is choked and husky. "Boy, I'm right proud of you. Always have been, but this day, you were mighty brave seeing to the safety of your sister. I'd call you a true hero," I tell him with great sincerity.

His little chest puffs with pride and his eyes light with that same fire.

"Are you sure neither of you are hurt?" I press. That's when I see his bloody and torn shirt. "Daniel?" I exclaim, indicating his shirt.

"Something hit Lailah's arm. I wrapped it in a bit of my shirt that I tore off." He pushes out of my arms to stand by my side, showing me the proof of his words. Next he points to Lailah's arm. Sure enough, now that I am thinking a bit clearer myself, I see the makeshift bandage wrapped and knotted around her upper left arm. Blood stains the material and more of it is smeared on her skin.

I turn to order Zeke to get Maggie and Sera but see that I didn't need to. Both have arrived carrying their travel medical bags. Elizabeth has joined them.

"Sheriff and his boys are here," Elizabeth tells me. She's a bit breathless from hurrying. "I'll take her." She reaches up to lift Lailah from my arms.

"Nooo, I want Daddy," she wails, intensifying her hold, clinging to me like a vine.

"I got her," I tell Elizabeth, patting Lailah's leg while still trying to hold on to her. "Why don't you go sit with the kids whose parents haven't yet arrived." Chin lifting toward a group of youngsters trying hard to look brave, frantically searching for any sign of a mom or dad.

She nods. Elizabeth gives Lailah a soothing pat on her back before taking herself off.

Sera sees me and takes in the children. The worry on her face disappears but returns when she sees the bloody wrap on Lailah's arm. She makes her way over.

"How bad is it?" I indicate the other kids.

"A few cuts from flying glass. All minor."

I blow out a breath of relief.

"Here, let me see to Lailah," she says.

Together we unwrap the makeshift bandage. It isn't serious. When Sera goes to treat it I stop her, hastily retying the cloth.

"Not yet. Go take care of the other kids," I tell her swinging Lailah away from her grasp.

Sera furrows her brow and gives me a bewildered look.

"A ranch rule. Slayers put all others before themselves. Go see to the others. She can wait a bit longer. Lailah's been given first aid by Daniel, Paradise's very own superhero," I tell her, placing a hand on his head affectionately before pulling him in close against my side. "Besides, the three of us are enjoying being in each other's arms just now."

Sera gives Daniel a look that makes him puff up again. She doesn't argue with me, instead, moves off to finish tending others. A few parents come over to talk to me or I go to them before they take their child home.

"We'll cancel school tomorrow. There will be a parent meeting in the afternoon to discuss everything," I tell them. Hopefully, the damage will be cleaned up and repairs made. Whether or not we use this building again will be a joint decision made by the parents, not just me.

However, I do believe in that old adage about what one should do when bucked off a horse. I know we're dealing with children and a traumatic experience, but the only way to fight trauma and fear is to look it square in the eyes and refuse to give it any power. We'll fix the school building, sweep up the mess. The kids will return. Soon we'll have a new one ready across the way.

"Hey there, faerie whisperer," Sera croons to Lailah who has laid her head on my shoulder. Sera rubs gentle circles on Lailah's back, picks up a hank of Lailah's hair that has fallen over her face. "Are you in there? Oh, there she is," she teases.

Lailah can't help but give her a bit of a giggle.

"Can I take a look at your arm, Lailah?"

Lailah nods.

Sera motions to me to follow her. I sit down on a bench and place Lailah in front of me, holding her securely in my lap. Sera sits next to us to better access the arm.

"Let's see what we've got here." Untying the makeshift bandage.

"I got shot," Lailah tells her.

"Shot?" Sera furrows her brow and speeds up the unwrapping of Lailah's arm.

"Daniel, you did a fine job in wrapping this wound," Sera praises. "Ever think about becoming a vet or a doctor?" she asks.

He shrugs. "Sometimes," he admits.

"This isn't a gunshot wound," Sera says.

"Is too. The bad guy shot his gun and the bullet came in thwough the window. Then it hit my desk and I got this," she explains.

"Mm-hum. This is called shrapnel. It's a kind of wound that one gets when debris is kicked up by the bullet. It isn't the bullet but the stuff that got broken up and flew apart when it was hit by the bullet. The bullet hit your desk and bits of glass from the window or wood from the desk flew up and hit your arm," Sera explains.

"Now I'm going to clean it and see if there is anything left in your arm," she keeps calmly talking to Lailah.

"Might sting a bit, but it won't last long so hold as still as you can."

"Ow!" Lailah screeches.

Sera snickers. "I haven't even touched you yet, you silly goose."

"I'm not a goose. I'm a faerie whisperer," Lailah retorts.

"Fair enough. Call on Violet while I see to your wound," Sera tells her.

Lailah nods, leaning her head back against me, then closes her eyes. Her little lips silently move as if she's speaking inside her head to her faerie. Sera and I share knowing smiles, though I watch Sera examine Lailah carefully as if she were sensing something that I am not. I shake off the thought as I sit holding my child while her wound is properly tended.

When all is done, I hoist Lailah back in my arms and the five of us make our way back home. cleanup has already started. The sheriff and his boys have already completed their investigation.

"I sure hope you have insurance," Sera says after we tuck the kids into bed for a nap. I give her a frown. "Already there has been damage to a number of your buildings. What worries me more is the damage being done to the kids, the people, and families that live here."

"Are we back to this topic?" I challenge. "You aren't going anywhere. Sure, I'm not happy that this thug has gotten away with doing what he's done. It bothers me on multiple levels knowing that my children were here, potential targets, that Lailah was injured and her brother, a seven year old, had to act as her white knight."

I drag my hands through my hair and vigorously rub my face.

"He may have increased my workload and that of others who have to see to cleaning up his mess, but I won't allow his scare tactics to intimidate you into leaving. That's what he's hoping for. He's counting on you leaving and then he will strike like the henchman of Satan he is."

Chapter 16

Sera

"Then let's let him think he's done just that," I argue, earning a blink of surprise then a possessive growl from Gabriel. "Hear me out!" Reaching out a hand to pat his chest and soothe my warrior angel. "Each time he acts, he gets closer to the children, to those who should be immune to suffering and attack. They're the very ones he goes after. You're right, it's calculated. So why not let him think he's won?"

"Set him up in order to trap him?" Gabriel stills. His eyes fixed while thinking.

"Exactly. He has to have eyes on the place, watching. Is he hiding on the grounds or is it more than one working together? The only way we'll get them is if they screw up the next time they try something or if we trap them," I reason. "Look, I know there is danger in this. But sometimes, risks must be taken in order for better things to come out in the end. I'm willing to put myself out there more than I'm willing to sit back and hope this guy doesn't get it in his head to hurt someone else." I'm feeling desperate. "I'm what they want. So use me as bait."

Gabriel's eyes snap and his mouth takes on a grim line. I can tell he wants to tell me no, but he knows that what I am saying makes the most sense.

"Call the sheriff, see if he can help set something up. Do it, do it quickly so all of this can be over and we can all get on with our lives." I cup his face with my hands and look deep into his eyes. "You and your family have created a real paradise here at Paradise. Don't let Devlin and his minion-thugs turn it into a purgatory. Don't let them sully and destroy the goodness of this place, leaving their taint, their mark. It isn't right that they should do so."

Gabriel lays his forehead against mine. Our breaths intermingle. I lift my face up inviting his lips to press upon mine. His tongue swipes across the seam of my lips. I open for him. Our tongues touch and engage in that all consuming dance. Oh, how I love his kisses. I could kiss him for hours, days, forever. I never want this to end.

His mouth breaks away from mine, moving to rain more kisses over my face. His teeth tug gently on my ear and down my neck. I arch, giving him greater access.

"Please," I whisper my plea.

He knows what I want. I pray he wants it too. He captures my lips with his before lifting me in his arms and carrying me to his room. *His* room. The master's bedchamber. I have not been in this room before now. It's the one room I've deliberately avoided.

His inner sanctum was not for me to trespass in unless invited. I am not a wanton woman and do not want to be seen as such, not by him. That isn't who I am. I'm no angel. I'm merely a woman. I feel no shame in giving him my body. It's mine to gift to whom I choose. I choose him.

Could I be falling in love?

I am hit hard by the realization. Love has struck me when I least expected it, hitting me hard. An Angel falling in Paradise, crashing head over heels for archangel Gabriel, my guardian angel, who has vowed to protect me and keep me safe.

"What is it?" he asks. He's sensed my mood.

I have never lied to him. I won't start now.

"It's just…it's just that I have come to realize…"

He stops, placing my feet on the floor next to his over-sized king bed. He gives me an expectant look.

"What is it you have only just realized?" he whispers huskily.

"G-Gabriel," I stutter. "I think I love you."

I search his face for a response, a clue of what he thinks, what he feels. The look of wonder reflecting on his face is one I only thought to see in my dreams.

Blinking. "No, that isn't right," I say in a rush, my giddy smile dissolving.

His beaming smile turns to confusion. His brow knots.

"I don't *think* it. I *know* it. Gabriel, it might be too soon, but I know I love you. I love you." I lay my heart bare before him.

His face softens, then radiates joy.

I throw myself into his arms, wrapping my own around him and bury my face in his neck. I'm laughing and crying at the same time. Gabriel holds me tight against him. I hear him muffle the same to me. He pulls away, removing my hair that has gotten caught on his lips.

"I love you too," he declares.

I search his face for the truth of his words. It's clearly there for me to see. Jubilant kisses are exchanged as we begin to fumble with our clothing.

"Hurry," I urge Gabriel. I can't wait to feel his skin on

mine.

His naked arms twine around my body pulling me down to the mattress. My body is pressed deep into the bedding as he covers me with his own. He braces up on his elbows and looks down the length of me. There is no shyness as I let his gaze roam over every inch of naked flesh.

"So beautiful," he praises, as he leans down to kiss my nipples and pluck them with his lips and teeth. Each breast is drawn into his mouth where he sucks each tip in turn until he releases the pearled nub with a pop.

"So soft," he murmurs, his lips grazing the soft skin under my breast.

His oral exploration of my body continues. When he reaches my navel, he spears it with his tongue. After extracting it, he blows a gentle breath over my dampened skin. Gooseflesh rises over the area and a delicious shiver overtakes my body. I can feel my core clenching in delight as my lady parts moisten in anticipation.

Gabriel isn't finished. Onward his lips travel, ever downward toward my core. My legs fall open automatically, inviting him in. The feel of his tongue on my clit causes me to gasp in utter delight. I close my eyes and moan. It seems to fuel Gabriel as he explores every bit of me with his mouth.

All too soon I feel that tightening in my inner core as if I am about to explode. And then I do. My orgasm is so much more than the others he has brought me. I'm completely undone.

"So responsive. So luscious," Gabriel croons as he moves over my body.

I feel him slide between my legs. The head of his cock pierces my opening. My greedy muscles eagerly pull him in as he pushes until he is fully embedded. Now he is the one that moans.

My turn comes when he rocks his hips and begins to thrust.

"Yessss," I gasp. "More." Arching into him, I surrender all.

Harder, Gabriel thrusts, increasing his tempo. Skin slaps against skin. I can hear the juicy sound of his cock retreating before plunging back into my wet channel. Again the pressure begins to build. I'm gasping and groaning, desiring the delight that is just out of reach. Then it hits me. Wave after wave washes over me. I crest and explode as he throws back his head, roaring as he spills his seed deep within my womb.

Gabriel's spent body drops onto mine. His weight is actually comforting. I wrap my arms around him to keep him anchored to me while my breathing and heart rate return to normal.

"Are you alright?" he asks as he rolls to his side and gathers me protectively along his length, careful of my booted leg.

"Am I alright? Are you kidding? I've never been better than I am at this moment. It's amazing how free and light I feel. It's the best feeling in the world. I enjoyed our joining before, but this time..."

"Sex is always better when there is love. It's no longer is simply fucking and relieving the body of lust and passion, it becomes lovemaking. There was attraction and affection before. Now there is more. It's the joining of hearts, minds, and souls along with the merging of two bodies."

My lover has become a poet. His words please me more than any simple declaration of love.

"Beautiful words for a beautiful sharing," I praise. I gift him with a sweet kiss.

Gabriel grunts in satisfaction. I place another kiss over

his heart and let my lips linger there. I flick his nipple with my own tongue, delighting in watching it bud.

He captures my cheeks in his hands, drawing me up to nibble and place love nips on my lips. "Minx," he says playfully. "I can't get enough of you," he says with a groan.

I can feel his cock growing where it lays pressed between our bodies. He grabs a hold of my buttocks and squeezes, urging me to scoot up the length of his body so I'm straddling his hips.

"Take hold of me and direct me into you," Gabriel instructs.

I eagerly comply. There is a heady sense of power that comes from taking charge and watching one's lover surrender. Fisting his cock I guide the head into my opening. I ease myself down over him until he is rooted fully inside me once more.

Balancing myself by placing my hands on his shoulders, I begin to move. Taking hold of my hips, Gabriel aids me. When I get comfortable with the movement, he moves one of his hands to play with my free swinging breasts.

Every time I lower and buck over his shaft, my clit comes in contact with him. The friction of our bodies rubbing together eliciting moans and groans. Gabriel moves his free hand down to where our bodies are joined and teases my clit even more. Soon, I feel myself building up for another release.

My muscles clamp onto his cock, squeezing him as he and I both climax together. His cum fills me again as my body convulses from the bliss of my release. Both of us are left gasping. Gabriel grunts as I land on top of him. I giggle in response but am disinclined to move. I sigh as my body melts into his.

"I could stay here for an eternity," I whisper.

Gabriel rubs his hands over my back and buttocks, caressing every inch of my sex-heated flesh. I sigh once again.

"Mmm, that feels good. You can do that as long as you like," I murmur.

He turns his head glancing at the clock. A few choice words are uttered as he comes to full awareness.

"Sera, as much as I regret this, there are things I still need to see to before this evening. Then we need to have a conversation about where this—us—are heading. What we want. What we see happening," he tells me as he moves from the bed and begins to dress.

"Okay," I yawn. "It's a date."

"What are you doing?" he demands as I make to rise from the bed.

"Getting up. If you get up, so will I."

He urges me back beneath the sheets and presses me back down. "Stay," he gently orders. "Rest as long as you need."

"Wrong," I challenge. "I want to check on the children."

He nods his consent.

He waits for me to dress, which I do in record time. Together we head down the hall toward the children's rooms. Halfway there, we hear them down below. They're with Elizabeth and Zeke.

"There they are," Daniel gleefully shouts.

"Sleepy heads." Lailah giggles. She's coloring and Daniel is playing with Legos at the kitchen table.

Lailah's brow furrows in thought. "How come Sewa was sleeping in your bed with you, Daddy?" she asks.

"Shhh, child. That's none of your concern," Elizabeth admonishes. I see her smirk.

Zeke turns beet red, but I can see the twinkle in his eyes as he looks over at Gabriel. Red is creeping up Gabriel's neck as he swallows, searching for an answer.

"But how come?" Lailah persists.

"Because I was too scared to sleep by myself," I supply a reason. "Besides, it put me closer to you two and I wanted to make sure you were alright too."

"Was Daddy being a hero too?" she asks, pausing in her coloring.

"Most definitely," I tell her. Lailah nods her head, returning her focus to her coloring. I was curious because I never heard the door open. The thought of one or both of the children peeking in, seeing us— "How did you know...?" Hmm. Not sure how to or what to ask.

"Violet told me," Lailah says before I can finish. She selects a new color and continues coloring in her coloring book. She pauses, handing me a crayon, an invitation to join in. I do just that.

"Violet?" Gabriel asks.

"Yeah, she told me that Sewa would be sleeping with you fwom now on and that evewything was going to be okay," she tells us.

"Would you have a problem if Sera stayed with me and shared my room?" Gabriel asks his children.

Daniel shakes his head. "I like Sera. I want her to stay forever."

"Me too," Lailah speaks up. "Violet thinks she should stay. She told me so."

That has the adults chuckling.

Gabriel turns to me. "I intended us to have this talk later," he says a bit apologetically. "Now that the cat's out of the bag, so to speak, and the subject has been brought up..." He swipes a hand through his short cropped curly-blond hair. I take it as a display of nerves.

I stand there looking at him expectantly.

"Sera, what I'm trying to ask is, will you?"

"Will I what?" Picking up a different crayon and helping Lailah with her coloring book.

"Will you stay forever? Will you marry me and become my wife?"

Swallowing the lump that has gathered in my throat, I try clearing my throat as the crayon drops from my fingers. I move to a standing position and face the man that I love. I can feel myself blinking back the tears that threaten to fall.

"I know this is sudden. You'd be taking on a lot more than just a husband," he says, glancing over at his children. "You know how they feel, and I've already told you that I love you. It's the truth. I love you and would be honored if you would consent to being my wife."

I look on the four faces eagerly waiting for my response. There is only one answer.

"I never thought that the day caught up in a storm only to be cast from the heavens," I glance over at Lailah, "crashing down into Paradise, that what I would gain was so much more than what I lost. Who would have thought that I would land amongst a host of angels who saved me, healed me, protected me, and gave me more love than I thought I would ever find."

"What does that mean?" Lailah leans over, whispering to Daniel.

I laugh. "That means, cherub, that my answer is—" I look directly at Gabriel, "yes!"

"Yes! Yes, I will marry you. Yes, I want to be your wife and be part of your family, if they will have me." Exuberantly, I grasp Gabriel's cheeks and pop him a kiss on his lips. Turning to Daniel. "I take you," I say, kissing him on the cheek. "I take you," Repeating the process with Lailah. "I take you and you," I say, kissing Elizabeth and a crimson faced Zeke. Facing Gabriel once again, I say softly with all the love I can muster into sound, "And I will take you as my one and only husband for now and all eternity." Sealing my vow by pressing my lips against Gabriel's.

Daniel and Lailah cheer. Elizabeth claps her hands and wipes a tear before Zeke pulls her into his arms for a hug and an exuberant kiss of his own. The astonished looks on both of their faces is hilarious to behold. Elizabeth looks delightfully taken aback while Zeke keeps holding her hand refusing to relinquish it. Gabriel swings me up in his arms and twirls me around in joyful abandon.

We laugh and shout our mutual joy.

"When?" Gabriel demands. "When will you marry me?"

"As soon as possible," I tell him.

"Done," he says, then proceeds to kiss the breath right out of me.

Chapter 17

Agent Johnson

"**S**he's what?" Devlin roars. I hold the phone away from my ear until he quits yelling and screaming.

"I thought you should know. I just learned of it myself," I tell him.

"Why haven't you brought her to me? Where is Peter? Have you found him? Terminated him? Well, have you?" he thunders.

"Sir, there have been some complications. Dr. Angel is heavily guarded. Rarely is she left alone."

"You're a God damned FBI agent. How much easier could it be to simply go onto the property and take her? Have you no creativity, no imagination? There must be something you can come up with where she would leave with you. Call her into questioning, or set up a meeting to go over the latest report and findings."

I sputter an answer but am cut off by his next words.

"You have forty-eight hours to bring her to me. If you're incapable of doing that then I won't be needing your services any longer," he tells me.

"I understand, sir. I won't fail you," I tell him.

"Good to know, Johnson," he says in a controlled calm

before hanging up.

I blow out a breath and use my pocket handkerchief to blot my brow. Just talking to the bastard makes we sweat. God, how I hate that motherfucker. I hate Peter even more. And when I get my hands on that asshole, I'll take all my anger out on him.

Got to come up with a plan and quickly. My life depends upon it.

How does one capture an angel? A wicked smile appears on my face. I've got the answer. Now I need to put it into play.

Sera

"Sera, this was just delivered. This has your name on it," Elizabeth says as she hands me a long white box.

I recognize the box for what it is. If I didn't, the Department of Agriculture seal on it is another clue.

"Flowers?" I can't quite hide the awe in my voice. Rarely have I received them.

Elizabeth chuckles and gives me a sappy smile. "Don't look at me. I don't know anything about it. Gabe must have done this on his own. That man is sure head over arse in love with you, girl," she says.

She watches as I open the box. My delighted expression quickly fades to one of horror. Instead of roses or some beautiful bouquet, there are a dozen dead black flowers and weeds.

"Mercy," Elizabeth gasps, pressing a hand against her mouth. Her shocked eyes search out mine.

"Ill wish. This is an ill wish," I whisper in horror. Tears

gather in my eyes. My lips tremble. How cruel.

"Who sent these?" I demand, becoming increasingly angry.

"I have no idea," Elizabeth says, appalled.

The two of us look around the box searching for a card or anything that will identify the sender. Tucked into the black tissue paper is a card. It reads: *A gift for the bride. May your special day be memorable in many ways. I wanted to be the first to kiss the bride, but this will have to suffice until then.*

"*What the fuck?*" I want to scream. My face pales as I collapse onto a nearby chair and stare blankly out into space. So absorbed in my horror that I don't hear Gabriel approaching nor the exchange of words between him and Elizabeth.

"Hey, Sera," he says, kneeling down beside me. "Let me take a look at that," he insists, prying the card out of my fingers.

Panting breaths puff between my slightly parted lips as I watch him read then re-read the card. When he is done he looks at me, taking in my haunted expression. Tenderly, he wipes away a fat tear that's fallen from my eye, then cups my cheek.

He turns, seeking out Elizabeth who's remained in the room but discreetly to the side. "How did this get here?" he demands, his anger simmering near the surface.

Elizabeth shrugs. "I found the box on the back landing near the kitchen door. There was no delivery vehicle. I never saw who placed it there." She wrings her hands, sorry etched on her face.

"I'll ask around," Gabriel murmurs.

"But you'll find nothing," I say. "It's the same with all the other incidents. Someone gets in and out without anyone noticing. How can that be?" Instead of pity and fear, I discover that it's my anger that is blooming.

"What are you saying?" he questions crossly.

I am taken aback. Gabriel has never said a word in anger to me since we first met. Why now? Have I offended him? Done something wrong?

Instead of backing down, I rise. "I'm saying that this is another verse of the same song and I am getting damn tired of it. And if the motive was to get us to be at each other's throats over something being done to all of us, then he was successful," I bark at him in frustration.

Gabriel takes a step back. I see him thinking on my words. He blows out a breath. "You're right," he apologizes. "We can't let these things drive us apart. That has been the goal, in part. And your question is a good one. How does this guy get onto and off the ranch each time and nobody sees him?"

"Because he isn't coming on or leaving. He's here already. He's hiding in plain sight," I answer.

Elizabeth and Gabriel stare at me. They obviously believe what I've said is the truth. It's the only answer that makes sense. Gabriel moves quickly to his office. Elizabeth and I follow behind. He sits behind his computer and hits a few keys.

"I'm bringing up a list of new hires. We keep a digital record of all those that work and live on the ranch. The information includes photographs. Accidents are rare, but some can be extreme. We keep photos of everyone just in case there is a need to identify someone after..." Enough said. He doesn't have to finish. "My Dad wanted everyone to wear dog tags. You know, like they do in the military."

"You should also keep DNA records," I suggest.

He nods after considering.

Gabriel holds out a hand to me. "Come around here and take a look."

He pulls me onto his lap. I take control of the mouse and move through the database, carefully looking at the names and photos that pop up. It's surprising to see the number of people whose livelihood comes from Paradise.

"This one." I tap the screen. "This is Peter."

"Peter Yale—"

"The picture shown me by the FBI had him listed as Peter Schlange," I hastily say."

"Hired the week you were in the hospital. I didn't spend much time here at the ranch. When I did, there was so much to see to that I didn't meet the new hires as I normally would," he says, admonishing himself.

"Hey, this isn't your fault." I place my hands on either side of his face so he would meet my eyes. "Look at me." I give his cheeks a bit of a squeeze to emphasize my demand.

"You are *not* at fault. *Nobody* is at fault. There has been so much going on to distract everyone. It's a testament to you and those who work here that we have this information and operations continued on so smoothly," I tell him.

Elizabeth nods her head in agreement. "Gabe, evil finds its way in. There is no sure way to keep it totally away. It finds the cracks in doors and windows left open. It creeps in when least expected. What person would think to sneak in such a way as this guy has?" Elizabeth reasons.

"One who thinks it's a matter of life or death. The man is desperate," Gabriel says.

"Agreed. Peter often told George that their lives were on the line if I was not brought out from the crash. Often they debated if Devlin would leave them alive if I was dead. Dead or alive, my body would be demanded in order to satisfy Devlin." I feel Gabriel's anger building once again. "Call the sheriff. Tell him what we've learned and let him apprehend Peter. Let him do it,"

He nods and does just that. I push off his lap so he can tend to the call. Elizabeth surprises me by coming up to me and enfolding me in a motherly hug. She gives me a few pats on the back and then heads off to the kitchen, the center of her domain.

"The sheriff is on his way. He's running the name but he thinks that Peter Yale will be a bogus name. He'll run a search on Peter Schlange as well. The Peter may be accurate but he wouldn't be that dumb to supply his real last name."

"With these guys it's hard to say," I scoff. I tell him a few idiotic things I witnessed when I was with them. "Peter was the brightest of the three, but the man has to be more than and little desperate at this point."

"That's my main worry. People don't always think logically when they're desperate. If Devlin is half the badass the papers make him out to be, he won't forgive Peter after all this time and you being here," Gabriel says.

"So we wait," I say.

"Yes, we wait," he agrees. "Oh, I nearly forgot. The reason for me coming in just now was this just arrived," he says handing me another package.

I give him a questioning look while taking it.

"I took the liberty of contacting your sister Grace. She said that your personal effects had been returned in Albany from the cathedral. That included your purse. She sent it here so there would be no complications when we decide on our big day," he tells me.

I rip into the package. There they are, my purse and wallet. My driver's license and even my passport are inside. I pull Gabriel to me.

"Thank you," I gush.

"Now we can have an official ceremony, not something that is simply symbolic. When we marry, I want it for real, for keeps, not just a token marriage," he says in all seriousness.

"That's what I want too," I assure him. "All or nothing. No in between."

My words please Gabriel. The kiss he gives me tells me so.

∞∞∞

"What do you mean he didn't show up for work today?" Gabriel barks.

Evelyn, the manager of the buttery, takes a swift step back from Gabriel's anger.

"Sorry, Mr. Slayer. He called early this morning saying he was feeling under the weather. We don't need anyone sneezing and coughing around open vats of cream and the product," she explains.

"If he calls or comes in, I want you to notify me immediately," he orders.

"Yes, sir Mr. Slayer." Evelyn quickly nods her compliance.

"Gabriel!" I hiss. "Ease back. It isn't her fault. We probably should have checked," I tell him. "Ah, Evelyn, do you know where he's staying?"

"Yeah, he has quarters in one of the bunkhouses. Bunkhouse C I think," she supplies.

The sheriff, Gabriel and myself head in that direction. On our way, one of the teenagers comes running over.

"Dr. Angel, you're needed," he says breathlessly. "Nancy Taylor is going into labor."

"Is she here?" She is one of my appointments later today. She's scheduled for a check up. Her records indicated that she was getting close but wasn't that near to delivery.

"No, she's at her place," I'm told.

Nancy lives away from the main compound. It will take about twenty minutes to get there.

"Did something happen?" I ask.

"Don't know. I was just told to find you and ask you to come over," he says.

I look over at Gabriel.

"Go. We've got this. I'll come over later. Birthings take longer than most people suspect, especially the first one." He smiles and chin lift to go with the boy.

"Okay, I need to get my medical bag..."

"Got it in the truck already. It's been loaded up. Driver said. All you need do is hop in and the driver will take you there," the kid tells me.

"Wow, that's unexpected and fast," I say, tossing a confused look at Gabriel who shrugs.

I give Gabriel a quick kiss then follow the teen. Hobbling as fast as I can, the boy leads me around the side of the bunkhouse, where there's a parking lot of sorts, to a waiting truck. The teen waves as I jump in and quickly fasten my seatbelt. I turn to smile and greet the driver then freeze.

"Peter!"

"Miss me much?" He greets me with a devilish grin.

Before I can react, he punches me in the face and pushes me back. As I recoil from the blow and scramble for the door, I hear a click. Peter is holding a gun and is pointing it directly at me.

"Sit still. Don't move a muscle, Dr. Angel, or you will be singing with a new host of angels in a matter of seconds. I saw what happened to George. Wouldn't want the same for you," he threatens.

I close my eyes and lean my head against the window in surrender.

Peter crows victoriously. "I'm taking you to Devlin. Not sure how he's going to take it when he finds out that you've been banging Slayer," he tosses out as he drives through the main compound.

"Shouldn't *you* be worried about that yourself?" I smirk.

His initial growling response is replaced by a smug grin.

"Oh, surprised we aren't taking the main way out?" he asks, off handedly. "There are always more ways on and off a ranch. This is a bit longer, but we'll not have those pesky local cops hounding us either," he comments.

I open my eyes and take a resigned breath. When I focus outside the window, I can't believe my eyes. It's Zeke! He looks up when the truck passes by. He squints in an attempt to identify who's in the truck. Slowly I place my hand on the window and give him a desperate look. I mouth, 'help me.' I hope he gets my message. I press my battered face against the window. I see a slight nod before he turns a shoulder giving the impression that he's disinterested in the passing vehicle.

Angling my head so I see Peter and out the back window, I notice that Zeke is already heading back toward the big house. He's pulling out his cell.

Hang on, I tell myself. A host of angels will soon come to rescue me. They will see me safe. Please let it be soon.

∞∞∞

Gabriel

As the sheriff and I walk quickly toward the bunkhouses, I glance over. And who do I see? It's Nancy. She's waddling her way toward the clinic. I stop and stare to make sure I am see- ing correctly.

"Nancy," I call out.

She pauses as she hears her name. "Oh, hey Gabe," she says in the tired voice of a woman who is nearing their time.

"I thought you were in labor out at your place," I tell her.

She tilts her head and gives me a bewildered expression.

"Ben just came by to get Sera. He was told to fetch her as you had gone into labor and needed her at your place," I explain.

She shakes her head. "Gabe, I don't know what you are talking about. I have an appointment to see Sera here. I'm a bit early as I wanted to share this knitting pattern I have with Maggie." She holds up a stapled set of papers she's pulled from the knitting basket she carries.

"You didn't send Ben to fetch Sera?" Sheriff Dobbins asks her just to be sure.

"No, sir, Sheriff. Sera thinks I have a couple weeks still to go," she says, rubbing her extended belly.

Any other exchange is cut off when I hear Zeke yelling.

"Dang gum cell phone," he curses, as he attempts to run in our direction.

My eyes widen. Zeke isn't one to use colorful language when women and children are present.

"Zeke?" The sheriff and I hoof it toward him.

"Gabe, Sheriff," Zeke wheezes. "I just saw Sera. She was being driven out the back way in a Paradise truck. Couldn't make out who was doing the driving. It wasn't anyone I recognized. Her cheek looked bruised. Her face was pressed to the window. She was asking for help," he rushes out.

The sheriff and I run to his car to head out in the direction we think they're going.

"Get the chopper up," I yell at Zeke as I climb into the patrol car.

The sheriff is already calling it in, requesting back up. Looks like things are in play. I just hope that Sera isn't further injured by the time we reach her.

Sera

"Where are you taking me?" I demand.

"I'm taking you to the one who has already claimed you," Peter tells me.

"Luther Devlin." I say his name as if it were a disease.

"Yes, Luther Devlin," he says as he drives through the last gate. He must have left them open when planning this move.

"You already told me that. I didn't ask *to whom* but

where. Where is Devlin?" I press as if addressing a moron.

"Reno."

Too soon we've reached the paved road. From the looks of it, it isn't a main road, but one of the backroads that the locals know about and use. Peter must be anxious as he hits the gas a bit too soon, causing the truck to fishtail before all the tires hit the road. I find myself holding on to anything I can reach to keep my balance.

"If you keep driving like this neither of us will be arriving in Reno." I deliberately insult Peter.

"Shut the fuck up, bitch," he spits at me.

I turn to look out the window to hide my smirky grin.

I'm not sure how I nod off. But at some point, the stress must have been too much. With the silence that descends between Peter and myself along with the motion and sound of the car, it must have been enough to lull me to sleep.

"Shit. What the f..." Peter roars.

In a snap, I am jolted awake.

There had been a pop just prior to Peter losing control of the truck. Slamming on the brakes does nothing to aid in his gaining control. We keep swerving. Peter oversteers until finally we run off the road coming to an abrupt halt in the ditch alongside the road.

We hit the culvert hard. The impact slams us forward with enough force that the airbags deploy before the truck tips over on its side. My side. Peter's crushing weight bangs me even further into the door.

I lay motionless, stunned by the crash. Peter begins cursing, kicking and pounding his fists and feet. When he finally calms down, he wiggles his way off me pushing against the door in an attempt to shove it open.

"What happened?" I whisper weakly.

"Tire blew," he says through gritted teeth.

His door flies open. Someone has wrenched it open from the outside.

"Son of a bitch," I hear Peter shout happily as he pulls himself up. "Give us a hand," he says to whomever is there.

I hear grunts and groans then he's gone. The sound of congenial slapping of shoulders is heard. Muffled human male voices reach my ears. Does Peter know the person outside? I lever myself so I can push up with my good leg and reach up toward the open truck door.

My arms are seized by two individuals and I find myself hauled up and out of the truck. When I gain my balance on the ground, I look up to see who has arrived to help us. Finding myself rooted in shock.

Agent Johnson.

My eyes dart between the two.

"Where are you all headed?" Agent Johnson asks.

Is he playing at being a friendly bystander? Do the two men know each other? These are the questions rolling through my head. This is all too convenient, too suspicious. Best not to say anything and reveal too much to the wrong person.

"Reno," Peter replies with a snarky smile as he looks back at me.

The two share a look. The hairs on the back of my head

are standing up straight. I remain quiet, hoping to learn more, and trying to remain as invisible as possible. The longer we're delayed, the sooner help may come if Zeke comes through.

"Tire blew," Peter says with a shake of his head. One of his hands runs over the back of his head.

"Anyone hurt?" Johnson looks to Peter. Peter shakes his head. When he looks over at me, I do the same. "Good," he heaves a relieved sigh. "Come along then. I'll take you where you need to go," he offers. He motions us toward his waiting car. It's up the way a bit almost hidden by a clump of pines that are sitting close to the road.

"You going to Reno too?" Peter asks. I notice he's hanging back a bit.

Johnson glances my way.

"I think we need to return to the ranch," I finally have the courage to say.

Both men look over at me. I notice their twin frowns. Johnson's disappears quickly. He gives me a slight smile. I'm not sure how to interpret it.

"I'll see that you both get to where you need to go," he announces. He takes out a handkerchief from his jacket pocket and mops his brow then returns it.

Johnson gives Peter the come along hand movement. Peter hesitates then grabs my arm and begins to tug me along.

"Let go of me," I shout at him, pulling away from his grip.

"Dr. Angel," Peter growls through his clenched teeth. "You're coming with me and we are going to Reno. This is not open for debate."

I back away from him. I won't get close enough to enable him to easily grab me again.

"What is open for debate is whether or not I will return here after dropping you off and pay a visit to...oh, let's say, Daniel and little Lailah. Would you like that? I'll make sure to sprinkle them with pixie dust that will never let them grow old," he threatens.

I shake my head. I can feel the blood draining from my face. This man is threatening those two precious cherubs, those innocent children who have done nothing to him, who mean nothing more to him than some pawn or bargaining chip.

Without another word I start walking toward Johnson's car. Maybe he has a plan. He hasn't yet revealed himself to be an FBI agent.

Peter laughs.

It's cut short by a bang. I startle when I hear that all too familiar sound. Right before me, as if in slow motion, I watch as a dot of red begins to bloom in Peter's belly. He instantly grabs his middle. With wild and bewildered eyes he raises them to the one with the gun. Agent Johnson.

"Why?" Peter whispers.

"Devlin told me to deliver a message. Peter, you screwed up. Devlin doesn't like failure. This is how he rewards incompetence. Consider yourself terminated," Johnson tells him.

He points and fires the gun again. This time it hits Peter in the head close to where I had struck him with the stone. I cover my mouth with my hands to hold back my gasps and screams. This is all becoming too much. Too much. My horror filled eyes race to Johnson.

"Sorry you had to see that, Dr. Angel," Agent Johnson says, placing his gun back in his waistband.

Calmly he walks over to Peter and nudges his lifeless body with the toe of his shoe. Peter's body flops over on its back. Blood pooling from the exit hole behind his head. As I watch, Johnson takes out his phone and snaps a picture.

"He'll want to see this. The bastard always wants proof," he mutters as he fiddles with his phone.

"Who?" I ask in a trembling voice, fearful of the answer.

Johnson looks over at me, shrugs, then ignores me altogether.

He holds up his finger as he takes a call.

"It's Johnson, sir. Just sent you the picture, sir. Glad to know you received it and viewed it. Yes, sir, she's with me now. Sir, I'll turn the phone so you can see her," he says to the person he's talking to.

"Dr. Angel, smile for the camera. No? How about a little wave. No? Come on. Smile a little. You're going home. You should be happy. I'm taking you to your man," he says.

"Peter wrecked the truck. Ran it into a ditch. Maybe she has a bump on her head or is in a bit of shock," Johnson suggests.

"Who are you talking to?" I demand.

Johnson merely holds up his finger again.

"I'll take very good care of her, sir. We're leaving as soon as this call is concluded. Yes, I understand your instructions and will follow them to the letter, sir." Then he ends the call.

Johnson lets out a heavy breath, tucks his phone in his breast pocket then backhands me. The force of the blow is powerful enough to land me on the ground. I cup my bruised cheek and split lip.

"This is your definition of taking good care of me?" I scoff.

With a growl, he pulls me to my feet, then proceeds to

drag me toward his car. I dig my heels into the ground, trying to make it hard for him to move me along. When he tires of that, he tosses me over his shoulder.

"Put me down!" I scream as I kick and beat on his back. He ignores me.

When we reach his car, he roughly sets me on my feet. Twirling me around, he binds my hands with handcuffs then shoves me into the back of his vehicle. I struggle, pushing myself up into a sitting position.

I note the direction we're headed. "You're not taking me back to the ranch? Where are you taking me?"

"Reno."

I sit back and lean my head against the back of the seat. Briefly, I close my eyes. *Think*, I order myself. *The night is darkest before dawn. This is almost over. Believe it.* I have to keep my spirits up and my mind alert.

As we leave Paradise farther and farther behind, I realize that it's the place I most want to be.

I will return, I silently vow to myself. Somehow, some way, I will make my way back to where it is I'm meant to be. To Gabriel. Home.

Fate has given me a new opportunity. I won't be a coward and allow this moment to simply pass me by.

"You're taking me to him, Luther Devlin." I break the silence. "It's been you all along. You're the mole. How can you sleep at night or live with yourself selling out your country the way you do? For what?"

"Luther Devlin pays me a lot for my services. More than good ole Uncle Sam," he sneers. "With the money I've saved up, I'll live like a king for the rest of my life. Got me a place down in the islands. Bought a boat. I'll take myself fishing every day or lay in my hammock near the ocean beach drinking rum. Hot, naked babes in the bed and I'm a happy man." He tosses me a lopsided grin. "If a few schmucks get iced in the process...?" He shrugs. "That's life."

I snort and sneer at him in disgust.

"Hey, life isn't fair. You should know. How have you benefited from doing the right thing as a humanitarian, a citizen, a fiancée?" he challenges.

"Maybe if everybody tried to do the right thing, this world wouldn't be so screwed up," I retort.

Now he is the one to snort.

"And just what is 'the right thing?' Who's to be the judge? You? Devlin? Reverend Moneybags?" he scoffs. "Jeez you really are naïve." He shakes his head and chuckles in a way that makes my skin crawl. "And don't say anything about the Golden Rule," he continues. "Honey, I've seen what people want, and most of it ain't pretty. Why do you think people frequent back rooms and dank alleyways?" He shakes his head again.

I just stare blankly at him.

"Ever hear of the Underground? People delight in the macabre, kink, enjoy receiving and inflicting pain. They *crave* it. The world is fucked up *because* people follow the Golden Rule," he derides.

I sit in shock. What can I say?

"The problem with living a life of goodness, Angel, is that people like you don't seem to understand that not everybody wants that sort of life. Get your head out of the clouds, place your feet firmly on the ground, and open your eyes. Paradise isn't for everyone."

"It certainly isn't," I concede. "So are you saying that Peter acted the way he did because he wanted to be on the receiving end of it?" I challenge.

"Peter was an idiot. He got what he deserved," Johnson says, spitting out the window.

"And you?" I press.

"I'm no idiot. I got into the game knowing that life isn't fair. There will be winners and losers. I just even out the odds in my favor so that I don't remain in the shit pile all my life," he explains as if he were talking to another idiot.

"And your reward for winning is, let me get this straight, lots of money, a place in the islands with a boat, a bottle, and a banging babe," I recite as if memorizing a lesson for a teacher or a test.

"Exactly. Angel, looks like you're finally seeing the light." He chuckles.

I laugh along with him. "Now who's the idiot?" I quip, giving him a look of disgust I know he recognizes in the rearview mirror.

I see the fire of his anger as he growls. I think I've hit a nerve. I can't resist pressing on it.

"You're no better than Peter," I admonish. "A fall guy for a scummy mobster. Retiring and living like a king as you've described? Now who's delusional?" I taunt. "You and your kind will end up like David, Frank, George, and now Peter."

I give him a few minutes to digest that nugget. He taps his fingers angrily on the steering wheel. Yeah, I've hit a nerve. Can't resist gouging deeper.

"Name me one, just one person who worked like you have for Devlin and is now living the dream. Name one. You can't. Can you? Know why you can't? They all ended up dead. D. E. A. D. And I'd bet money that most of them became fish food or were ground up as some tiger chow supplemental food sold to zoos. Dead meat, man."

His neck starts turning red. "Shut up, bitch," he barks.

"Famous words spoken by a man who knows he's lost the game and beaten by a woman, no less." I can't seem to help but rub it in.

Without warning, Johnson slams on the breaks. My safety belt isn't fastened. In accordance with the laws of inertia, I slam into the metal cage that separates the back from the front seats before ricocheting around the back. The force of the blow and the whiplash leave me momentarily stunned.

"Golden Rule, Dr. Angel," Johnsons says with an air of satisfaction, "I'm just giving you what you wanted. After all, you did ask for it. Didn't you? Be honest." He leers.

I moan and curl up into a ball on the backseat. If I believe in Johnson's philosophy, then I'm to blame for my predicament. Have all my life's choices lead to this point? If I answer yes, that means I'm the master of more than my own fate. It means I control the destinies of others. That's hogwash.

I reject what he says. My life's philosophy has always centered around the principle of, 'Do as thy will so long as it harms none'. I am not not naive or unworldly. There's a lot of ugly I've witnessed first hand in my travels with Global Medicine. Discovered that though we make look and sound different, people are not all that different. People have lives and desires. It's how they go about living and satisfying those desires that's what makes us different, even unique. Everything else is geography. *"Judge not, lest ye be judged."* Those are words I've tried to live by.

Tolerating and accepting another's quirks is one thing, engaging in behavior that deliberately harms others is wrong. By any standard, it's wrong.

"My soul is free," I murmur.

"What? What did you say?" Johnson barks.

I hadn't realized I'd spoken out loud.

"I said that at least I live a life where my soul is free. My mind is my own. Willingly, I have tethered my heart to another. When I sleep, it's the sleep of angels. I'm at peace. Can you say the same? If we go with your pie mentality or your dog-eat-dog philosophy, you'll still end up no better off then Peter," I tell him. "Like Peter and all else who work for Luther Devlin, once you sign on with him, you've sold your soul. He'll never give it back. So maybe it's you who needs to get their head out of their ass and smell the shit pile you're truly in. Agent Johnson, you know very well there will be no island living for you. You've already sealed your doom and by your own hand. Who's the real idiot?" I scorn.

Johnson suddenly swerves the car to the side of the road, throwing it into park. Swiveling around, I see the barrel of his gun pointed directly at my head. His finger is looped around the trigger, ready to pull. What's holding him back?

"You're not thinking straight, Agent Johnson," I say. "Pulling that trigger will only make your end that much sooner than you originally supposed."

He gives me a questioning look.

"How do you think Devlin will reward you when I turn up dead? Hmmm? He's seen me alive and relatively undamaged. Killing me...why you might as well turn the gun on yourself. Weren't you the one who told me he likes to make those who displease him suffer?"

The barrel of the gun begins to waver. Sweat pebbles on Johnson's brow. He's breathing huffs of air through his teeth. His lips are pulled back in a maniacal grimace that makes him look more insane than feral.

This is it. *Gabriel, I love you. I will love you forever.*

I allow my mind to fill with images of my sisters and

parents and of my new Paradise family. Images and memories of Gabriel, Daniel, and Lailah fill my heart.

Please, I pray to all that is sacred and good. *Don't let Gabriel suffer when I meet my death. The man has such a huge capacity for love. Find him someone he can cherish and who will cherish him in return. A person he can grow old with.*

There's a pop, a shattering of glass. Blood and brains splatter over me. At the same time, Johnson's gun fires before his body slumps.

As I feel myself slipping away. I give my thanks to the universe. *Thank you for my life. Thank you for allowing me to know love. Thank you for Gabriel.*

Chapter 18

Gabriel

"I've located it, Mr. Slayer, Sheriff Dobbins," the copter pilot radios. He rattles off the coordinate information. I remain silent as the sheriff relays the intel to his men.

The sheriff presses on the gas as we race toward the where the truck has been spotted.

"Thanks, Keith. Keep an eye on it," I tell him.

"Will do, sir," he replies.

"Why have they stopped?" I look over at the grim faced sheriff.

The sheriff pushes back his hat and scratches his brow with his thumb.

"Could be lots of reasons, son. What fool in their right mind would come onto a ranch filled with so many people and do the things he did? There's no telling," he states.

I clench my jaw.

"Boss, looks like the truck is sitting in a ditch. Driver's door is open. I can see a body lying in the road a short distance from the front of the truck," Keith radios us.

Worry, regret, loss, and anger seep into me, each attempting to possess my very being.

"Pilot, this is Sheriff Dobbins," he says. "Do us a favor and fly around the area some. See if you can't spot anybody else. If not, move ahead, follow the road and see if you can spot another vehicle."

"Copy that," Keith replies.

My mind races with what we will find. Desperately, I try to close off dire images lest they haunt me for the rest of my days. But this I vow, if so much as a hair is harmed on her head, I will seek vengeance.

"There!" I shout, pointing to the truck. It's as Keith said. I can make out the tire marks. Whomever was driving it somehow lost control.

Before the sheriff's car has come to a full stop, I am unfastening my seatbelt and jumping from the vehicle.

"Sera! Sera?" I call out. No response. I keep yelling for her as I run toward the truck.

"Hold on there, son," Dobbins barks. "We'll find the little lady, but you might make our task harder. There may be plenty of evidence or clues and you stomping all over tarnation may be destroying some of that," he warns.

He's right. I must keep a cool head. We're soon joined by a few more police officers. The sheriff approaches the body. He bends down and feels for a pulse.

"Dead," he says in a flat voice. "Shot. Twice: once in the belly and once in the head."

He looks up at me and asks, "Can you ID him?"

I follow the path the sheriff took getting to the body. I look at his face. I nod my head.

"He's name is Peter Yale from the records we had on him at the ranch. This is the guy we called in to you."

"Yeah, he looks like the picture you showed me. We'll interview the person who hired him," he says.

"And I'll be looking over our hiring practices," I reply. "Now, where is Sera?" I search the scene and the surrounding area, looking for some telltale sign. Maybe she got away and is hiding.

"Steady, son. Slow and steady wins the race. Go too fast or if you're in too much of a hurry, you're bound to miss something," the sheriff advises.

He stands up and surveys the scene. I follow suit. "Clearly there is more than one set of human footprints. The mess of them tells me that Peter and Sera both got out of the truck. Don't find any blood smeared in or around the truck save what is pooling around the body. We can assume that Sera wasn't hurt in the accident," he says.

I wonder if he is speaking out loud to hear himself in order to think it through or for my benefit. Regardless, it does make me calmer. It has me doing my own inspection, using my head instead of reacting.

As a rancher, one learns to read the signs, all sorts of them. Sometimes it's the little things that most people overlook that become your best clues.

"I see two sets of men's footprints leading away from the truck. They mingle at first, but then they part. These," I say, pointing to a different set of prints, "must be Sera's. See, she has one shoe and her boot-cast on her left foot."

"Boss," Zeke calls out after several ranch trucks have pulled up. Each truck is filled with men from Paradise. They're toting rifles and grim looks of determination.

"Zeke, Jeb, Hunter, come take a look at this," I call them over. "Sheriff Dobbins, these men are my best trackers. Mind letting them take a look?"

Dobbins gives me a look of respect. He and I know that even though it's my woman that has been taken, he's the one in charge of this investigation. It's my way of telling him that I will not tread where I'm not invited.

"More eyes the better is my way of thinking," he says, motioning for my men to go ahead.

Several of Dobbins' men join in. They walk around the area setting down cones to mark the perimeter. Photographs are taken to preserve the fragile evidence before Mother Nature takes it upon herself to erase it all.

The men squat, study, and eventually gaze further down the road. Some even venture farther away toward where a wide bend in the shoulder lay just behind a clump of thick pine.

"What's the story, boys?" Dobbins asks though Jeb and Zeke are just as old if not older than himself.

"Two got out of the truck: one man and one woman. The tire was shot out. Bullet was fired down around there." Jeb points back down the road. "Yup, can see where someone lay in the ditch, concealed from oncoming vehicles."

"Skid marks, loss of control can be seen in the remaining pavement and gravel until the truck comes to rest here in the ditch," Zeke adds.

"Two sets of men's tracks. Seems as if one helped open the door and together they got the woman out." Hunter takes over.

The others nod their agreement.

"Then they head down this away," Jeb says, pointing farther down the road.

"But here's the interesting part," Hunter can't contain himself. "Looks like one, I'd say this guy here," he points to

Peter, "gets close to her. I'd say he's got her in some sort of hold and forced her down the road. They break apart."

"That's when he's shot by the other guy. He was standing here," Zeke says. A marker had been gently placed there on the ground. You can follow his tracks back to the woman. Now you can see scuff and drag marks for a bit. Then there is only one set of prints. Those belong to the man. No more female tracks."

My gut clenches with the telling of the story the prints tell. "She was carried."

I see the nods.

"After she was hit. You can see where her body lands on the ground," Hunter tells him, eyeing me carefully.

Another marker had been placed on the spot.

"Appears there was another car up ahead." Jeb motions up the road aways. "Must have been concealed just beyond the pines."

"Goes along with your theory that there was more than one: Peter and the mole," Zeke comments.

"Boss! Boss, I've found something," Cob calls out. Heads come up as if sniffing what new thing has been discovered.

I break out in a run. The others follow.

I turn to my foreman. "Zeke, see if you can hail Keith on the radio. See if he has spotted anything. Can't be too many other vehicles on this stretch for a while before hitting a main road into Reno," I order. "Whatya got?" I call out to Cob.

"Business card, boss. Used my fingers on the side. It belongs to the FBI...

"Agent Johnson." My nostrils flare. Rage pumps into my muscles. I hear Sheriff Dobbins barking orders as he runs back to his vehicle.

"Boss," Zeke rushes over. "Keith says he needs to head back. He's nearly out of range if he doesn't use his reserve fuel. But he says there's a black vehicle he's spotted. Only one on the road coming from this direction. Its making a beeline for CA-99. My guess is they're headed to…"

"Reno." I fist my hands. "Son of a b…" I grit out, searching out Dobbins.

"Sera is being taken to Devlin in Reno."

Dobbins motions that he hears. He has been switching from cell phone to radio, sometimes using them together. I've got my own forces to call upon.

I flip out my cell. "Isaac," I urgently say when my call is received. I tell him everything. "Thanks buddy. I'll owe ya. Once I get Sera back, you and your's are invited to the wedding," I tell him before hanging up.

"Load up, boys," I call out. My men freeze and look at me like hounds waiting for the go signal. "We're headed to Reno. We're bringing back our stolen angel. Nobody takes one of ours from Paradise and definitely not our angel."

The men whoop and holler as they run to get into place.

"Now, Gabe. Hold on there, son. You can't go all vigilante on me now," Dobbins warns.

"Sheriff Dobbins there is no harm in citizens visiting a fine city like Reno, now is there?" I challenge.

"Well, son, there's visiting and then there's visiting. Just need to know what you intend." Dobbins gives me a steely look.

"My angel was taken away from Paradise against her will. I aim to get her back with or without your help." I look him dead in the eye.

"I don't have jurisdiction in Reno," Dobbins reminds me.

"Sheriff, you are in pursuit of a fleeing kidnapper and murderer. He is a suspect in an array of federal, state, and local crimes. Don't tell me you're not within your legal rights to remain in pursuit until he has been apprehended. Call your buddies in and around Reno and get them to join in on the hunt," I tell him sharply.

"What did ya think I've been doing on the horn, boy?" He motions to me. "Come along, son. You're riding shotgun."

I smile faintly as I hurry to his vehicle.

Dobbins stops as he's placing a leg in his car. He encompasses everyone as he yells out. "Consider yourselves deputized."

He slides into the car, adjusts himself in the seat before fastening his seat belt, then starts the engine. He looks in his mirrors and then pulls out onto the road.

"I'll deal with the damn paperwork when I get back," I hear him mumble. "Nobody is coming into my jurisdiction and getting away with this kind of shit. Messing with those under my protection, not happening. No siree. Someone's gonna get their due. I guarantee..." He keeps muttering to himself. He flips on the lights and takes off like a bat out of hell. That's fine by me as hell is probably where we're headed.

Chapter 19

Sera

I wake with a start. A moan escapes my lips then a whimper. I feel a sting. It makes me flinch and hiss from the burn that remains.

"Shhh," I hear a male voice close to my ear.

Someone brushes my hair away from my cheek and brow. I feel something cool being pressed against my battered cheek. I know Gabriel's touch and his voice. These do not belong to him. I inhale, just to be sure. The scent does not match Gabriel's.

Slowly, I open my eyes. Focusing is a challenge. I blink until the fog seems to dissipate and images no longer blur.

"Hello there, angel mine," says a voice I'd hoped to never hear again.

I turn toward the voice. There sitting on the edge of the bed on which I have been placed is Luther Devlin. Nope, this is not Paradise. I'm in hell.

My lips part as I rapidly intake air. Desperately I try to steel my reaction. Instead of responding or looking at the man, I scan the room in which I'm placed. I feel hot color rushing to my cheeks when I discover that I'm naked and laying in a huge soft bed not my own or Gabriel's. The room has been darkened. The ceiling-to-floor, wall-to-wall drapes have been drawn closed. Not a bit of outside light enters. Everything in the room, for the most part, is black. Black. There are a few pieces of decor that are not. Those things are red. Blood red.

Devlin chuckles. "Welcome to Devil's Den. Deluxe living spaces for the elite in my highrise casino and hotel, Lust," he tells me.

My eyes swing to him.

"You looked like you were wondering where you were," he explains. "Don't want to keep you too much in the dark." He gives me a charming smile.

I press the covers tight against my naked chest.

"Now, don't be shy," he gently admonishes. "I promise you, we'll become intimately acquainted in little time."

I can't help but flinch when he reaches out to flick away a bit of hair that has fallen over my face. I see his face take on a hard look. He's not pleased by my reaction to him.

"I'm sorry," I whisper softly. "This is all so new to me." I hope my answer satisfies him.

"Ah." He pulls back a bit, considering me for a moment.

I take several settling breaths to keep from squirming under his questing perusal. I sense this is a man who sees more than most. Curiosity has me wondering just what it is he sees in me. Why does he think he must have me?

"I keep forgetting how young and innocent you are, darling. It's not often that I encounter such in my line of work. To be sure, I've had my share of women. Some were even younger than you—barely legal," he leans to say in sotto voce. "Even they had an edge, a hardness to them by the time they entertained me between the sheets or wherever I had them," he says flippantly with a wave of his hand.

"Never have I thought about being the one to break in

a virgin angel. Now, I find myself filled with anticipation and eager for the challenge."

He laughs. "To think I have snatched from the very heavens an angel of the highest order and brought her to, what you must think, is the pit of hell. No matter. Over the time we have together, I plan to introduce you to a whole lot of sin and evil that will have you renouncing heaven and embracing a new status as a fallen angel of my making and for my pleasure." His smile is one of cocky confidence.

Devlin picks up my hand, kissing my knuckles lavishly. He sucks and licks my fingers and hand. It's all I can do to keep from wrinkling my nose in disgust. He raises my palm to his nose and breathes in deeply before sweeping his nose up the length of my arm.

"So sweet. So mine," he says, congratulating himself.

His eyes find mine.

"When I came to fetch you, you were covered in filth." He wrinkles his nose. "I bathed you myself. No other's hands have touched your skin nor has any other seen your naked body, yet," he tells me in a voice laced with desire. "I rather fancy keeping you all to myself, though I have shared my pets and toys with others. I've even given a few away. But there is something about you that makes me a bit more possessive."

It sounds as if he is speaking to himself, unaware that I am a sentient being who is listening and understanding every word. I want to vomit.

"Y-you came and fetched me?" This is news indeed.

Immediately, Devlin presses a finger to my lips.

"Shhh. I know I haven't gone over the rules with you, so I shall be lenient with you for now. My dear," he says in a deceptively sweet tone, "never, *ever* question me about anything." His eyes have gone hard. "All you need to know will be what

I decide." The sweetness is gone. It has been replaced with a stern warning voice.

Truly, it's amazing to see this man transform from a solicitous lover into a near raving monster in a blink.

"Do you understand, my dear?" he asks in a new calmer voice.

I nod my head.

He boops my nose. "Words, pet. Use your words *always* when addressing me." Steel has returned to his eyes.

"Yes." His eyebrows lift. "Yes, I understand," I alter my response.

He continues to look at me as if he is waiting for something more. I give him a puzzled look. Then, "Yes, I understand, Mr. Devlin," I whisper.

He holds up a finger. "Master. You shall address me as your master," he reprimands. "Now try it again."

I take a huge breath. "Yes, I understand, Master," I dutifully parrot.

I know I'm not going to win a battle over words. I don't feel quite strong enough to cause too many waves right now. I must bide my time before I figure out what to do. Surely, Gabriel knows that something is wrong.

Gabriel, I'm calling on my warrior angel, my guardian angel. Oh, how I need you. Please send help. I need your help. My soul and heart call out to the one I love. Please hear me!

"Well done, pet," Devlin croons. "Now for another lesson," he says, flicking a glance over my form. His eyes linger on my exposed shoulders. Some inner fear compels me to tighten my grasp on the covers that shield my naked flesh.

Devlin runs a finger around the edge of my face, over my ear, and down my throat. He draws his fingers backwards and forwards over my exposed collar bone. Gently, he cups my chin, turning my head toward him.

"Look at me," he commands in a whisper.

Though I long to ignore the order, I obey.

"Don't turn away. Remain still. This is your next lesson. You belong to me now. You are mine. I expect you to always welcome my touch. We shall practice now," he says, shifting his eyes from my skin to my face and into my eyes. The slight narrowing of his eyes tells me I am remiss in remembering his earlier command.

"Yes, Master," I dutifully reply.

I see his slight smile. He is pleased.

Devlin tugs the covers from my clenching hands, pressing my hands flat against the bed.

"I want to look at you," he says. "Do you know how long I have desired you?" He isn't wanting my answer. He chuckles and shakes his head. "Ever since I first saw your face in that bridal magazine, I knew I wanted you. Had to have you. You were destined to be mine. Mine," he emphasizes. "I've already seen you. Now I desire a lingering look at my new pet."

He reaches for the edge of the sheet near my shoulders and begins pulling it down. Quickly, I move my hands to intervene and prevent his actions.

"None of that," he says in a voice normally reserved for children or pets. "You don't want to make Master angry on our first day together, now do you?" he cajoles.

When he reaches for the covers again, I squeeze my eyes tightly closed. I am not able to contain the sobs or the whimpers of distress that escape my throat. I maintain a death grip on the sheet and twist away from him in an attempt to shield myself.

In an angry movement, he grabs my shoulder, shoving me on my back. With a vicious yank he completely rips the covers from my grasp exposing every inch of my naked flesh. I instantly react by letting out a screech from the fear that seizes my body, rapidly covering my breasts and the apex of my thighs with my arm and hand.

What proceeds is a match of strength and will. Laughing cruelly, Devlin lands on top of me, using his body and his hands to restrain me and pull my arms away. I thrash and scream as I fight to free myself from his weight.

"Stop this foolishness," Devlin bellows. "Acting this way will not get you what you want. You must surrender to me. The sooner you accept this simple fact, the easier your life will be. Defy me, become more a burden than I wish to deal with, and you will regret it."

"I will never yield to you," I shout.

"Very well, have it your way," he snarls through angry lips. His face has turned a deep shade of red in his fury. "I shall enjoy taming you." He binds my wrists with a zip tie. Too tight. It cuts into my flesh, a deliberate maneuver to make me understand how helpless I am.

My bound hands are anchored to a hook above my head. The hook is such that it allows him to flip me over so I am belly down upon the bed. My naked backside is fully exposed.

With all my might, I try shifting to my legs in order to put some weight behind my effort to pull my arms free of the hold. Devlin has no intention of allowing me to do this. Grabbing my booted ankle, he pulls it out from underneath me. This too he ties to the bed, repeating the process with the other.

I keep thrashing my head screaming. Surely someone will hear. Devlin shoves a cloth into my mouth before binding another around my mouth and head.

"I assure you, my pet angel, I have vast experience in subduing reluctant pets. Now cease your struggles. You will only wear yourself out and then where will we be? Humm?"

Again, he crushes me with his weight by laying on top of my body, pushing me deep into the bedding until I think I might suffocate. My breaths are coming in pants. I need to calm down in order to draw sufficient air through my nose. If it fills with tears and mucus I will end up suffocating or blacking out.

Stay alive.

Those words become my mantra. What am I willing to endure? What am I willing to give up? What am I willing to lose? Is this how so many hand over their souls? My own question stuns me. Momentarily I freeze, ceasing all movement and resistance.

"There now. That wasn't so hard. Was it?" Devlin says wickedly. I can feel his growing cock pressing against my bottom. That alone increases my fear once more.

My muscles quiver. My legs and arms quake. I can feel the burn of the plastic ties as they abrade my skin. Blood trickles down my limbs tickling my flesh in its wake. My head pounds. Breathing is increasingly difficult. In truth, I'm exhausted. If I plan to rally to my own defense, I must regain my strength. Surely he will not rape me as I am now.

He means to punish me, show me he is dominant. Though I know he can force me at some point, I believe that is not his game. This is a man who needs to believe that his female conquests come of their own accord. He will want me to give myself to him. Beg him. Invite him. His ego demands this. Power is what he is after but of a different sort than what he is normally used to welding.

"Oh, little dove," he croons softly and sweetly. "Your heart races like that dulcet bird of Noah's fame after her flight around the world seeking that space where man could once again flourish," he says in a silky and suave voice.

He straddles my body. I press my face into the pillow to smother my sobs. His fingers caress my back moving ever downwards toward my bottom. I flinch at his touch.

"Be still," he admonishes in a commanding voice.

He brushes the hair away from the nape of my neck. I sense him leaning over my body. His breath is coming out hot and heavy against my flesh. Devlin swipes his tongue over my skin then viciously bites down on the back of my neck. I scream and buck in a natural instinctive attempt to dislodge him from my body. Like a rutting monster, he holds me down until I am thoroughly exhausted.

Relinquishing my skin from his teeth, he moves off my body.

"We will repeat this lesson as many times as it takes, Angel pet," he says while wiping way the blood that stains his lips on a crisp white handkerchief. Though he warns me, I hear the note of excitement in his voice.

I gulp in air, desperate to calm and steel myself from reacting to his sadism.

"Now for your punishment." My eyes widen at that. Dear God! What does he consider punishment if that was not a display? "I will go easy on you this time. But I promise it will become worse for you the longer you defy me and refuse to accept your fate."

His hand skates down my back until it has descended to my bottom. Devlin cups and caresses me there then cruelly squeezes my flesh.

I cry out through my gag from the pain and unwanted

touch.

Devlin laughs.

The man craves my response. He's seeking a reaction. I vow to not give one unless it becomes impossible to contain.

With a crack, his hand lands on my bottom. Again and again his hand makes brutal contact with my skin. When I do not give him the response he desires, he moves away opening a panel.

"Your tolerance for pain is greater than I had anticipated," he says in a conversational tone. "How about we try something else? How about the strap?"

I don't know what is more cruel, to be told of one's torture before it commences or to be totally taken by surprise. At least, this way I have time to prepare. The key is to stay calm, to not flip out. If I engage my mind elsewhere, sort of placing myself in a meditative trance, I should be able to withstand much more than I imagined. I pray this is so.

Nothing. I mean nothing ever in my life could have prepared me for the strap. Now, I have treated people who had been caned and whipped. Such things happen in many parts of the world. Treated patients who thought it was a form of foreplay. To see the damage is one thing, to feel it is altogether something different.

In all honesty, I don't know how much I'll be able to withstand. The pain is all consuming and terrible in the extreme. It isn't just my bottom that is struck. My back and thighs are not spared. I know that I will bear these marks for some time. I force myself to think about anything other than about the new wounds or the pain.

So deep into my attempt to remove my mind from my body, I'm not immediately aware that the beatings have stopped.

"Amazing. Simply fucking amazing," I hear Devlin say through his labored breathing.

The man is out of breath. He stopped because it had tired him. For me this is a victory.

Devlin lets out a weary huff as he sits heavily in a large cushioned chair near the bed.

"This is better than a work out in the gym," he says with a satisfied voice. He leans his head back and shuts his eyes momentarily as if seeking a bit of rest. Or...

What? He's enjoying this, the bastard. What sort of sick pervert is he anyway? No. I don't want to know the answer to that question. I've already seen some of what he does or orders others to do. This can't be normal. Can it? Or am I really naïve as so many people of late have commented? Silently, I weep into the pillow.

I must have fallen asleep or maybe I simply blacked out. Tugs on my limbs bring me back to awareness. The hell I am in is not over. That alone makes me want to weep some more. My body aches to the point where the pain is nearly all consuming. My muscles quiver and shake uncontrollably.

No longer am I face down on the bed. Devlin has rearranged my body once again. A dog collar encircles my neck. The metal swivel is attached to a long chain that is connected to a hook by the head of the bed. The zip ties around my wrists have been replaced by metal cuffs, each with a circular metal swivel.

A quick glance down the length of my body confirms that I am still naked and very much exposed to Devlin. My ankles have cuffs similar to what is around my wrists. I am no longer laying longways in the bed. He has shifted me so my bottom is at the side edge. My arms have been drawn over my head and my wrists secured by a chain to another hook. The same has been done to my ankles which have been anchored keeping my knees drawn up and spread wide.

"I've enjoyed watching you as you sleep," Devlin tells me now that he has noticed I am awake.

"When I play rough with my pets, I smooth the stings with a soothing salve afterwards. I will not do so with you this time. You need to learn your place. Something tells me you will need many lessons." He gives me a lazy smile. "I look forward to our sparring, Angel pet."

His face and eyes harden. I can see why others would be easily intimidated by him. There is just a hint of crazy behind his eyes. One never seems to know if he will laugh or yell, shake hands or shoot your head off. I've seen him go from gallant to demonic. He has caressed me then beaten me, crooned then raged. He seeks my surrender, yet thrills when I resist. Is he unstable? Is this what I am witnessing?

Frist David, then Peter and his cohorts, and now Devlin. Dear God, how is it that I always seem to be thrown into the company of crazy males?

Chapter 20

Gabriel

"**A**re you fucking crazy, bro?" Isaac, my longtime friend and FBI agent, growls. "Don't you understand all the potential trouble I would be getting myself into by allowing you in on this operation?" he challenges, though to my ears it sounds more like a whine.

"Isaac, that's my woman in there being, God only knows, brutalized by that monster mobster Devlin," I bark back.

We are nearly nose to nose. "Isaac, what would you do to get back your woman if she were taken?" Instantly, I see the telltale sparks flash in his nearly black eyes. "If our positions were reversed, I'd let you in," I tell him in a calmer voice.

I turn away and run a hand through my hair. "Man, I don't want you losing your job over this. Besides, Sheriff Dobbins already deputized me and my boys."

I see his brows wing up with that statement.

"Well, then why didn't you say so in the first place. Let's get you some bullet proof vests and go over basic protocols," he says, giving me a slap on the shoulder in reassurance. And just like that we're back in.

When our posse arrived in Reno, Isaac was there waiting for us. Dobbins had contacted the local authorities. It was at their headquarters that we met up. I'm pleased to see that Isaac has moved so quickly and has come himself.

We exchanged bro hugs when we first met up. It's good to see him again. It has been too long.

"Gabe, your call was just the break we needed, man," he says. He's got my attention. "We've known that there was a mole in the agency for a long time. Identifying the traitorous bastard was another thing. The guy was too good at hiding in plain sight. Too much of a chameleon. Anyone who got too suspicious ended up gone or damaged. He even covered up such hits by having others killed too, motherfucker," he spat.

"Once you called and gave me a name, it was easy to put the pieces of the puzzle together. It was there the entire time. Nobody seemed able to see it, me included," he admonishes himself. "Found a few others he suckered into aiding him. They'll spend the rest of their lives, or at least most of what's left, behind bars. Even there, their life expectancy will diminish. Most likely they'll be taken out," he says, though there's no sympathy.

"So tell me, how are we going to get Sera?" I cut to the chase.

"First we need to verify that Devlin's the one who has her then where exactly she is being held," he says.

Isaac's cell phone sounds. He holds up a finger and turns away to answer. He speaks in rapid Spanish. The looks he flashes my way clue me that the call involves Sera.

"Gracias. Buen trabajo. Avísame si aprendes algo más que sea útil. Mantente a salvo hasta que te contacte." Translated, "Thank you. Nice job. Let me know if you learn anything else that is useful. Stay safe until I contact you," I hear him say as he ends the call.

Isaac gives me a predatory grin. "Devlin isn't the only one who has moles conveniently positioned," he tells me in a low voice. He motions me to follow him to a more private location.

I don't hesitate.

"That was one of the eyes and ears I have placed within Devlin's organization." I motion him to continue. "That person just informed me that Devlin received a series of calls today. The timing is most interesting," he says with meaning. "After one particular call Devlin himself took off. When he returned a few hours later, he was not alone."

My entire body has come alert.

"A woman that matches Sera's description was brought in. She was carried. She appeared to be unconscious." He grips my arm. "She was covered in blood."

I can feel my anger building up once again.

"Gabe, she's alive. Devlin would not have bothered to recover her body if she was dead. He rarely fouls his nest that way," he reasons. "Devlin must really want her. He seems to have gone to a lot of trouble to obtain her," he adds.

Okay, I reason with myself. *Sera's alive.* That's one less worry. Now to make sure she stays that way and isn't hurt.

"What is he doing to her and what are his plans for her?" I throw that out at him.

He gives me a look of sympathy and pity. "Gabe, don't go there, man. You'll just drive yourself mad that way. What could he do to her that would push you away from her?" he counters.

"Nothing." I am adamant on that score.

"That's your answer. So don't dwell on it. If you do, I'll have to keep you here. Your emotions will only make you a danger to yourself and others. That I can't allow, bro," he tells me honestly.

"I hear you and respect what you say." I need to change the subject. "So did your contact tell you where to find Devlin?" I press.

He flashes me a brilliant smile. "Come, I'm gathering everyone in the conference room so we can make plans. There's no time to lose." He's moving down the hall even as he speaks.

I'm hot on his heels.

My own cell phone vibrates. As soon as I answer I hear Lailah's voice. "Daddy!" she calls out desperately. I can hear the tears and fear in that one word. I also hear a bit of hope.

"Hey, cherub. Daddy's very busy right now." Desperately trying to not sound impatient.

"I know, Daddy, but this is important. So important that Nana Elizabeth said it would be okay to call you and tell you."

"Okay, darling. What do you need to tell me," I urge.

"Violet says you have to hurry. Our angel is in danger fwom the Devil himself. He's hurting her. Sewa is twying to be bwave but she's scared, Daddy. I'm scared too."

"There are a bunch of people here with me that are working on getting her back. It will be okay. I plan on bringing Sera back to Paradise." The vow isn't only to her, but one I make to myself.

"Violet says that in the end it will be okay but you have to hurwy. *Hurwy*, Daddy. You don't have much time." I've become more alert than before. Isaac and a few who know me are watching me closely. They sense something is about to be revealed.

"Lailah, tell me…"

"Violet says that Sewa has been taken to the Devil's den. It is like his home, Daddy," she says in a quivering voice. "Violet showed me pictures inside my head of his home. It's scary there."

"What makes it scary, cherub mine?"

"Its dawk," she whisper-whimpers. "His favorite colors are black and wed. He doesn't like the light fwom outside to come in. There's a dog collar on Sewa. She doesn't like it. Sewa's chained down and naked. Violet says that Sewa is trying hard to be bwave but she cwied and scweamed sometimes when he was spanking her with a belt."

I can hear Lailah starting to cry.

"You did a good thing telling Nana Elizabeth and asking to call me, Lailah. I'm very proud of you and I know Sera will be too when she hears of it," I tell her.

"Weally? I like it when you and Sewa are pwoud of me. It makes me happy," she says in a watery voice. "Is Sewa gonna to be our new mom?" she asks pointedly.

"Yes, if you and Daniel are fine with it," I amend with my fingers crossed. "We will always love and remember your mother but I think she would want us to keep Sera and make her a part of our family. Don't you think so?" I ask.

I hear her muffled voice. She is shouting to her brother. I hear the joy that's returned. "I take it you approve."

"Yes, Daddy. Daniel and I want Sewa to stay. We picked her to be our new mom. Can we call her Mom?"

I chuckle. "I think Sera will love that."

Lailah giggles with excitement.

"Lailah, did Violet tell you anything else?" I probe.

"Umm," she thinks. "Violet says that Sewa will bwing other angels to Pawadise. She won't be the only one. But you have to bwing her home first, Daddy. You are her warwior angel, her guawdian angel. Violet says it is a task that can't be done alone. It will take a host of angels to bwing our Sewa safely home," she says as if she were reciting something word for word given to her by another. It's one more way I believe that someone is communicating to and through Lailah.

"Lailah, tell Violet thanks for the information. I'm hanging up now. I need to share this with the others and then we're gonna bring Sera home. I love you, cherub. Tell Daniel I love him too."

"We love you too, Daddy. Bye."

I look over at Isaac. "My contact," I see Zeke smirk, "says that Sera was taken to Luther Devlin's personal home in a place called the Devil's Den. Have you heard of the place?"

Isaac nods. Maps are displayed on screens around the room. He points out the location. Immediately schematics are also displayed. I am rather impressed by how much information Isaac seems to have at his fingertips. Then it dawns on me.

"You've been working on trying to break into Luther Devlin's organization and find enough intel to have him arrested," I say.

"Someone's been using their brain," he replies. When I remain silent he fills me in. "For about five years I've been assigned to a special team that has been focusing on bringing Luther Devlin to justice. Yeah, we were able to bring in some of his employees but could never get enough to pin on the man himself. Very little goes down in his crime organization without his knowledge, his say so. The man is dirty, but knows how to clean up and present himself real good in a courtroom."

"Nobody was willing to flip on him or do a deal?" I ask, a bit surprised.

"Nope. Those we had enough to put away in prison would rather do their entire time then spring for a deal. They wouldn't last long on the inside or the outside even if they were in witness protection. Devlin's that good," he tells me. "We had a few takers." He grimaces. "Devlin made swift examples of what happens when you double-cross him. Look at what he did to David, Sera's ex."

"True enough." I nod.

"But over the years, we watched and learned. Little by little we got closer and closer until we knew how to slip people into his organization without him suspecting a thing," he says.

"Dad always said that slow and steady wins the race."

Isaac nods.

We share a grin.

He picks up the volume of his voice. "Okay people, listen up. This is the plan," he says, then proceeds to lay it out.

If there is a place lower than hell, it will have a new resident come tonight. Trusted agents will be going in undercover. Some will go in as customers of the casino, others as servers and workers. Others will simply go in as the FBI and police agents they are.

I'm impressed by the plan. Nothing seems to be overlooked. Every exit will be covered. In one fell swoop, Devlin and many of his bad boys will be caged.

I make my way to my Paradise team. "Men," I say, "I'm proud and honored that you would volunteer for this mission. If any of you feel you want to hang back and wait, it's your right and your decision to do so."

"Ain't playing out that way, boss," I hear one of my men say.

"We're all sticking together. Can't have a host of angels with just one or two. You heard what Violet said," Zeke says with a determined light in his eyes.

Can't say I'm not a bit choked up by all the support. These guys are putting their lives on the line for my woman, my angel, for me.

Zeke places his hand on my shoulder.

"We all know you would do the same for us. Paradise men look out for one another. Sera isn't just your angel, son. She ours too. Paradise just wouldn't be the same without our own seraphim. We got cherubs. We even got our own archangel. We ain't losing our seraphim. Sera's ours and we aim to get her back."

Though I recognize Zeke's attempt to bring some levity into the situation, he and the others are quite serious.

The truth is, Paradise has become something more since Sera's arrival. If she left, it *wouldn't* be the same. It says something when others know this simple truth as well.

"Let's go rescue our angel and kick some devil ass," I say, receiving whoops and hollers.

Chapter 21

Sera

I must be hallucinating. My mind must be preparing me to survive this next round of horror. I believe this because the distinct scent of violets fills my nose. As strange as it sounds, it somehow comforts me.

When I was a child and visited my Granny Flowers, I loved to spend time in her bedroom. Granny Flowers had an old fashioned dressing table. On top sat an exquisite set of perfume atomizers and bottles. My favorite was the one that smelled of violets. It pleased my granny endlessly when I told her. I didn't know then that her name was Violet.

I allowed that scent to lull me. It would serve as my armor, my mental and emotional guard against the rape I knew was coming. Devlin may take my body, but I would never surrender to him my soul, heart, or mind. In God's hands, I've placed my soul. My heart I have gifted to Gabriel. It was now in his keeping. My mind is my own.

A sharp smack lands on my cheek. "Ah ah ah, Angel pet," Devlin admonishes. "Can't have you drifting away. Come back. I must insist that you be a full participant. If you like, you may consider this another lesson, pet." He chuckles indulgently.

My gag has been removed. I wonder why. Would I be punished if I spoke? He told me questions were not permitted.

I know he enjoys my vocalizations particularly when he has been cruel. For him, it seems they, along with the play, are part of his fun. Devlin needs it in order to become fully aroused.

"Master, may I speak and ask a question?" I ask in a breathy voice. I give him what I hope is a bewildered look.

"Ask your question," he consents.

I give him a slight smile. "What are you doing? Why the chains and collar? Master, you are ever so much more power-ful than I. Surely you do not mean to woo me through means of forced restraint?" I ask in mock affront and feigned shock.

Now it was his turn to give me a look of bewilderment. I take it as an invitation to continue. At this point, I'll do any-thing to delay what he has in mind to do.

"Luther. May I call you Luther, Master?"

He studies me then gives me a slight nod of consent. "For now."

I give him with another smile. "Thank you, Luther. Lu-ther, obviously you are a man of great strength and power. You have mastered many men and women and can master all that comes before you," I tell him, hoping to stroke his ego.

"Go on," he says, intrigued.

"It is obvious you use such props because women have been false with you in the past. How many throw themselves at your feet a day? Hmm? Chains, whips, and such...toys only serve to make them deliver a true response, to show them that you are the one in charge and will not be manipulated by them." I give him a few minutes to absorb my words.

"What is your point?" he asks at last.

"Luther, I am not used to such antics. These chains, being held down and positioned, exposed in this manner truly frightens me. I do not enjoy it. Sex, intimacy, foreplay is all new to me. I haven't the experience that you have. Maybe other—pets have come to life in such a situation as this, but not I." I take a deep breath. "You said you were drawn to me. I was different than all the others you have had. Why treat me the same? That is all I am asking."

Giving the air of being resigned to my fate, I lay my head down on the bed and look up at the ceiling. How I long to watch and observe the emotions that play over his face. But I dare not deviate from the path I have committed myself to.

First I hear his approach. I caution myself not to flinch, to not react to his touch, recoil from his brutality if it comes down to that. Instead of being pounced upon, I am surprised to find that he is in fact releasing me. First my ankles than my wrists. Quickly, sitting up, I wrap my arms around my chest bringing up my knees to sit sideways to shield my nether region.

Devlin next releases the chain but does not remove the collar. Then he brings me a robe, placing it gently around my shoulders. Quickly, I slide my arms in and hastily secure it shut.

"Thank you, Luther. That was very nice of you. I very much appreciate the comfort of the robe. Never have I worn such a finer one as this." I look coyly at him through my lashes.

There is a bit of preening at my praise.

"What must I do to gain your total compliance?" Devlin asks.

He offers me his hand. I take it without hesitation. To refuse him, I decide, would not be the wise move. I need him to trust me.

"Treat me as the girl of your dreams." I tell him with a slight giggle.

In turn he gives me a wicked smile.

"We Angels may look delicate and love a gentle hand, however we were raised to be sturdy. There is much I can withstand by way of cruelty, but I am better persuaded by kindness and good faith." I flutter him a glance that is meant to flirt. "I have always dreamed of being wooed by a handsome man." A blush stains my cheeks as I cast my eyes around in a deliberate attempt to evade his gaze.

Swiftly but ever so gently, Devlin catches my chin. Holding my head still, he forces me to look into his eyes. "There now. No need to be shy when you're with me," he tells me huskily.

When I give him yet another smile, he releases my chin, but not before swiping my lower lip with his thumb.

"Ask another question," he says, leaning in to me so his lips nearly scrape against mine. "I find I rather like your questions.

"Why did you decide you wanted me?" My question surprises me. I don't know where it came from.

Devlin purses his lips as if he is considering his words. He then flashes me a speculative look.

"I'm a wicked man who lives in a wicked world. I have worked my way through the bowels of mankind's depravity, using man's need for sin against those with such afflictions. It has brought me riches and a life of splendor and indulgence."

He places his hands in his pockets, walking slowly toward the curtained wall. He draws back the drapes revealing a purpling sky as the sun begins to set behind the mountains to the west. Neon lights are aglow. The city is coming alive with the dark pleasures to be had here with the rising of the moon.

I join him there when he motions to me by holding out his hand. Again, I dare not defy him.

"Behind the bright lights and polish lays a world of dirt

and decay that the headiest perfume can never cover up." He stops to analyze the effect his words are having on me. "I see you do not fully believe what I have said."

As if debating with himself, finally he grabs my hand. "Come, I wish to show you something. Words can say much, but, as they say, seeing is believing."

He takes me into a room that must be an inner-office void of windows. There are numerous monitors attached to the walls. A control station is placed just beneath a bank of them. Devlin picks up a remote control and in a flash turns them all on.

"There is a private club that I own and house within this complex," he begins telling me. "We provide services for those who are willing to pay extra for the pleasures they seek."

I must have given him a perplexed look for he further explains. "People like to be, let's say, entertained in a variety of ways. Some ways are not socially acceptable. So, for a fee, we discreetly provide what our clients desire."

He points to one monitor. "Recognize this fellow? He's a senator who's held office for nearly two decades and this is how he finds release from all his stress."

I look on aghast while I watch as the man is bent naked over a table and restrained while a man wearing nothing more than leather chaps rams his cock into the senator's ass. Over and over this plays out to the painful joy of the elected government official.

Devlin directs my attention to another monitor. "Here is a very famous outspoken TV evangelist. This is one of the many fetishes we help him satisfy," Devlin says, giving me a crooked smile.

Though I long to pull my eyes away from the screen, I cannot. There he is. the man who has a holier than thou fire and brimstone style of preaching subjecting himself with relish to a dominatrix. Dressed in a diaper, he is on his knees licking his mistress's needle point six inch heels.

On another screen I watch as a famous female singer is fucked by animals of varying sorts. Large breed dogs appear to be her favorite. Each screen is more shocking than the other.

I turn horror filled eyes toward Devlin. "Why do you show me this?" I ask in a voice filled with anguish.

Devlin pulls me into his arms in an awkward attempt to give me comfort.

"Nothing will remove such things from my memory." I shudder. I can never unsee all that has been presented.

"Even angels from heaven must have their eyes opened to the horrors of humanity. I thought for sure as a doctor you had seen your share," Devlin tells me as a father would a child who refuses to grow up.

"I have treated the results of such things and worse. Never have I been required to watch them being inflicted. Even still, they always were a small part of the medical issues I encountered. But this," I flourish my arm toward the monitors, "this is…" I shake my head in disgust.

"These are mild," he tells me. I think he delights in my growing horror.

"If you don't believe it, I can show you more, live. Would you rather I tell you of a few?" He leads me from the room.

"We've had those who desire the experience of killing another." He chuckles when I gasp. "Don't fret. We select people who wish to end their own lives or, in a few cases, people who had it coming," he says in a hard voice. "There have been a few who wish to perform, shall we say, *sex acts* on those under age or who were less than willing. Sex of some sort seems to be the most popular request," he tells me.

My mind is reeling.

As he begins to describe one horrible session, I cover my ears. "Please stop. I don't wish to hear any more. Cease this torment, I beg you," I plead. "Why? What is the purpose of exposing me to all this...filth?"

"I am simply trying to answer your earlier question, my dear. This is only a part of my world over which I reign," he explains innocently.

"What? You're the king of a dunghill? Why do this when you could be king of something much more enriching?" I challenge.

"That's the point, Angel pet. This is something I quite enjoy and I am quite good at. This is my passion. The same way you chose being a doctor. This life called to me, resonates with me," he tells me with impatience.

"I'm not ashamed of what I do," Devlin tells me honestly and I believe him. "But there are times when I want something different. I find myself craving a bit of light in my darkened world, something more clean and pure. When I began to realize that my current lover bored me, that was when I first saw your image in that silly frivolous magazine. At first glance I knew I had to have you. I knew you were the one that my soul craved," he tells me.

There is a part of me that feels sad for him. Here is this physically beautiful man who has chosen and relished a life as a beast, yet even he desires the good. Can he be all that bad if he craves what is clean and wholesome?

He turns me to face him. We have returned to his inner sanctum. Night has fully descended. The sky is pitch black making the neon seem all that more luminescent. The brilliance of the colors is almost shocking. Gaudy.

Devlin follows my gaze. "I have a special coating on my

windows that allows me to see out and nothing to see in," he tells me. There are times I like to watch what is happening below or simply gaze out toward the mountains," he says as if he is revealing a part of his soul shown no other. "Tonight I shall feast on many things. I now desire food. Come," he commands, as he leads me to a private dining alcove.

The table is covered in a black linen cloth over which a smaller one in grey is laid. A service for two all in black except for the crystal glassware and brushed silver cutlery has been set out. Devlin presses a buzzer. In seconds, a door opens up and in walks two men pushing a food trolley.

Neither man looks at me. They sneak glances at Devlin who waves them on to lay out the food. Each man wears a similar black suit with a crisp white linen draped over their left arm. With swift elegant moves and nary a sound, the two men place plates in front of me and Devlin. Other dishes are set out on the table. Our water and wine glasses are filled in a manner seen in a five star restaurant. Devlin flicks his fingers. Instantly the men bow and hastily retreat.

As the last man to leave turns to close the door, I see him glance our way. Was it my imagination? I would have sworn that he deliberately allowed his eyes to linger on me, catching my eyes then giving me the slightest of nods.

"What have we here?" Devlin asks as he surveys the food.

Quickly, I recover myself and refocus my attention on Devlin.

"One of the perks, Angel pet of living in and owning such an establishment is access to the finest cuisine money can buy. And it looks like the kitchen is at their best. Rare beef with *au jus*, steamed asparagus with hollandaise, loaded baked potato, fresh baked rolls. This wine is from my private reserve," Devlin says as he waits for me to begin eating.

I sample everything. "Delicious," I say. In truth, I am

very hungry. It could have been a burger and fries or a grilled cheese sandwich for all I care. But I understand what Devlin is doing. The man is trying to impress me as a young buck wants to do when he's taking his girl out on a date. This is his attempt at wooing. Impressing the opposite sex is his method.

Silently, I wonder how long I could drag dinner out.

"I must commend you, pet," Devlin says in between bites.

I pause while lifting my fork to my mouth when he breaks the silence. I place it down when I sense he has more to say and wants, no demands, my full attention.

"Good, my pet," he praises. "I do wish to go over a few basic rules that will help ease your transition. You seem to be a quick learner and one who knows proper behavior and etiquette. One day I shall tell you some stories about some I had to train." He shakes his head. "Ghastly, to say the least, but some were a bit more...what's the word," he ruminates while rolling the stem of his wine glass between his thumb and fingers, "engaging. We'll leave it at that."

"Rule one you already know. No asking questions unless given permission. Rule two: do not engage the help in conversation and that goes for any guests I bring in here or whom we meet in other locations, unless of course, I direct otherwise."

I am not about to remind him he has given me a different rule number two.

"Never make eye contact with the help," his voice hardens slightly. "That is rule three. Rule number four: always give me your undivided attention when I am speaking to you. There are others but we shall get to them as needed," he instructs. He peers over at me, waiting.

Ah, yes, another rule he has given me that didn't make this grouping. Dutifully I respond with, "Yes, Master."

Triumph registers on his face. He leans in, placing a kiss on my closed lips. Neither do I respond nor pull away. I just sit there immobile. A frown darkens his visage. Just as he is opening his mouth to speak, a buzzer sounds and a light blinks from a phone set near the table. Devlin is clearly irritated. He heaves a sigh before picking up the phone.

"Yes," he bites out. He falls silent and listens. His handsome face becomes distorted with rage. "And you are unable to handle this?" I hear the veiled warning. I wonder if the person to whom he is speaking does as well.

"Did you remind her of the consequences? And she still refuses?" Devlin taps his fingers on the table, the only sign of his irritation as he continues to listen. "Enough," he barks. "Set her up in the naughty room. I'll see to this personally. I expect you to be there too."

When he hangs up, he wipes his mouth then pushes back his chair, rising from the table. I don't move a muscle. As he begins to walk away, he stops as if coming out of a stupor. Turning around, he blinks his eyes and looks at me. He motions for me to join him.

"You might as well come and see how I deal with some of my naughty workers," he tells me. "Who knows, maybe we'll get to see your medical skills in action."

With reluctance, I join him. I have no desire to see more of what seems to be standard in his establishments.

Chapter 22

Sera

The naughty room is a special chamber located deep in the bowels of Casino Lust. It's a place where workers who are on the wrong side of Luther Devlin are taken to have punishment meted out. From the looks of it, the room must also come in handy for those paying clients who want some kink or are into all levels of BDSM.

When Devlin and I arrive, there's a guy with arms crossed standing in front of a naked girl whose wrists and ankles have been strapped to a large metal frame erected in the middle of the room.

"Remember the rules, Angel pet," Devlin softly warns as we enter. Snapping his fingers, he points to a place in the room he wants me to stand.

Without hesitation, I obey.

In one swift motion, Devlin picks up a leather whip with four lashes and brings it hard down on the woman's bare bottom. Immediately, I see welts begin to rise across her abraded skin. Again, Devlin lashes her. Each time she arches her back and screams.

"Do I have your attention, Connie?" he barks.

"Yes, Master," she screams her reply, her face contorted with agony.

"Word has reached me that you have been very naughty," he says, striking her flesh again, making Connie scream some more.

"Your unacceptable behavior has interfered with my evening plans," he admonishes her administering several additional blows. These are delivered with much more force, a punctuation of his irritation of having been interrupted. An interruption I am cognisant of that has given me a reprieve from his undivided attention. Poor girl!

"Now tell me, Connie, what is the one word you may never use with a customer?" he prods the sobbing girl. "Come on, Connie." He runs his hand over her marked and reddened ass. Devlin laughs cruelly when she flinches and whimpers from the new pain. "Let me hear it."

"No," she sobs. Her head hangs low, her hair a tangled mess curtaining much of her face.

With a single finger beneath her chin he raises her head, peering into her eyes. "Once more, Connie." His voice demands, reminding her, and myself, that he will not be denied.

"No," she repeats. Her red painted lips quiver. Mascara has made black streaks down her flushed puffy cheeks.

"Okay, Bennie, take Connie back to the customer if he still wants her. I think Connie has learned her lesson. Tell the customer that time with her is on the house. Either way, take the fee out of her pay," he directs, never sparing a glance at the girl. She is now violently sobbing.

Devlin puts back the whip, washes his hands in a nearby sink then comes over to me, taking me by the arm.

"You remembered your rules," he praises. "That one did not." He indicates Connie with a chin lift. "Instead of just doing what the customer wanted, she now has a sore ass and less money as well. Employees such as Connie are not permitted to deny customer requests. They have rules, as do you. One of hers is to never say no," he tells me. "You look a bit pale." Devlin says after examining my face with a critical eye. "Let's go back and finish our supper."

"Boss," Bennie calls out as we are about to leave. "Cal says that Joey has been caught with his fingers in the till again."

He heaves a sigh. "How much?" Devlin asks darkly.

"This time he was found with a thousand in cash and another five hundred in chips," Bennie tells him.

"When it rains it pours," he says, rolling his eyes. His words belie the fact that he is extremely pissed.

Devlin escorts me to another room. This one is sound-proofed and vacant of almost all furniture except a single chair, a table that sits in the middle of the room, and a locked metal cabinet. A man with combed back, greasy hair and a sweaty face sits in the chair. Two other men stand beside him. Another remains at the door. The seated man's eyes flare with fear as we enter.

With a flick of his finger, Devlin indicates where I am to stand. Once again I obey. The three other men glance in my direction then quickly avert their eyes. Who I am is clearly none of their concern. What I am is plain to these men. I belong to Devlin. Realization hits hard. All in this room are owned by Devlin. I will not allow myself to be one of them. The other four clearly are and know it.

"Joey," Devlin says, his voice laced with disappointment. Though his hands are hidden in his pockets, it makes Devlin seem more formidable. Devlin clicks his tongue and shakes his head at the seated man.

"Bbb...Boss," Joey stammers out. He isn't even permitted to finish his sentence. Devlin flicks a glance at one of the men who reacts by backhanding Joey.

Devlin sidles over to the table and sits on one of the corners as he continues to look down at the now quivering man. It's safe to say Joey is consumed by fear and dread.

"First you diddle with women who are off limits, reserved for special clients. Did you learn your lesson when I was lenient with you then? No," Devlin calmly says. "No, Joey, you had to keep sampling the merchandise. Show and tell my pet what your punishment was for breaking contract rules."

Joey glances in my direction. He darts his eyes to the men who continue to flank him. I can see his face go from pale to crimson.

"Quickly, Joey. I don't want to take all night," Devlin warns. "Shall I have these other gentlemen do it for you?" At his nod, the two men move as if to grab Joey.

"I'll do it. I'll do it," Joey says hastily as he rises to his feet. With his eyes averted, he unzips his trousers, letting them drop. He peels down his boxers.

"One of my balls was removed," Joey says in a dead voice. "Boss, promised to remove the other and my dick if I fucked another one of his whores."

"Go ahead and look, Angel pet. Take a good long look. The man signed a contract of which he broke more than once. I can assume that he has broken it countless times but was only stupid enough to get caught with his prick in the honey pot twice," Devlin says.

My hand covers my mouth as I look at the man's private parts. Clearly his penis was left intact but his testicles are a different story. They no longer are symmetrical. A ghastly scar is visible where the second one should be. I turn toward Devlin.

Clearly he is carefully watching me, gauging my response. I vow to show him as little as possible. I drop my hand from my mouth and give him what I hope is a stoic nuetral expression. I barely catch the winging of his brows before he turns back to Joey.

Joey pulls up his pants. The two guards place a hand on his shoulders forcing him to sit. Fear has taken over the man once again. A strange stench fills the room.

"So what is it that brings you here this time, Joey?" Devlin asks too casually.

"Cal is accusing me of stealing, boss," Joey whines.

"Did you steal money and chips? Did you take money that belongs to the House, to me?" Devlin's voice has gone hard.

When Joey would have opened his mouth, Devlin raises a warning hand. "Careful, Joey," he cautions. "Be careful that you don't get caught in a lie. Crime hidden behind lies will not be tolerated."

Fear consumes Joey's face making his already wide eyes even wider and wilder. Everyone can see him visibly swallow. His breaths are shallow and rapid.

"It was the first time, boss. Honest. I was going to return it later. It was more like a loan. For God's sake, boss, I needed the cash in a hurry. I was going to tell Cal and you, but Cal must have seen… Before I had a chance, he slammed me up against the wall and searched my pockets…" Joey's words die out when he hears Devlin snort and sees him shake his head.

A deadly gleam has entered Devlin's eyes.

I find myself recoiling inwardly from the emerging beast.

"What was the sudden need for all that cash?" Devlin asks. "You know I have a standing policy that any of my employees can obtain a loan. If you'd done that, we would be sitting in my office going over the appropriate paperwork, deciding on acceptable terms, sipping a glass of brandy like real men," Devlin reasons. "But you didn't do that did you, Joey?" Devlin didn't wait for a reply.

"I have to ask myself why. Why would one of my employees who has been caught doing what he shouldn't treat me this way? What have I done to you to deserve such disrespect?" Devlin asks in a considering voice as he rubs a finger and thumb over his chin.

"Nnn...nothing, boss."

He stops and pivots to look over at Joey. "Exactly. Maybe it isn't what I've done but what you think I am. Obviously you believe that you are so clever that you won't be caught or that nobody within my employ will give a damn or will notice the missing money."

Devlin walks around Joey, the guards move out of his way. When Devlin places a hand on Joey's shoulder, Joey jolts as if he was hit by a live wire.

"Joey, you always have been overly cocky. Stupidly so. You think your swagger and good looks make up for your lack of brains. That ego of yours you stroke as if it fondling your dick gives you the impression that everyone around you is a rube, easy pickings, too stupid to catch on to what you are truly doing. That's your biggest mistake. Now you have to own up to your mistake," Devlin says as if he feels a bit culpable for Joey's plight.

Devlin turns to me.

"See, my pet?" All in the room are taken aback when Devlin begins to address me. "This is what comes of being kind and generous. When I am merciful to those ill deserving, do they give me thanks? Do they learn the errors of their ways and seek to change and atone for their misdeeds? No! Do they respect me? Hardly. They think it gives them license to continue down that road of deceit and manipulation."

Devlin moves to stand in front of me. Slowly he pulls the tie loose of the robe I am wearing. With a flick of his hand the robe opens leaving me bare and exposed. This must be some sort of test. I know well the rules he gave me. I steel myself but also must remain pliant. Gently, almost reverently, he fondles my breasts. Before all, he places a kiss on each nipple before taking one into his mouth to suckle. His hands move around clasping hold of my buttocks. Fingers of one hand slither further down between my legs where they probe in between my thighs.

The room is dead quiet. The sudden and complete silence must have penetrated Devlin's mind. I watch as he visibly shakes away his momentary mental fog. Leaning in toward me, he licks the side of my neck then pivots around to focus once again on Joey.

With less than steady fingers, I close my robe and tie the sash. Quietly, I let out a shaky breath. A quick glance shows that the three thugs have averted their eyes from me. Joey is a different case altogether. His sexual leer is slow to dissipate. Hastily he covers his crotch to hide his growing erection. What a fool to think his expression and movements would go unnoticed.

Devlin extracts a black cloth bundle from a cabinet. In an unhurried, almost lazy, fashion, he lays it on the far side of the table. It looks like one of those cloth tool cases. My curiosity is piqued. It has also gained the attention of all the men in the room.

Joey must suspect what it contains within. I see him trying to move away. The two men come forward, placing a restraining hand on each shoulder. His movements become frantic as he gives pleading looks to all in the room.

When his eyes linger on me, I look away. Sure, there is a bit of pity in my heart for this man. I harken back to words

I learned in my youth. Reaping what one has sown. This man has made his life among the wicked and the evil. He made his home among a den of thieves then has the gall to whine about the injustice of being caught doing as he pleases.

With a bit of impatience, Devlin flicks open the black cloth revealing several sharp knives and saws. He takes out a cleaver and examines the tool in front of Joey. He replaces it and picks up a sharp paring knife of sorts. Joey has seen this before. The man is now squirming earnestly in his seat. Only a sharp bark from Devlin has him stilling.

"Joey, it is now time to pay up accounts. Since I'm in a good mood this evening, I shall grant you a choice. Listen and choose well," he advises. "First, you may select to become a total eunuch and lose the remainder of your manhood," Devlin says, pointing the knife close to Joey's crotch. Joey pales. "Or you can lose your fingers. This way, I will atone for not taking firmer measures with you. In future, you will not take me for a fool and break the rules or my trust. Lastly, you will atone for your errors and go on living with whatever parts of your person you will have retained." Devlin glances back at me then turns a raised brow toward Joey. He waits for a decision.

Joey's mouth falls open. The three thugs flare their nostrils. Only one of them smirks. Poor Joey. He will not be leaving the room the same person he was upon entering. This, I believe, he fully understands. I'm not sure what is more cruel, the punishment or the choice in determining what part of your working body is to be permanently severed.

"Joey, your time to consider and decide is fast eclipsing. If I have to decide for you, it will be both," Devlin warns.

It's as if you can really hear precious time tick, tick, ticking away and Joey's brain click, click, fizzling into nothingness.

"What do you value more: your prick or your hand?"

One of the thugs tries to be helpful. "Joey, you're taking up more of Mr. Devlin's valuable time. The sooner you decide the sooner the pain will end and you can get out of here and be on your way."

"Let's take a vote," Devlin says. He points to each thug one at a time.

"A man ain't no man without his dick. I'd choose the hand."

"Hand," says a second. "No contest."

"I'd get me one of those hooks or claws, make the whores ooh and aww...hand. I'll keep my member fuck you very much," the third man says to the laughter of his buddies.

Devlin looks at me. "Angel pet?"

"From a medical perspective, save the hand and it can be reattached. I don't have a dick so I shouldn't comment," I say, holding up my own hands.

That makes Devlin chuckle appreciatively.

"Hand," Joey whispers.

In the next moment, one thug restrains Joey while another seizes hold of his left hand, pressing it down flat on the table. Devlin has swapped out the knife with the cleaver. When Devlin said hand I thought the entire hand. I never thought he would do what I witnessed.

There will be no chance at attaching the severed appendage. Devlin begins the amputation at the tips of the fingers. It's as if he's a top chef chopping up a length of meat. By the time Devlin has reached where Joey's fingers met his palm, it takes all three thugs to retrain Joey. His screams crescendo until I am forced to cover my ears.

The last chop cuts Joey cleanly at the wrist. All that is left of his hand is a mess of butchered confetti of flesh, muscle, bone, and blood. Never in my life have I been grateful for being both a doctor and having worked for Global Medicine. The gruesome sight does not turn my stomach. I allow my mind to linger on what I would do if I was treating such an injury.

At some point in the chopping, Joey passed out. It's then that I uncover my ears and resume my stoic stance. Surprise flickers across Devlin's face when he glances over at me. He busies himself with wiping down the blade before replacing it carefully and precisely back in the case. Then he returns it to the cabinet, securing the doors.

"Boss, what do you want done with Joey?" asks one of the thugs.

Devlin barely gives the man a look. "See him to the clinic we use, then let him go. His employment is now permanently severed. Make sure he understands he is never again to step foot in one of my establishments. If he trespasses he will lose more than his hand."

Devlin thoroughly washes and dries his hands before coming over to me. Grabbing my arm, without a word, he escorts me back to his private penthouse suite. By the time we return, I'm feeling rather exhausted. All the emotional demands and trauma of the day are adding up and taking their toll. Something inside me warns that things are not yet over.

In my exhaustive state, I stumble.

"We've done too much," Devlin remarks. "We shall rest, have a light snack, some wine and see where we are led," he tells me.

He directs me to a wide cushioned chair facing a hearth that contains a small crackling fire. Under normal circumstances, the scene would be utterly comforting and charming.

In this context, it merely makes me more wary.

"Pet, you may ask any questions you may have," Devlins invites solicitously.

I sip the wine hoping it will settle my stomach and my nerves. I shake my head. "I have no questions, Luther," I softly say.

"None? Not after where we have been? What you have seen?" A note of surprise is in his voice.

Again, I tell him no. Devlin seems puzzled and a bit taken aback.

"Then humor me for I have my own," he says.

I tilt my head inviting him to ask what he will.

"You have no problems with what you saw this evening?" he asks me incredulously.

"I don't understand what you mean by problems," I say after some thought. I see his continued puzzlement. "Luther, I have always lived by the motto: 'Do as thy will, but do no harm'. I imagine that those people you...punished, signed contracts before you employed them, that they had a trial period to understand just what they were getting themselves into."

He nods, sitting back, pleased with my statement.

"Well then, where is the problem? I assume that they knew fully and well what the consequences would or might be for breaching their side of the terms. That is just business." I flip-wave my hand as if it was nothing of great concern.

I think I have thoroughly surprised him. I may be the first. Keeping my smile contained is extremely difficult. I feel it tugging at the corners of my mouth.

"Exactly," he says decisively. "But the flogging, the blood and..."

"Chopping?" I finish, hastily excusing myself for interrupting him. I shrug. "As a doctor I have seen what humans do to each other out of spite and to themselves for pleasure. The outcome can be the same though the reasons differ. My granny would say that each was reaping what they had sown."

"So you believe each got what they deserved?" he challenges, intrigued.

"I don't fully know the context and therefore should reserve judgement on all fronts," I say diplomatically.

"Huh. You intrigue me, Angel pet. I must say, I am pleased that I have pursued adding you to my personal collection," he tells me.

"You have racked up quite an expense in adding me to your stable," I comment. "The loss of manpower, plane, and your mole... A lot of time and effort over acquiring little ole me. Aren't you afraid you may have expended too much capital in obtaining your new...pet?"

"There is very little I wouldn't do to obtain my heart's desire," Devlin tells me.

With the press of a buzzer, the door opens. In walks two more servers. One places a covered tray down on the small table between our chairs. With a flourish the lid is lifted. Inside is a dish of fresh strawberries and smaller bowls of whipped cream and chocolate sauce and a variety of extras in which to roll and dip the berries. The other server pops the cork on a champagne bottle then proceeds to pour the bubbly wine into flutes. Both leave as discreetly as they arrived.

"Allow me, my pet," Devlin says.

He selects a choice berry, rolling it in whipped cream. Though I cringe inside, I know what is expected. As his hand moves toward me, I open my mouth like a baby bird accepting the offering. I close my eyes, not in appreciation of the flavor as Devlin supposes, but in supplication to be rescued.

"Now try one this way," he directs. This time he dips the berry in chocolate. Passion flares in his eyes as he brings the berry toward my lips. "Extend your tongue," he orders.

I obey.

The third one, he dips in chocolate then whipped cream. As he nears my lips, he bobbles, seemingly accidentally, grazing my cheek and neck with the luscious coating. With the berry still captured in my teeth, he pulls me closer to him with a hand captured behind my neck. He tilts his head and spears the berry with his teeth, essentially pressing our lips and mouths together in a kiss. After he passes the berry back and forth between our mouths, he lets me have it and proceeds to lick the cream and chocolate from my cheek. When this is done to his satisfaction, he continues to lap up the sticky sweetness from my neck and face.

Satisfied with the effect he thinks he is having on me, he pulls me up from the chair. He holds the flute of champagne to my lips. "Drink," he commands.

I take a sip. When I take my lips away from the edge, he pushes the bottom of the flute up toward me again.

"Drink all of it," he orders.

I comply. If I'm to be raped, then maybe this will help ease my pain and help me to forget.

When there is nothing left in the glass, he takes it from me, setting it down without looking away from me. His eyes glow with some strange light. This is a masterful seduction. Any normal woman may have been flattered, pleased, and filled with desire for this man.

I am no such woman. I feel no such desire. My heart belongs to another. Gabriel. He is who I wish to share such moments with, not some other man. No matter how ruthless, powerful, wealthy, or handsome, the only man for me is my own warrior angel.

As Devlin pulls me against his body, caressing me through the thin fabric of the robe, he tugs on my hair to better plunder my lips and neck. When he does this, I close my eyes and utter one word. It's for me both one of prayer and one of hope.

"Gabriel."

Instantly, Devlin pulls away. A snarl is on his face distorting his dark *GQ* looks with such ugliness I would have sworn that a demon lived just underneath his skin.

"What did you say?" he seethes.

I blink in confusion.

"As I am romancing you, treating you like the devil-damned angel you seem to be, you utter another's name?" Grabbing hold of both my upper arms, he shakes me until I think my teeth may be rattling in my head. With a vicious move, he casts me away. I fall heavily on the floor.

It takes me a moment to regain my full senses. Not quick enough. Devlin hauls me up by my hair. Gone is the gentle man. Gone is the gentle lover, the romancer. The monster has emerged.

In the darkened room that is eerily lit by the neon lights out side, Devlin takes on a demonic appearance. His lips are snarling and his teeth bared in an animalistic growl. His face contorts with his unleashing rage. Muscles stand out prominently on his neck and ripple beneath his shirt.

In one fluid motion, the monster Devlin is on me.

The robe proves to be no barrier. It's too quickly torn from my shoulders. It slithers down my arms and remains hooked near my elbows as I in turn away while defensively shoving my hands against Devlin's chest to ward him off. Simultaneously maintaining my balance becomes nearly impossible. The robe is loosely held together by its knotted sash. My breasts are exposed and just a bit of my belly until it widens further near the apex of my thighs.

My hair is a tumbled mess. My eyes must appear wild and frantic. I open my mouth to let out a scream as I continue to struggle against Luther Devlin.

"I will have you, pet. Here and now, I shall claim you. I thought to woo you and win you over with romance, but now I think I rather like the ravished angel look you have about you. I have never known a woman who evokes such a duality in my soul. Both the man and the monster desire you. Each craves to claim you and make you ours. Long, I have tried to keep one at bay. Now I know that I must set them both free and allow each to have you as they will together and be damned the consequences," he says huskily before plundering my neck and breasts with his lips.

As one of his hands snakes down my body to grab me between my legs, I scream and fight. I am pleased that it takes Devlin a bit of effort to keep me contained. But instead of dissuading him from his goal, it only serves to fuel his desire.

Devlin chuckles maniacally. "You're such a wild angel. I rather like that."

He tumbles me onto the bed following after me, holding me in place beneath him with his heavier form. Still I continue to fight and squirm. In my bid to be free of him and his assault, I put by voice behind my efforts. Screaming over and over, I vow to not stop until I have no voice left.

My screams turn into one word, a name. "Gabriel. Gabriel!" I cry.

I call for the protection of the mightiest of archangels, my warrior angel, my protector, the love of my being. Just when I feel the energy within me begin to fail and Devlin crows his victory, shouts followed by pops, then a crash sound.

The door to Devlin's room bursts open. There in the backlit space is my own true angel. Gabriel. He has come at last. He has come for me!

In that moment of stillness, Gabriel takes in the scene. Throwing back his head, Gabe lets loose with such an unearthly sound that it stuns Devlin. In that moment I scramble away from my tormentor. Hastily, I try covering my exposed body. Tears course down my cheeks as I attempt to put distance between me and Devlin.

As agents, police officers, and ranch hands begin pouring into the room, Devlin and Gabriel lunge toward the other. This is a match of two otherworldly beings: one of light, the other of darkness. Both have been cast down from heaven. One has made his empire through sin and vice, the other through toil and love of the land and his fellow men and women.

A flurry of fists and kicks happen in a blurr. Body slams punctuate the room along with growls and grunts. Blood freely flies as does sweat and spittle. The adrenaline that is pumping through their veins is waning. Each is sporting split lips and I suspect a few bruised or broken ribs. Neither is willing to concede. I know that this will be a finish to the death.

A blanket being gently placed around my shoulders is the only thing that momentarily distracts me from the fight.

"Zeke," I breathe out the man's name in relief. "Am I ever glad to see you."

"Not nearly as glad as I am now that we have you once again." Zeke blushes with his words.

"Why don't the agents step in and arrest Devlin?" I'm unable to take my eyes from the fight.

Seeing my worried look as we watch the battle, Zeke

seeks to ease my concern. "Gabriel will win, Sera. The man has everything riding on this fight and everything to lose," he says, using his chin to point toward where the two men are circling each other. "Gabe needs to do this. Isaac," Zeke chin lifts to a man in a suit, "understands this. Besides, Gabriel has a secret weapon that Devlin lacks. It makes all the difference."

Again, I momentarily redirect my attention from the fight to fix my eyes on Zeke with a questioning look.

Zeke leans in close, whispering, "You. Gabriel has found love. Nothing's more powerful than an archangel fighting on the side of love. Not even the Devil himself can defeat such a force or power and will."

I notice that Zeke has positioned himself slightly in front of me, willing to protect me if there is a need. Other men from Paradise are doing the same thing, surrounding me, keeping me out of harm's way. Tears blur my eyes. So many from Paradise have ventured from home into the depths of the Devil's Den to rescue me.

The scent of violets fills my nose once again. The soothing scent fills me with calm and courage. It clears my head. I know what I must do.

"Gabriel, I love you. I am yours and you are mine," I yell. "End this!"

My words seem to startle the two men. Devlin frowns. Gabriel smiles. Light seems to pour from his being, blinding Devlin in his darkness. Enraged by my words, Devlin lunges for Gabriel. Gabriel lets out a roar, hoisting Devlin up in his arms, bodily tossing him. Devlin's flying body slams into the window. The glass shatters behind where Devlin hits. We all watch transfixed as the window falls away and Devlin plunges thirty-eight stories to his death.

A sob tears from my throat as I fly to Gabriel. I climb his body until I feel his arms wrap around me, holding me close.

My legs twine around his waist and my arms wrap around his neck. I vow to never let go.

"You came for me," I sob against his neck. "You came for me."

I peer over Gabriel's shoulder when I hear someone clearing their throat. There stands my champions, all from Paradise. I give them my brightest smile.

"Thank you all," I say through tears of happiness and relief. "I've never seen so many angels gathered together in one place. You all risked your lives coming to free me, to rescue me. My very own host of angels."

Finally, Gabriel extracts his face from my neck. "Are you hurt, Sera?" he asks, his voice still rough from the fight.

"Just a few bruises. Nothing serious," I tell him. "Can we go home now?" I plead. "Please, Gabriel, take me back to Paradise. That's where I want to be, where I'm meant to be."

He places his lips on mine. Before all his men and everyone in the room he kisses me like a lover, like the soulmate I know him to be.

Chapter 23

Gabriel

Hearing Sera screaming my name over and over again gives me a strange strength that has me flying down the corridor and bursting through every door until she is before me. It is as if something otherworldly has taken hold of my body. Instead of possessing me completely, we seem to work in concert. Our mutual goal—rescuing Sera and seeing her safe.

When I see Devlin forcing himself on Sera. I go crazy. There is my angel fighting with all her might to keep him at bay, an angel versus a devil from hell. God only knows what she has endured. There she is nearly naked and that demon is on top of her.

I can't help but roar my rage and lunge at the monster. She is mine. *Mine!*

I'm determined to protect her at all cost. The feel of my fist making contact with his face is very satisfying. He dares to put in danger someone I love? He stole her away and intends on abusing her, making her his.

There is much he owes for such offenses. In truth, I'm sure even he doesn't have the means to pay and atone for all he had done. Then again that is not my concern. I'll leave Isaac and the various law enforcement agencies and courts to decide.

All I want is my pound of flesh for the hurt and harm he has reeked on my ranch and on my people, my family. Punches to his kidneys and gut help with that. He gets in a few hits and kicks himself. I felt my lip split when he got one in under my watch. It only serves to fuel my fire. As the fight goes on, I know that we are well matched. I also know that only one of us will prevail and walk away.

As both of us begin to drag, our strength diminishing, I hear Sera yell out her love for me. Those words energize me, fueling me with renewed strength and purpose. With a roar I go for him again. How I manage to lift him up over my head, I'll never know. Next thing, I'm tossing him aside like he is yesterday's news. Instead of bouncing off the wall and landing on the floor, he hits the window. The weight and force of his body smashing into the glass must have been too much. A quick cracking of the pane is heard before it gives way, causing Devlin to fall to his death.

That is one fall he won't be walking away from. They will have to scrape his remains off the pavement below. I have barely breathed in a settling breath when Sera comes barreling into me. She throws her arms around my neck and climbs my torso, wrapping her legs around my waist like a baby koala. I do what any other red blooded male would. I pull her closer still and hang on for dear life. So overcome by emotion, I bury my head in her neck and breathe in her calming scent.

With hands I keep hard from trembling, I search my woman, inspecting her from head to toe. Noting the bite on the back of her neck, as I move aside her hair. Lifting her chin, I examine her bruised face.

Sera captures my hand and my gaze. "All superficial. They will keep until we are gone from this place. Then you or a medical professional can treat them."

Tucking the blanket Zeke had given her more securely around her shoulders, I nod, giving in to her request. Placing a protective and possessive arm around her, I pull her into my side. I'm never letting this lady out of sight again.

As she speaks to my men, calling them her host of angels, I look up at my old friend Isaac. There is a satisfied look on his face as he speaks first into a radio then several cell phones. Yeah, now that I have Sera in my arms, the only thing left for me to do is to get her and the boys home and make her my wife.

For Isaac, his work is just beginning. He'll be the one to clean up this mess. I don't envy him. But hey, this is the life he chose. Maybe this is what he's called to do.

When Sera asks to be taken back to Paradise, that's music to my ears.

"Bring the trucks around boys," I holler joyously.

All go to see it done save Zeke. I know that old coot will hang back and not leave my side until we are firmly back on Paradise soil.

"Isaac," I hail my friend. "Sera, I'd like you to meet a real good friend of mine. This is Isaac. We grew up together, about as close to being brothers you can get without blood. He's the..."

I stop my words, when Sera turns to the man without leaving my arms. She leans over, grasping his face between her hands and kisses each of his cheeks. "I know who Isaac is, Gabriel. He is a member of the family. Isaac, thank you for all you have done," she says. "You've been too long away from home. I insist you come by and spend time with us at Paradise," she says.

Isaac shuffles his feet and gives me a brotherly look that speaks volumes. We're both a bit choked up. "Yes ma'am," he acknowledges Sera's open invitation and mild scolding. "You'll be seeing me quite soon. We'll need to get your statement and go over a few details, but I would love to spend time with everyone. I'll give you a few days to get back your equilibrium. It will take that long just to get things set up here to process through all of this." He gestures to all of Devlin's property and businesses.

As we head out, we speak briefly with Sheriff Dobbins. By the time we make it down to the front of Lust, I have Sera swaddled in a blanket like a baby. I chose the back seat so I can continue to hold her on our drive home. Nothing can separate us and nothing ever will.

∞∞∞∞

It's well after midnight by the time we pull into Paradise. The place is peaceful. All is still. All is quiet. The moon seems fuller and the stars brighter. Even the nighttime animals are bedded down or roosting for the night. Sera has fallen asleep in my lap. I hold her tightly and place tender kisses on her head and stroke her hair. She needs rest. I intend to see that she gets it and more. Tomorrow, I will insist her doctor examine her mending leg. Still wearing the boot, her leg still hasn't fully recovered.

After being let out at the big house, I take her to the only bed she will ever sleep in, ours. I will see to having her few meager belongings moved to our master suite later today. I lay her on the bed and undress her. She's so exhausted, she doesn't even stir. It's a testimony to how safe she feels when she's with me. Bruises on her arms are clearly visible. When I see the damage to her bottom, I nearly lose it. I want to throw Devlin out another window for what he's done to her.

Gently so as not to disturb her, I place her under the

covers after a quick sponge bath. Quickly, I shed my clothing and slip in next to her. Pulling her close to me, I hold her with one arm anchored around her waist. Sighing in contentment, she snuggles further into me. No sooner after closing my eyes, I'm out.

When I wake the next morning, the sun is shining brightly through the window. I can hear birds chirping in the garden. Everything will be fine now that I have Sera beside me. Reaching a hand out lazily in search of my love, all I encounter is cold sheets.

My eyes fly open. I roll to my side for a better look. The imprint of her body remains so I know that it was not a dream. We've recovered her and brought her home. I bury my face in her pillow, inhaling her scent.

I need to find her and make sure she's safe. Rushing out of bed, I pull on sweatpants and a T-shirt then bound out of our room. The sound of voices coming from the kitchen has me heading there. I come up short.

There is Sera all clean and fresh as bright as the morning sun, despite the dark bruising on her face. She and my cherubs are sitting at the breakfast table. Pancakes are this morning's fare. Sera is listening to each one as if their words are the most spectacular things she's ever heard. No wonder they love her. She truly is interested in each and everything they do and say. She loves them and they understand that.

Daniel looks up and sees me. The joy that lights his eyes nearly brings me to my knees. I hope that we will always have that special bond.

"Daddy," he calls out, causing my girls to look up and Lailah to holler out the same as her brother.

I join them at the table, planting noisy kisses on their bed tangled heads. Sera pours me a cup of coffee and places it in front of me when I take my seat. Scooping up her hand, I pull her so she sits in my lap. My cherubs giggle. They have never seen me show such open affection for a woman in public and in front of them. I've not lived a celibate life since Mary died but neither have I brought those women home. Now I understand why. Paradise was not for them. We've been waiting for our angel, for Sera.

Without hesitation or bashfulness, Sera lets me kiss her full on the mouth in front of my children. I want them to know that we love each other and are happy to display our affection for one another. Sera sighs when our lips part. Her arms are wrapped around my neck as I rub her outer thigh.

"Cherubs," I say, breaking eye contact with Sera and looking over at my kids, "Sera and I love each other. As you know, I asked her to marry me."

"And she said yes!" Lailah cheers, holding her arms up in victory. "She's gonna to be our new mom," she adds, clapping her hands in glee.

"That's right." I beam at her. I look over at Daniel who has been quiet.

"Daniel? How are you taking this, son?" I ask.

"Does this mean that our other mom won't be our mom any more?" he asks a bit sullen. "I like Sera...I love Sera. I don't want her leaving, but I don't want to forget our first mom."

Sera reaches over to clasp Daniel's small hand. "Mary Slayer will always be your mother. Nothing is ever going to change that. She's the one who carried you under her heart. She loved you. You love her. In your heart she should always live. Never shall we forget her. She is a part of you and should always remain so," Sera tells them. "Oh, I know... How about after breakfast, we go speak with her at her resting place. We'll plant beautiful flowers to brighten the spot reminding us and telling her how much she's cherished?"

Lailah's game, eager to lend a hand.

Daniel mulls over Sera's words. From the look on his face, I think he's coming around.

"My granny, Violet Flowers," sneaking a smile over at Lialah, "always told me that the more we love, the larger our heart grows, allowing us to love even more. So...maybe you could find room for me? I would love to have some corner of your heart for myself. Heaven knows, I already love you lots," she tells them both. "If you want me to be your friend and continue to call me Sera, that's fine by me. If you want to call me mom, I would be honored. Either way, we are now family. Okay?"

Daniel seems satisfied. "Okay," he whispers.

I ruffle his hair when I see his smile growing wider and wider until he is giggling with glee.

Sera claps her hands to gain our attention. "Okay, who's ready for another round or pancakes?"

"Me, me, me," my cherubs chorus.

"Daddy, Sera made us special pancakes," Daniel tells me. "These have chocolate chips in them and those have blueberries. There are lots of toppings to put on them," he says, pointing to each of the bowls that held nuts, banana slices, fresh mixed berries, whipped cream, chocolate sauce, and the standard maple syrup and butter.

"Sewa... I mean Mom made bacon and eggs too," Lailah says, not to be undone by her brother.

"Well pass me some of that over," I say.

I load my plate with a little bit of everything and eat companionably with my children. Soon we are joined by Elizabeth and then Zeke. Zeke takes one look at the fare and readily accepts Sera's invitation to join us.

"So when are you and Momma Sewa gonna get married?" Lailah asks.

She keeps right on eating, not noticing that all the adults have stopped. Sera looks at me, blinking her eyes as her cheeks pinken enough to match her lips.

"As soon as Sera can find a suitable dress," I tell them. "Getting the license and preacher won't take any time at all." I wink at Sera.

"Where were you thinking of holding it?" Elizabeth asks.

"Right here at Paradise. Everyone here will be invited. Kind of silly to have everyone drive somewhere else now wouldn't it?"

"There's a lovely field full of wildflowers not too far off. It would be lovely there and the reception could be held in one of the indoor rings," Zeke adds. When he catches Elizabeth looking at him with her mouth ajar, he turns beet red.

"Cookie could roast us up a beef or a hog. Jeb's wife makes the most beautiful cakes. I'm sure some of the ladies would love to help prepare other dishes," Elizabeth adds. "We have wine from the vineyard and cheeses from the creamery."

"Perfect!" Sera exclaims.

Elizabeth takes Sera's hand. "I know just the place in Bridgeport. There's this delightful boutique that sells the most wonderful gowns, one of a kind. I think they would be stunning on you..."

I shake my head. Seems everyone is eager to see us wed. Truth be told, so am I. The sooner the better. I have a few calls to make.

∞∞∞

Gabriel

Sera and I have been relaxing in the private garden outside our bedroom. It's good to see her fully relaxed. I don't think she has been until now. Though I know she is happy, there's a sadness that lingers. Maybe less of a sadness but more of a yearning. I long to find a way for her to set her sorrows and troubles aside.

The faint sound of footsteps can be heard. I watch as Sera turns toward the sound. She startles. Squeals from multiple sources have me flinching. The sound hurts my ears. In a flash, Sera is up and limp-racing across the veranda, flinging herself into the open arms of her sisters.

I've come to my feet to watch the greeting. My smile is as wide as California is long. Sera turns her tearful face toward me.

"Did you do this? Did you arrange to have my sisters brought here?" she asks me.

I nod and give her my best smile. I revel in the love that pours from her.

"I wanted you at your happiest on the day we wed. It was only right that your family be here for our special day. I know how much your sisters mean to you," I tell her.

She turns to her sisters who have not quite yet released their hold on her. "See what type of guy I'm marrying?" she boasts. "He's the best."

She sighs dreamily, as her sisters giggle in delight.

"Come," she says. "Come meet the man of my life." She draws her sisters toward the patio chairs.

I meet them halfway.

I can't imagine raising five girls. That's what Sera's parents did. Five beautiful girls, each one different and unique in their own way. Each has their own talents and interests. To see them all together is simply staggering.

"How did you pull it off?" Sera asks me. She still seems to be in a bit of a shock.

"What's so difficult about it?" I challenge playfully. "You just pick up the phone, talk to one and quickly they get the word to the others. I reserved plane seats for each and had their tickets waiting for them at the airport. They checked in and flew across the country. When they arrived I had one of my guys pick them up and bring them out here." I shrug.

With twinkling eyes, she slowly advances on me, capturing my face between her hands and then proceeds to kiss me soundly before all of her sisters. They cheer. When she pulls away, I'm the one with the crimson face.

"Ladies, I shall leave you to yourselves. I imagine you have much to discuss. I'll see you all at supper if not before," I tell them, touching a finger to the brim of my hat as I take my leave but not before kissing Sera once more.

Chapter 24

Sera

Elizabeth has been a bulldog, relentless in her desire to help me find the perfect dress for my wedding. Lailah, Elizabeth, and I made a day of it. We traveled to Bridgeport to visit the boutique that Elizabeth swore would be the place to find just what I wanted.

She was right.

After modeling so many bridal dresses, I had already determined what I fancied and what I didn't. In the end, I selected a strapless lace bodice dress with a full A-line skirt. Lavender and wildflowers will be my bouquet. We purchase Lailah a violet colored dress as she will be one of my maids. She is thrilled.

"My faewie will be vewy happy when she sees the color," she exclaims.

"Yes, and you must tell her she is invited to the wedding. I selected the color in honor of her," I tell a shocked Lailah.

"Weally?" she asks with a child's enthusiasm.

"Oh, indeed," I confirm. "Didn't she tell you? She came to me twice to give me comfort and let me know things would work out."

"Did you see her?" Lailah asks with large round eyes.

I shake my head. "No, but I smelled her." I wiggle my

nose. "A soft hint of violets was all it took for me to know that it was her."

Gabriel and I told a gentler tale of how their father managed to save me. We wanted them to know the truth, but they didn't need to hear all the details.

Isaac did what he promised. He gave us a couple of days to ourselves before arriving to ask questions. With Gabriel's encouragement, I had sat at his computer and typed out my memory of events starting with when I found myself kidnapped. I started with the hoax of being needed to help with delivering a baby.

Gabriel had taken pictures of my various injuries in case they were needed for the official record. We are confident that all participants in the plan to bring me to Devlin are now dead. Isaac confirmed that his team had arrested two more people within the FBI who were Devlin's informants. Casino Lust is now closed as investigators comb through every room, computer, and file in order to dismantle his crime organization.

I can only imagine what the fallout will be.

That chapter, for us, is now relegated to the past. It's finished. Our future now awaits. I'm almost giddy when I think about it. I will have the rest of my life with Gabriel, living here in Paradise.

In less than two weeks I will be marrying Gabriel. How is this all possible? We will be husband and wife. My sisters will be here too. I will be the first to marry, though I'm not the eldest. The only downside is that my parents will not be coming. Spain is too far away to drop everything at such short notice. If I push that aside, everything is perfect.

Though my life seems to be getting back on track in a fast and furious but glorious way, I can see that it is not so for two of my sisters.

"Grace? Pre? What's going on?" Finally, I can no longer hold my tongue.

They exchange looks then give me anemic smiles.

"That's not going to do."

"We don't want to add to your troubles," Pre says.

"Nonsense," I retort. "We are sisters. We've always stuck together. Remember, we are our own host of angels. Whatever is bothering you is of my concern. I want to help you, to be involved, not an outsider looking in."

I insist that they tell me. Whatever it is, I can tell my other sisters knew of it. Their pinched lips and sad eyes tell me that it isn't good. Finally they relent.

"Sera, there isn't anything to be done." Grace finally breaks down. She tosses Pre a sour look. "Don't give me that face, Ms. Grumpy. Someone has to tell Sera. It isn't right that she doesn't know, isn't told," she scolds.

"For about a year now, a developer back in Albany has been pestering me to sell what's left of the farm," Pre tells me. Anger rolls off her. The pain is still too fresh.

"You told him no, didn't you?" I quickly respond.

It was the collective funds from most of us, including me, that purchased the land and main part of the farm when my parents decided to retire and sell everything and quit the country.

"Of course I did, many times in fact," Pre fumes. "The man wouldn't take no for an answer. Letters kept coming. I ended up getting an attorney to write a formal decline to get him to quit."

"That didn't work?"

Pre shook her head no. "The jerk started showing up at

home or at the restaurant. I even caught him on the property surveying as if he owned the land," she tells me.

"I hope you gave him heck for it when you caught him," I say.

She gives me a wily grin.

"I chased his ass off my land with a pitchfork and told him if he ever came back on without an invitation I would get my shotgun."

That's my sister, glad to see her spunk returning.

"So?" I prompt.

Pre heaves a sigh. "So, the next thing I know, I'm getting this notice that the county fathers are seizing the entire property by right of eminent domain." She bit out the last words as if they tasted foul on her tongue.

"Eminent domain?" I ask, a bit confused.

I know what it means. The US Constitution, in the fifth and fourteenth amendments, gave the government the right to confiscate private property for public use in exchange for compensation. Many cities are doing this as a means of getting rid of blighted areas or from property owners who either haven't paid their taxes for a while or have allowed their property to become derelict. Neither is the case for what was left of the family farm.

"We appealed the decision and were awaiting a ruling when you came home," Grace tells me.

"Why didn't you tell me then?" I ask, a bit dismayed.

"We were planning on doing so but wanted to give you some time. You already had so much to worry about and we really thought we had this in the bag. Our attorney was confident that the ruling would be in our favor."

"But it wasn't," I conclude.

Grace shakes her head. "The very day we realized you were missing and David...well, that was when we got the final word. Not only did we lose, we also found out that the city had turned around and sold the property to the developer who had been pestering us for so long."

"Why? What reason did they give you?" I demand in outrage. "Didn't they know that the property was a historic heritage farm? It has been in our family for generations. It provides food and income and jobs that benefit the community, enriching the community."

Pre nods. "You're saying everything that our attorney said. We showed them the history and how keeping open agricultural land in the midst of urban development enhances the value of all the property and enriches the lives of those who live around it. We had figures, pictures..." Tears overwhelm her. Obviously, the pain is still very raw. Knowing Pre, I'm not surprised.

"They said that the revenue from the property tax on the houses that would be built there far outweighed other considerations. We were going to fight the ruling and take it through the courts but when word got out that night, someone threw Molotov cocktails through the windows of the house and into the barn," Pre whispers hoarsely.

I can only sit and stare in shock and growing grief.

"We couldn't save everything. We barely got out with our lives. Much was lost. Personal possessions, the family antiques and mementos. Gone," Grace adds.

"I had installed a sprinkler system in the barn in the case of fire," Leigh says. "The fire was so hot and burned so quickly because of the accelerant used, everything was turned to ash, including animals and produce."

"That's when Pre decided to protest. She chained herself

to what remained of the house and some of us took up residence in the tree fort built in the old oak in the yard. We all got hauled off to jail and fined for trespassing. Trespassing on our family farm," Leigh exclaims.

"As soon as we posted bail, we headed back out to the farm. When we got there it was too late. The developer was there personally seeing that everything was demolished. We stood there with the police blocking our way and watched as ancient fruit trees were uprooted and all the other buildings were torn down," Grace went on. "Well save for those they didn't get their hands on, but that's another story.

I look over at Pre who is silently weeping.

"It was too much for her," Grace says, laying a motherly hand on Pre. "She couldn't handle it, not after all she had done to try to save the land, the farm, our history from that... that..." Grace couldn't finish.

"There he was, the developer, Simon Konig. All high and mighty himself, gloating over his victory and what he was able to accomplish. 'Can't stop progress, ladies,' he chortled as he ripped out another productive plum tree. He just didn't get it. Pre collapsed." My eyes swung back to my sister. "We had to call an ambulance. She spent two days in the hospital."

"I've closed the restaurant," Pre whispers flatly.

"What?" I exclaim.

"What other choice did I have? My eatery was based on the notion of food being locally grown on our land and on surrounding farms. I can longer provide that. Grace lost her businesses, I lost my business, we lost our home. Our family history is now lost and buried beneath new ticky-tacky homes that will look old and ugly in less than half a generation. All of our employees at the farm and at Angel Fare had to be let go," Pre tells me.

"I'm so, so sorry, Pre, Grace. There simply aren't words..."

We are all silent for a bit.

"Where are you living? Do you have any plans?" I ask softly.

"We're all camped out in the old hunting cabin or in one of the old travel trailers. Part of the protected zone on account of the crested caracaras that have nested there. At least King Konig can't touch that land," Leigh tells me.

There's more to this story, but I'll wait to hear it.

"Well then that's settled," I say. I rather like the shocked looks that swivel toward me at my too cheery a voice. "No use in crying over spilled milk, as Granny Flowers always liked to remind us. I need some fabulous food at my wedding and was wondering if Angel Fare Catering might want the job? There's a lot that is raised and grown right here on site."

I'm delighted when I see Pre's interest start to rise.

"Would you be interested in taking charge?" I ask her?

"I'd love that," she says.

Yes, life is coming back into her eyes. The fire that was missing is returning.

"But now, I want to take you on a tour of Paradise. You'll love to know that this is a historic and a heritage ranch too. Gabriel tells me they have always embraced the sustainable philosophy. He's looking to expand on that in a new and modern sort of way..."

We move off together. I'm excited about seeing my sisters' reactions to what they see being done here at Paradise.

Chapter 25

Gabriel

"Dearly beloved, we are gathered here today..." Pastor John Sutton officiates the vows Sera and I exchange.

I look over at my bride. A woman never looked more beautiful than this one who will shortly be promising to be mine in front of family and friends. We've already weathered the worst. During that time, we discovered love. We found each other, discovering in the mix that love made us stronger. If that was the worst, I look forward to what the best will entail.

As I wait for her to come to me down the aisle, a sense of pride fills me, having my Paradise family out in force. As they've done my entire life, they stand behind me. It's a humbling truth and one I have never fully taken stock of until recently. Never did they hesitate to aid me in reclaiming my angel when she had been taken. They were willing to risk their lives so that my love and I would be reunited.

On the bride's side, stands Sera's sisters. All are dressed in shades of violet. My son and I exchange grins when we see it. Daniel stands in as my best man. When the girls had gone shopping for their dresses, we men had done a bit of shopping of our own, for our tuxedos. This was my second marriage but Sera's first—and my last. I want this to be the wedding of her dreams and one that will live long in our memory.

Now that Devlin is no longer a threat and his crime organization being dismantled, Sera and her family are no longer in danger. All of her sisters were eager to be present when the first of them tied the knot. We had a few days to get acquainted. I can say that I easily accepted them as my sisters. My own cherubs are thrilled to have so many new aunts.

Our family is already growing. A couple of Sera's sisters have decided to remain here at Paradise. I know that will make Sera happy to have her sisters so near.

Sera is taking charge of our clinic. Grace will help us expand our organic farming operation. Pre will be opening a cafe and catering business. She's even thinking of teaching a few culinary classes to local foodies.

My only regret is that Sera's parents did not join us from Spain. Hopefully in the near future, they will make the long flight to come visit with their family, old and new. In the meantime, there's Skype and email.

As I wait at the makeshift altar for my bride, I see a flurry of activity down at the other end. A pretty older woman dressed in pale blue that accents her silver-white hair rushes down the aisle. She seems a bit embarrassed that she's late and flicks me a glance that is both apologetic and curious. When she reaches her destination, instantly I know who she is.

Sera's sisters leap to their feet and enthusiastically hug and embrace the woman. This must be Rose Angel, Sera's mother. When I see Zeke saunter down the aisle to sit by Elizabeth, I have my full answer. Zeke shoots me a nod before tipping his chin down where the bridal procession has assembled.

At first I see my cherub Lailah dressed up all pretty in her new dress as she leads the procession when the music begins to play. Sera is being escorted by a man who must be her father. He is beaming a broad smile as he looks down at his daughter. Tears sparkle in both of their eyes.

Then as if she hears me calling her, Sera looks my way. Her eyes lock with mine. She simply takes my breath away. I am more than ready when her father hands her off to me. As the preacher makes his benediction and begins the ceremony, I feast on the one that will be saying 'I do'.

I was born in Paradise. In Paradise I have lived my entire life. Though I have seen much of the world, Paradise is the only place I will ever call home. Once, long ago, I thought it was truly a paradise. Now with this angel by my side, I've come to understand that it's heaven on Earth.

Epilogue

Sera

Not so long ago, I thought my world had come crashing down. It seemed all I'd believed in was an illusion, an elaborate lie. Everything I loved was taken away. I found myself in situations I never could have imagined.

I woke up from a nightmare and found myself surrounded by a host of angels. Somehow acquiring my own archangel, my own warrior angel, who was more than willing to go to battle for me.

Angels brought me to Paradise and now I call it my home. Some of my Angel sisters have flown in and have remained, seeing the opportunities that living here in this community can afford one who shares in their vision and philosophy of living and of life. Now, they too will live in Paradise.

Gabriel not only gave me his name, he gave me his love and his two precious cherubs. And now we are bringing more angels into the world.

Not long after our wedding, I discovered that I was pregnant. I must say that not once did I suffer as some women do. No morning sickness or issues of any kind plagued me. No heartburn, no emotional swings. The only thing I suffered from was a peculiar need to eat strange combinations of foods such as grape jelly and dill pickle sandwiches, sardines mixed with blueberries on Ritz crackers spread with cream cheese, Twinkies dipped in ranch dressing, and sauerkraut and chocolate icing on pizza.

The gross looks on the faces of my family slipped into fits of giggles with some of my odd concoctions. Sometimes, I couldn't seem to stop laughing myself silly. Regardless of their faces, I simply couldn't help myself. I even got Daniel and Lailah to try shredded BBQ pork ala mode. Yum.

I opted to have a home birth with Maggie serving as my midwife. I wanted my child born in Paradise. With all the changes at the ranch, one more added community program has been a communal day care. Women—and a few men—now serve as caregivers for parents who wish to work part-time or full-time at one of Paradise's many agri-businesses.

Grace now works at keeping Paradise a responsible steward and partner with the land while expanding what it grows and raises. Poultry, heritage hogs, and mushrooms are three of the biggest additions.

Pre opened up a cafe where she serves almost exclusively ranch raised and grown items. First it attracted those who worked and lived in and around the ranch. Soon people began making it a destination. From there, she began a catering service that is now thriving. Her business morphed into a party planning business where Paradise ranch has become a destination spot for weddings and conventions. Interesting how many people are eager to marry and hold workshops, conferences, and retreats on a working ranch.

"Need more ice chips?" Gabriel asks, hovering anxiously next to my side in our bedroom. I nod my head as I huff out another breath. I open my mouth like a baby bird to receive the chips he feeds me.

I woke up early in the morning with my first clues that this baby wanted to be born. All day long I had been driving Gabriel crazy with my cleaning fits. Finally, he had taken himself off to do "ranch work" and left me alone to do my thing. Elizabeth, I suspect had been the one to shoo him off, understanding my nesting behavior for what it was, an early warning sign.

By bedtime, the sneaky woman had laid out all the supplies Maggie and I said would be needed for the long awaited event. My belly had become huge. Increasingly, it became difficult to get comfortable enough to sleep for more than an hour or two at a time. In exasperation, I finally decided to get up. When I did, that was when my water broke.

By the time my hyper husband came back from alerting people, I had mopped up the mess and changed the bedding, placing the plastic protective covering over the sheet. I pulled out the med cart with all the needed supplies and filled the tub with water.

As the rising sun peaked its head above the horizon beginning a new day, our son, followed by our daughter, were born. Twins. Even I was fooled. One hid behind the other. My sisters cleaned and wrapped each one in a receiving blanket before handing them to Gabriel. My warrior angel couldn't keep his tears from falling.

"Welcome to Paradise," I coo to our youngest cherubs.

Lailah and Daniel join Gabriel and myself on the bed as we hold and snuggle with our newest angels.

"What are you going to name them?" Lailah asks as I place one of the infants in her arms.

"It's got to be a good name since they are Slayers and Slayers are warrior angels," Daniel thought to add.

"How about Knight and Kingsley?" Gabriel replies.

"Perfect," I respond.

"Knight Slayer and Kingsley Slayer the newest, but not the last of our growing host of angels."

The End

Books By This Author

Aria: The Pride Of Lion's Pride, An Mc Saga

A contemporary romance about a group of people who believe in loyalty and following a code. In the end, nothing can overcome the power of love and family. When danger lurks, the males defend, the women hunt. Together, they protect what is theirs.

Find out more about Catherine and her novels at her website https://catherinelampshire.wixsite.com.books

Acknowledgement

Doug, you spoil me. Thanks for doing so much so I can spend more time in my writing room. Dad and Joyce, each of you, as does Doug, stepped up, eager to read the words I've written, giving meaningful feedback. It means a lot. Kristi and Greg, ever you have been my cheerleaders. A heartfelt thanks goes to you two. A shout out goes to Jennifer at Killion Publishing and to Dean for their editing skills.

About The Author

Catherine Lampshire

Catherine's curiosity and ecelctic tastes come to her naturally. Her love of travel and thirst to explore the world around her orignated from being into a military family. This semi-nomadic life helped foster a love of history, reading, and adventure. Years as a historical reenactor and interpretor fuled her drive to teach. For over twenty years, Catherine was a high school History teacher before retiring. She now writes. Spending hours in her writing room typing out the stories filling her head. When not writing, Catherine can be found traveling with her husband working in her garden or taking walks with Mr. Pickles.

www.ingramcontent.com/pod-product-compliance
Lightning Source LLC
Chambersburg PA
CBHW031550240626
47153CB00002B/450